THE
BODYGUARD

THE
BODYGUARD

Cherry Adair

Gena Showalter

Lorie O'Clare

St. Martin's Paperbacks

This is a work of fiction. All of the characters, organizations, and events portrayed in this novel are either products of the author's imagination or are used fictitiously.

THE BODYGUARD

"Temptation on Ice" copyright © 2010 by Cherry Adair.
"Temptation in Shadows" copyright © 2010 by Gena Showalter.
"Hunting Temptation" copyright © 2010 by Lorie O'Clare.

Cover illustration by Craig White
Photograph of dark alley © Denis Tangney Jr / Getty Images
Photograph of man © Shirley Green

For information address St. Martin's Press, 175 Fifth Avenue, New York, NY 10010.

ISBN: 978-0-312-94323-3

Printed in the United States of America

St. Martin's Paperbacks edition / July 2010

St. Martin's Paperbacks are published by St. Martin's Press, 175 Fifth Avenue, New York, NY 10010.

10 9 8 7 6 5 4 3 2 1

CONTENTS

TEMPTATION ON ICE

Cherry Adair

CHAPTER ONE

Decommissioned Soviet Submarine Base #15
Arctic Ocean
90 00 N, 0 00 E

Invisible, Sebastian Tremayne and fellow T-FLAC operative Anatoly Cohen silently followed the three physicists, two male, one female, down the long, dimly lit corridor of Decommissioned Soviet Submarine Base #15.

The casual conversation of the targets wasn't relevant and Sebastian tuned it out. Half of him prayed the woman wasn't who he'd been told she was. The other half felt a surge of hope. The question was, what should he hope for? He looked at her and the question became instantly moot.

Her glossy chestnut hair was longer than it'd been the last time he'd seen her. But the color, even in the crappy lighting, was instantly recognizable. For a second he remembered the heavy, silken weight of it as he'd held her head in his palm and brought his mouth down on hers. Her hair had draped like a spill of satin over his fingers. Sebastian remembered the feel of her slender body pressed against him. He imagined he smelled the heady fragrance of night-blooming jasmine as the heat of her wrapped about him.

The smell of meat cooking on the grill outside, the sound of glasses clinking and people laughing, faded to nothing. For a few incredible minutes, standing there in a back hallway of his best friend's house, holding his best friend's fiancé, Sebastian had felt an aching yearning that had gone miles beyond sexual desire.

He walked a different hallway now. Cold, dim, and smelling of mold. This hallway was far more danger-ous than being caught kissing another man's woman. *Turn around, sweetheart, he* thought, angry with him-self as well as with her. *Let me see those big, beauti-ful lying brown eyes.*

As if she'd heard him, the woman turned her head to answer one of the men, giving Sebastian a clear view of her profile.

Sebastian looked into the very much alive face of a dead woman.

His heart raced. Michaela Giese. Beautiful, vibrant *Dr.* Michaela Giese. Very much alive after being de-clared dead two years ago. He sucked in an inaudible breath, his heart manic with lo—*lust*. With unre-quited *hunger.* Beating fast, because just *looking* at her turned him on like no other woman ever had, nor, he knew, ever would.

It took every ounce of fifteen years of T-FLAC training not to suck in a shocked breath, not to grab her, not to . . . Fuck—not to demand answers, right *now.*

They'd been right. She *was* here and responsible for building a nuclear bomb primed to detonate in mere hours. Set to melt the polar ice caps into a world-wide slushy margarita, flooding coastal cities, and within a short time, raising ocean levels. Fast.

Millions would die because of her actions. Because of her piss-poor choices. Unless ridiculous billions of dollars were paid to the terrorist she worked with by midnight.

Sebastian and Cohen were here to stop her.

The beautiful, breathing, lying, gut-yanking bitch was obviously ruthless enough to do it.

"That her?" Cohen whispered into his lip mic.

"Hell if I know." *Oh yeah.* He needed some time to get used to her being back from the dead. Along with the pieces of him that had gone into that empty grave with her.

His fingers flexed at his sides as her glossy ponytail swayed against her slender back as she walked. It would feel like heavy silk against his skin. He knew . . . He shook his head, as if to clear away cobwebs. *Get a grip, Tremayne; what do you really know about her?*

Had she intentionally faked the plane crash to come and work with the terrorists? *Jesus. Jesus. How long had* that *been going on?* He hated to believe it, but the evidence was too hard to negate. The timing had been just too fucking convenient.

Two years ago she'd abruptly called off her engagement to his best friend, fellow operative Cole Summers, a month after their engagement party. No explanations. But there'd been plenty of suspicions, most of them tossed his way by Cole afterward. It had been a major blowout that Sebastian and Cole had eventually managed to overcome.

A few days later, the bits and pieces of her crashed

Cessna had been found on the shores of the tiny island of Diomede in the middle of the fucking Bering Strait.

There'd been no body.

Speculation had run rife at T-FLAC HQ. As far as anyone knew, Michaela didn't know anyone locally. She was an experienced pilot, but there were no signs of foul play. She'd simply . . . vanished. Drowned in the icy sea. Or so everyone had believed.

Her funeral had been a seminal moment in his life.

"Still with me, bud?" Cohen asked quietly in Sebastian's headpiece.

"Yeah."

The long, narrow cement corridor, painted half filthy white and half puke green, had a domed ceiling and metal-caged, bare lightbulbs. A track ran down the middle, indicating that during the Cold War heavy equipment had to be transported to and from the dock at sea level.

Even with just his face and hands bare, it was freeze-his-balls-off cold, and Tremayne was grateful for the protection of his LockOut suit worn beneath a thick, hand-knit gray sweater and charcoal jeans. The insulated boots with the no-sound tread developed by the science geeks at T-FLAC were doing a good job of saving him from frostbitten toes. If they stayed in this corridor much longer, though, the gloves and face mask were going to come out of their pockets. He wondered if he had ice crystals in his eyebrows. . . .

Michaela was similarly dressed in a bulky brown sweater and too-long black pants, rolled up several times to accommodate her walking. She looked like a little girl playing dress-up in her father's clothes. But she wasn't a child. Whose clothes was she wearing?

Sebastian felt a surge of unwelcome annoyance at the direction of his thoughts. Even though Cole was now happily married and father to a delightful little girl, Sebastian still felt guilty as hell coveting his friend's fiancé.

Ex-fiancé.

Dead, miraculously alive ex-fiancé.

And that guilt and anger was without the added component of her contribution to this particular terrorist cell. *Damn damn damn.*

"Think they're heading to the nuke?" Cohen speculated. "If that's the case, we can be outta here in thirty minutes tops."

"When has an op ever been that fucking easy?" Sebastian rubbed the back of his neck. He trusted that itch, and it told him there was plenty of shit and several fans before they teleported out, job accomplished.

Ahead, one of the scientists they were following pushed open a rusted metal door, which creaked ominously. Michaela and the other man followed him inside. "—just ask that you check my numbers," the man in front said to Michaela.

"I'm sure there's nothing to w—" The thick, insulated door closed.

"I'll go see what's up," Cohen offered.

Sebastian leaned against the corridor wall to wait.

Would Michaela recognize him when she saw him again? Hell, would she even *remember* him? They'd met five times. Always with Cole and a group of friends. Every *second* of every one of those encounters was fresh in Sebastian's mind. *Hell.* He'd better get his shit together before he confronted her. He was here to do a job. A job he'd volunteered for even though it was one he didn't want.

Like it or not. He was a trained counterterrorist operative with a directive. Clear. Nonnegotiable. There was no wiggle room in his orders; personal feelings were not only unimportant, they were also forbidden.

A brush of air nearby indicated Cohen was back. "They're splitting up until a meeting in an hour."

"I'll take care of her." Sebastian's heart did a triple axel. "Maybe the guys will lead you to the lab?"

"That'll save time."

A technopath, Anatoly Cohen's power was the ability to control technology. They didn't need to know how to shut the nuke down or how the damn thing was rigged; Cohen would use mind control to jam the signals and rewire the thing without ever touching it.

The door opened and Michaela preceded the men back into the corridor. She had several large black binders cradled in her arms. "I'll look these over," she told the older man with a nose like a strawberry and thinning gray hair pasted to his shiny scalp. "But I'm sure you have nothing to worry about." The sound of her husky contralto went through Sebastian like the first rays of spring sunshine after a long, dark North Pole winter. Oblivious to his presence, Michaela was close enough to touch. The heady fragrance of jasmine was a ghost of his imagination. She'd lost weight. Too much weight. Her face was hollowed, her beautiful eyes shadowed and troubled.

"Please confirm my findings, Michaela. You know Tongpan." The shudder shaking the man's skinny frame had nothing to do with the Arctic air blowing through the corridor. Who was Tongpan? His name hadn't been on any of the intel they'd received. Tremayne made a mental note to pass it on to HQ later.

The waiting fishing trawler had dropped anchor six miles away early that morning. In case things turned to shit inside the sub base. Sebastian didn't anticipate trouble. The place was manned with geeks and low-level security people; the principals would control what was happening here from a remote— and safe—location.

"I'll check and triple check. *Again*," Michaela told the man soothingly. "I'm sure you have nothing to worry about. After all this time, you just need a few more hours of patience. Then all any of us can do is wait."

"Dr. Gangjon will expect us to go with him when he leaves?" Sebastian heard an invisible question mark at the end of the sentence. Hope and fear painted a stark mask on the man's horse-like features. The tall and painfully skinny guy's puppy-dog eyes watched Michaela's every move through bottle-thick glasses. Another sucker bites the dusk. Was he bitter? Hell no. She should just wear a goddamned warning sign on her chest: HEARTBREAKER!

About to turn the opposite direction down the passageway from her comrades, Michaela paused. "I sincerely hope you're right, Dr. Ackart." Her tone indicated she had no faith in his supposition whatsoever.

"Gonna catch up," Cohen said softly into his lip mic. "Cover my ass. Hell—better connect in case we get split up."

The thought had occurred to him. He reached out and closed his fingers around his partner's upper arm. Sebastian's ability to maintain invisibility would last another hour unless he once again made physical contact with Cohen to rejuice the power.

Sebastian had no powers of his own. Unlike Cohen, he wasn't a wizard. He was more of a supernatural freak of nature. He had one power, and one power only. As a power chameleon, he could absorb powers from a wizard by direct physical contact. Transmogrifying was a handy tool in his T-FLAC grab bag, but it didn't define him. Not enough to be part of T-FLAC's paranormal unit anyway.

The transference of Cohen's powers was an adrenaline spike that had Sebastian's heart galloping pleasantly.

"Man, I'm getting the sucky end of this assignment," Cohen said, clearly amused. "I get to go play mind fuck with a computer, while you get to fuck her."

"Can't do much about your short straw, man." Sebastian forced a lightness to his tone he in no way felt. "Go," he whispered into the mic and immediately felt the absence of the other man's heat signature beside him as Cohen teleported after the two scientists.

For several moments Sebastian just stood there, icy air playing against his face as she walked away from him, her steps brisk.

His eyes burned and his chest hurt like hell. He'd been handpicked over psi guys because of Cole's recommendation. Now that the persistent itch on his neck was increasing he had a damn good idea why.

The mission had started out simple. Get in, use

any means necessary to prevent the nuke from detonating, then get the hell out. He'd had no idea that
might include one-on-one time with the woman whose
"death" had ripped his heart to shreds. Cole didn't
blame the breakup on Sebastian anymore, but he knew
damn well that Tremayne would recognize her if she
were indeed there. But there was a world of difference between "see if she's there" and "do what you
must if she is."

With Michaela in the mix, this wasn't just another
ball game; this was the Super Bowl. Winner take all.
And he was a piss-poor loser.

Why the fuck did it have to be you, Michaela?

CHAPTER TWO

Michaela removed the broom handle she'd used to bar the bathroom door. A necessary, if not lifesaving, measure she never forgot. There were twenty-five rusted showerheads on each of two cement walls, twenty-five urinals and washbasins on the third, and doorless toilets on the fourth. No doors, no curtains, no locks. It took the definition of no-frills to new heights—or depths. She wondered if the substation had always been this bleak or if the last troops had simply stripped it as they left.

Twenty minutes under a hot spray was one of the things she'd missed most since the kidnapping. Okay, she missed sex even more. But not enough to welcome the advances of anyone on base.

The bathroom stank of mold and desperation and was so cold she could see her breath. She pulled open the heavy metal door leading out into the corridor, carrying her kit bag and the broom handle, a thin towel wrapped around her wet hair.

As the only woman on base, taking precautions, especially when she was naked, was second nature. The security guys in particular were persistently horny and determined. She'd had several really bad moments over the past twenty-three months, so she was ever vigilant, and *always* prepared for the worst.

As a physicist on counterterrorist organization T-FLAC's payroll, Michaela had quickly learned to adjust. Especially since it was clear there was absolutely no way to leave. Not alive. Dead meant she couldn't sabotage the project. She had to stay alive and finish the end game.

So, while she hadn't been sent on this op, she considered herself deep undercover. There was no one to report to, no one who knew where she was. No one who gave a flying frick if she lived or died. The only unshakable certainty she had was that what she did here would eventually count. With that she was satisfied.

As a nuclear physicist she was an *experimentalist,* into designing and constructing experiments that led to observation and tests of theoretical prediction. Even though she'd been kidnapped to work on the nuclear weapon, she'd never had any contact with, nor interest in, nuclear weaponry while working for the counterterrorist organization. She'd applied herself diligently, however, when she hadn't been given multiple-choice.

There'd be the last-minute briefing in an hour. But Richard Ackart was wrong. Dr. Gangjon, Bingwen Ling, and Afanasei Popov had left the base in the wee hours that morning.

Tongpan could easily have teleported them out, but he never bothered to make it easy for anyone coming or going. They'd left, quickly and quietly, early that morning under their own steam. Michaela had watched the two-man submarines slip under the ink-black frozen waters and disappear into the darkness.

They wouldn't be back. It was one step up from rats deserting a sinking ship; in this case, the ship was going to blow up, and the rats not only knew it, they'd arranged it.

Gerald Malard, the British physicist, was somewhere about. She hadn't seen him leaving with the others.

Those who were left behind were justifiably scared, not knowing what the next few hours would bring. Unfortunately, as both a realist and a pragmatist, Michaela knew damn well what was going to happen. Had already happened.

She, the other two kidnapped physicists, and the security people had been left behind. They were expendable. There was no reprieve.

She never knew how or when Tongpan, the head honcho, came or went. With his long, white, cotton-candy fine hair, deep-set black eyes, and propensity for violence, he scared the living crap out of her. As did Kang Gangjon, his frighteningly, deceptively handsome second in command. Even though the next few hours here would be her last, she was grateful not to have to see those two monsters again.

She'd go to the last meeting in a little while. She'd smile and make small talk, and then . . . she'd wait for the end.

The last meeting.

This, she thought with gallows humor, was a day for lasts.

The air in the corridor was Arctic cold despite the thick sweats she wore. *Damn.* They had money for all the high-tech crap in the world, but one decent pair of warm pants that fit? Nope. She tried picturing a hot tropical beach as she jogged back to her room, but the sound of her own teeth chattering spoilt the dim image. Even though there was no chance of her getting out of this alive, her favorite fantasy involved hot sand, warm surf, and scorching sex with the right guy.

And Michaela knew precisely who she'd fantasize about. Cole's best friend, Sebastian Tremayne. With nearly blue-black hair, shoulders stacked out to there, and a smile that could knock a woman senseless at fifty paces, he'd earned a reputation at T-FLAC HQ for being a hotshot, not just in the field but in the sack as well. Not that she'd gotten to find out.

Her engagement to Cole had ended when she'd met the best man, Sebastian, at her engagement party. She'd seen him a few times before but hadn't actually spoken to him, looked into those eyes, or felt her entire body come alive the way it did as he shook her hand and congratulated her on the upcoming wedding.

It had been a revelation. She'd suddenly realized that her relationship with Cole, while comfortable, was no more than friendship with fringe benefits. Cole didn't rock her world.

Sebastian Tremayne had rocked her world. Just back from a long op in South America, they'd seen him *everywhere* those few weeks. In spite of herself, Sebastian had instantly and completely intrigued and captivated Michaela. Not just his dark brooding good looks. Not that single dimple in his right cheek. No, she'd loved the richness of his voice. The flash of humor that lit those piercing pale blue eyes. Blue eyes that had avoided hers when she'd glanced his way and caught him watching her through half-lidded eyes.

Meeting him had been bad timing. After she'd

broken off the engagement, she'd gone for that fateful solo flight to clear her head. She'd never gotten to explain to him why she'd ditched Cole or how attracted she was to him—enough to change the course of her life if he was interested.

Since then, Tremayne had starred in all of her incredibly hot, breathless fantasies. His dimpled smile, the heat in his blue eyes, and the phantom touch of his skin against hers had kept her sane for 703 nights.

Michaela glanced at her watch and picked up a bit of speed. . . . Half an hour . . . She smiled. "Sebastian, here I come."

She paused outside the reinforced metal door to her small cell of a room as the damp towel wrapped around her head slid to the floor. Bending down to pick it up, she was hit with a frigid blast of cold air and her entire body shuddered. Uneasy, she briskly towel-dried her shoulder-length hair, glancing up and down the dimly lit corridor until she was certain no one was lurking. Assured no one was lying in wait, she shoved open the heavy, reinforced door. No lock here, either.

The 75-watt, yellow hallway light spilled into black as the door swung open. She'd left the small lamp beside the bed on. *Hell.* The room was so small she'd have to go inside and close the door to reach the switch. Even the pale light from the corridor was better than nothing at all. Darkness had never bothered her before she'd been imprisoned in a hostile environment, against her will, three hundred meters beneath the ice pack.

Michaela swore under her breath. Everything was

either pitch-dark or deeply shadowed beyond the meager cone of light. She couldn't see a damn thing, but the hair on the back of her neck prickled a warning. Her instincts had saved her from rape and worse a dozen times since she'd been here. She wasn't about to doubt herself now.

"Whoever the hell you are, show yourself." She wanted to claim she was armed, that she had a 9 mm and would blow a freaking hole in his groin. But other than her handy-dandy, ever-present broom handle and her little kit bag, she was unarmed, and everyone on the base knew it.

The silence hummed.

She wasn't foolish enough to believe the lightbulb had died. If her room was dark now, it was because someone wanted it that way. If that someone was inside, running back into the corridor would just mark her as prey. And stepping *into* the confined space with an adversary was just asking for trouble.

Damned if she did. Damned if she didn't.

Either someone had finally found out what she had planned and was here to stop her or the tension of the impending countdown was too much and some idiot had decided he needed to nail her once and for all.

A surge of adrenaline sharpened her senses and reflexes. She dropped the towel and kit bag and tightened her fingers around the thick shaft of the broom handle as she shoved the door closed with her foot.

Now they were both trapped.

Instead of ramming the straight-backed, military-issue chair under the door handle as she usually did, Michaela wrapped her fingers around the cool metal,

ready to use the piece of furniture as a weapon if
necessary. Chair in one hand, stick in the other, she
felt like a fricking lion tamer.

Even with her excellent hearing, she didn't pick up
so much as a shallow breath, but she was 99.9 per-
cent positive she wasn't alone. "You've got five seconds to get the hell out, no questions asked." She
inhaled deeply and centered her body weight, the
way her instructor had taught her back in another
life. "After that I'm going to break your dick in half."

A muffled chuckle was followed by a quiet, "Shhh."
A large hand clamped over her mouth, shocking her
into dropping the stick. *Fricking hell. Assholes never
learned.* With her intensive T-FLAC training she figured she could handle any man on this base. Other
than Gangjor or Tongpan, who were too evil to be
mere men.

The minute the stranger touched her she dug her
short nails into his hand. With a soft oath he pulled
her hard against his chest. Six three or four. Rock-
solid abs.

Who was it this time? Sergei? Too tall. Richard?
Too solid.

Michaela managed to get her mouth open just
enough to bite down hard. She tasted his blood. Good.
A knock-down, drag-out fight would deplete the sur-
plus adrenaline surging through her body. But a fight
wasn't what he wanted, and she was suddenly terrified he'd prevent her doing her last-minute sabotage to
the nuclear device. Then everything she'd endured for
two years would be in vain. She fought him like a
wild woman. Teeth, nails, knees, and fists.

"Jesus, it's m—"

She wasn't in the mood for *chatty.* Wrapping her

fingers around the base of his thumb, she wrenched it back, trying to break his hold. No go. She chopped at his thick wrist. That didn't fricking work, either. Reaching over her head with both hands, Michaela grabbed the intruder in a headlock and attempted to throw him. Too centered. Dropping her hands, she shot a hard elbow into his gut, followed by a head butt backward, which made *her* see stars and elicited zero reaction from him.

She realized that the height difference had rendered the move useless—his face and throat were too damn high for her to reach that way. To be effective she needed to turn around and face him. The room was small, barely eight by six. The hard edge of the chair pressed against her knees, which meant the narrow bed was behind him. She couldn't get enough leverage to hit him with the chair; he was holding her immobile. If she could get a good grip, she could use his own body as a fulcrum and—

His warm, damp breath caressed her shower-damp neck. "I'm letting go, Michaela. Don't scream."

As if. She nodded. Hard to ID him from the almost inaudible whisper so close to her ear. Not that she cared which of her captors or fellow scientists he was. Not at this late stage of the game.

As much as she'd been thinking about sex, or the lack thereof for the past two years due to being fricking *kidnapped* by these terrorists, being raped mere hours before her death was unacceptable in every way. Michaela knew to the second when her time was up, and now wasn't when.

As much as she would've liked having hot, breathless sex one last time before she croaked, this wasn't how she wanted it.

He removed his callused hand. Her mouth felt numb from the pressure, but her mind was going a mile a minute as she slowly reached for the door handle a foot away.

Strong fingers closed around her wrist. "Stay." It was darker than a witch's heart and he unerringly found her wrist? That was serious training. Having no idea who she was dealing with complicated things, and suddenly her heart pumped even harder. She'd worked beside these men for twenty-three months. She *knew* them. Had studied their strengths and weaknesses. She still couldn't place the intruder.

"You imbecile," she spat out, keeping her body moving in the cage of his arms, keeping her mind jumping with possible escape scenarios. "You're jeopardizing the project because you want to get *laid*? Get the hell out before I emasculate you."

He muttered something hot and low, then spun her around so fast it made her dizzy. Disoriented in the darkness, she managed to close her fingers on his forearms for balance, then dug her nails into—a wet suit? Protective clothing of some sort? Someone *stupid* enough to think he could escape by swimming away from the base?

Nobody would give a damn if she screamed her lungs out. Everyone in the decommissioned submarine base had more exciting things to deal with right now than her. Still, he might not like having sex with a shrill, shrieking woman.

Yeah? part of her brain mocked. A man without sex for two years and he'd give a rat's ass if she were screaming like a banshee while he pumped into her? Not.

She opened her mouth to scream blue bloody

murder anyway. If he was Gromyko or Ackart, he'd run. Neither man was this confrontational. If he was Ling, Popov, or Malard, he'd rape, *then* kill her. And if this was Gangjon returned, she'd be praying for a quick death. Michaela managed to release a high-pitched shriek. There was zero chance of anyone hearing her. The walls were three feet thick. The conference room they used was clear on the other side of the underwater complex.

His mouth closed down on hers with no warning, effectively shutting her up. Stealing her air and her ability to scream. Iron-strong arms wrapped around her body, lifting her off her feet. He backed across the room.

No, oh no, oh fricking no!

His arms were locked over hers, but she wriggled and kicked like a wild woman. Legs, knees, feet. Anything she could use to make contact.

She was too close to her objective to allow anyone to stop her now. Two years of her life would be wasted if this caveman did worse than rape her. He was strong enough, determined enough, to kill her.

Too soon. She jumped up against him, locking her legs around his waist, her arms around his neck. A lover's position, but also one that could break his neck if she exerted just the right pressure here, and here—

He bit her lower lip. Michaela's heart raced and her adrenaline shot off the charts as they fell awkwardly onto the narrow cot. The springs shrieked, and the metallic taste of blood caused her heart to thunder in her ears as she battered whatever she could reach with her fists and heels. Her back slammed painfully into the concrete wall beside the bed.

Despite being a lab rat for T-FLAC rather than a field operative, she'd enjoyed her combat training, and had maintained that same level of fitness. Especially in the last couple of years. She was fit and strong. He was stronger.

Attack.

Counterattack.

The guy's powerful hips pressed down, trapping her crossed ankles at the small of his back. *Not good. Oh, God. Really not good.* Worse, she was straddling his groin. He was fully aroused as he rolled her under him, effectively pinning her body, her arms, and her legs.

"Stop. You'll hurt yourself," he said harshly against her ear in an achingly familiar voice that convinced her she was hallucinating. "Damn it, Michaela. It's me. Sebastian Tremayne."

CHAPTER THREE

Heat of a different kind flooded Michaela's body, even though there was no fricking way he could possibly be who he claimed to be.

Sebastian Tremayne?

Impossible.

Not out in the godforsaken Arctic, under three hundred meters of ice. There wasn't a snowball's hope in hell for T-FLAC to know where to start looking for her. And no way they would've taken *two years* to extract her if they did.

While she'd been thinking about Tremayne a lot lately, and in positions much like this one, a fantasy wasn't the same as a full-out physical manifestation, delicious as his body felt between her knees. Maybe she was having a psychotic break? "Liar!"

Had they watched her in her room at night? *God! Had they seen—* Furious, cheeks hot, chest heaving, Michaela aimed a punch to his face. Before it landed he grabbed her balled fist in his. His hand was enormous, enclosing her hand completely in the cage of his fingers.

"Engagement party," he said flatly, gripping her wrists to hold her bucking body still, his hips and the hard ridge of his erection pressing harder against the cradle of her pelvis. "Bozeman. May seventeenth two years ago. You wore a strapless little red number. Made me deaf, blind, and stupid the second I laid eyes on you. And the afternoon of the barbeque . . ."

She stopped fighting. *Oh, God. How could anyone here know about that life-changing night?* The reaction had been mutual and directly responsible for her breaking off her engagement a month later. One look at the tall and brooding Tremayne with his intense pale blue eyes and unsmiling mouth and Michaela had instantly forgotten her brand-new fiancé, Cole Summers.

They'd been walking down the same back hallway at Cole's house when Tremayne had said her name in that low, sexy rumble of his. He leaned in as the best man to give her a congratulatory kiss on the cheek, she'd turned her head at the last second, and they'd ended up kissing. What started out as an accidental brush of his mouth against hers had turned into an instant inferno that left them both breathing hard.

He'd braced his hands on either side of her head, his breath hot and heavy against her neck. "We can't do this."

Michaela had let her head drop against the wall, her heart beating so hard it threatened to burst out of her bra. "You going to say anything to Cole?"

She'd never seen a more forlorn look in her life than the one she saw flit through Sebastian's eyes. "Nope. This never happened."

"Good." She pushed away from the wall and held out a hand. "Friends?"

All he'd done was nod in agreement before turning on his heel and walking quickly away from her down the hallway. But that was then, and this was now. Sebastian wasn't some erotic figment of her imagination. He wasn't off-limits. He was hard and real and his heart pounded just as fiercely as hers.

In the dark she freed one hand and, with rising wonder and unsteady fingers, traced the rough planes of his face. His strong nose, the roughness of his jaw, the long, almost imperceptible slash of a dimple in his right cheek thrilled her.

They'd never touched again after that night, yet she recognized the texture of his skin, knew the *smell* of him.

Her heartbeat went from fear-frantic to lust-induced, manic tom-tom in a tenth of a second. "Sebastian." A frisson ran from her temple to her toes and the tight place inside her chest unfurled as she breathed his name. "Are you real?"

In response he plunged his fingers into her wet hair. Gripping her head in a hard palm, he took her mouth in a rough, carnal kiss that left nothing to the imagination. She knew precisely what he wanted because ever since that night, she'd been wanting it, too. She responded with equal passion, snaking her hand around to the back of his neck and holding him in place as she thoroughly enjoyed her first real-world kiss in way, way too long.

His mouth left hers, and she whimpered in protest. "Come back; I wasn't done."

"Patience is a virtue." He nibbled her earlobe, making her shudder, then swirled his hot, wet tongue in her ear until she arched her neck with a thick moan. His mouth, tongue, and teeth made her forget where she was for just a little while. Made her forget where she was and what was about to transpire.

Sebastian shifted his head the few inches required to plunder her mouth again. She saw fireworks behind her closed lids as he dragged his firm mouth back and forth across hers before plunging his tongue back to duel with hers.

Dizzy with lust and longing, heart about to burst out of her chest, Michaela couldn't—forgot to—draw a breath and ripped her lips from his to drag in lifesaving oxygen. "You're t-torturing me—"

"Breathing is highly overrated." With his free hand he gripped the hem of her sweatshirt and pulled away long enough to drag the garment over her head. Then his hot, avid mouth was back on hers before the chill of the room could compute in her muzzy brain.

Michaela surrendered to the kiss, stroking his face as he made love to her mouth. God, she wished the light was on so she could be sure this was real and not the usual graphic fantasy. Although God only knew her fantasies had been good, but never *this* good.

She stroked Sebastian's lips with her tongue, and he bit her lower lip. Her heartbeat skittered and pulsed as his other hand slid under her tank top to cup her bare breast as he continued kissing her as if he were starving and she a feast.

Her heartbeat, already manic with the adrenaline spike, shot into the stratosphere like a rocket as he caught her nipple, rolling and pulling it between his fingers as he devoured her mouth with teeth and tongue. Tears stung her eyes, and a rush of pain/pleasure hurt her heart—a reaction to being touched after so long without human contact. A visceral response to *him*. *God*. He was here. Like a hero out of some fantasy novel. The good guy sweeping in at the eleventh hour to save her.

She'd resigned herself to the inevitability of death.

He'd brought her life.

Love and unspeakable gratitude filled her chest to bursting.

His fingers bunched the thin top, gliding it sensuously up her back; then that, too, was discarded. Her nipples pinched tight at the brush of his hand. "I want to see you naked," he murmured, trailing his lips down her arched throat.

Yes. God, yes. She needed to see as well as feel his hot, satin-smooth skin. Wanted to see the crisp hair on his chest, wanted to watch as his pale eyes lost focus with desire. "Light," she demanded, her voice hoarse with urgency.

"Hmm." He slid down her body, then surrounded her nipple with the wet heat of his mouth and clamped down on the hard bud lightly with his teeth. Her hips bucked off the bed with the intense pleasure shooting through her body. Bringing her knees up, she clamped them around his narrow hips as he nibbled delicately at her painfully aroused nipples. First one and then the other, and then back again.

She started tugging at his clothing. The shirt was relatively easy—just a matter of disengaging long enough to deal with buttons and sleeves, and dispersal. The LockOut he wore beneath it required him rolling off her to strip. While he peeled off the skintight protective clothing, Michaela yanked off her drawstring pants and panties, and lay back to wait for him.

"I can't believe— Hmm." Sebastian blanketed her body with his, cutting her off. The feel of him on top of her made Michaela want to freeze time and stay this way always. She couldn't see him in the stygian darkness, but God, she felt every delicious battle-hard inch of him pressed against every sex-starved inch of her.

He kissed her deeply, lips and tongue avid until her mind disengaged and all she could do was feel, all the atoms within her gone wild in a fission chain reaction to his touch.

With surprise, she heard the rip of foil, then felt him shift as he rolled on a condom. "You thought to bring a rubber on an op? On a rescue missi—"

He pushed into her, his large body shaking with his attempt to control himself as he slid into her wet heat with ease.

Michaela instantly started to move her hips. His penis was huge. Long and thick and incredibly hard as he pushed up inside her.

"Don't," he managed to grit out, "move. Need . . . a minute."

She was a nanosecond from the biggest orgasm of her life, and he told her not to move? A keening sound reverberated deep in her throat as she tightened her legs around his hips and dug her short nails into his shoulders.

His entire body shuddered as he tried to keep control. But it was too late. With a feral growl he thrust into her, hard and deep, unable to delay the inevitable. For either of them.

Clenching around him, Michaela came hard. Once.

Twice. Three times in quick succession, every nerve on fire, every pore open and saturated with the feel of him on her, in her, until her entire body was as nothing more than light, air, and energy. Her muscles and nerves caught up in the nuclear explosion within her that torqued all her senses beyond bearing.

Silently Sebastian came, too. His face buried in her neck, his arms clamped around her body, his fingers gripping her ass. She'd have bruises there in an hour, but she didn't give a damn. He cupped her to him so tightly, as if he never planned to let her go. The good news was it was a perfect fit. The bad news, that it had happened too fast, for both of them.

The darkness of the room was filled with the sound of their rough breathing. Their bodies were slick with sweat; their heartbeats syncopated and still pounding at a wild pace.

He started to pull out of her, but Michaela imprisoned him with her arms and legs. "Wait; not yet." Reality would come knocking any minute, and after two miserable years, surely she was entitled to a few more moments of bliss.

Sebastian in her arms was infinitely better than Sebastian in her fantasies. Yes, it had been wild and almost desperate. Yes, it had been pretty damn fast. But she'd loved every sweaty, pulse-pounding second of it, and she'd been the one who hadn't wanted to hold on for even one more minute. It was almost unbelievable—she'd gone from thinking about having hot, breathless sex with Sebastian to *having* incredibly hot and completely breathless sex with Sebastian.

Powerful and primal, he hadn't "made love" to her. He'd mated with her.

Michaela wondered if he'd know the difference. She'd love to find out. Sebastian in primal mode was amazing. Sebastian making love would likely be mind-blowing.

Then, perhaps selfishly, she wondered if they could do it again before they both got back to the business of saving the world.

CHAPTER FOUR

Michaela slid an arm and shapely leg across his hip.
The glide of her silky skin poured a rush of testosterone-fueled heat through every sensitized inch of
Sebastian's body. Catching her musky scent, his nostrils flared. The cheap soap from her recent shower
smelled clean and fresh mixed with the natural
fragrance of her skin. And far more seductive than
a designer fragrance. The toothpaste she'd used reminded him of how she'd tasted as his body had
pounded into her.

Fuckit!

For those minutes, as her body clenched around
him, as her arms and legs had drawn him harder and
more tightly against her clenching wet heat, Sebastian had forgotten his directive: Allow Cohen time
to use his unique powers to disable the nuke; find out
what Michaela knew and why she'd turned rogue.
Get names, places, and dates.

Fuck her if necessary to allay any suspicions that
he was aware she'd turned.

Then kill her.

He'd wanted to prove them wrong. The woman

he'd known so briefly was incapable of pulling off a terrorist act so heinous.

But facts, supported by intel, proved he was a fool. A wrong fool who thought with his dick. *She* was the lead physicist on this project. *She'd* done "excellent work, and was to be commended."

That was a direct quote from one of the messages Intel had intercepted, a report from a Dr. Ackart to a Dr. Gangjon. The son of a bitch had gone on at length, describing the skills of the admirable, indispensable Dr. Giese and her immeasurable contributions to the success of the project.

Fuckshitdamncrap.

There were a thousand things Sebastian had wanted to do to Michaela. Killing her hadn't been— still wasn't—on the list.

Bad enough the one with the bull's-eye on her forehead was *her,* but he had serious misgivings when he'd insisted on coming on the op. Misgivings he'd kept hidden, because, fool that he was, he'd hoped . . .

He was a seasoned T-FLAC operative. Hope was not allowed to play a role in his professional life, and he didn't *have* a life outside of the profession these days. T-FLAC operatives were trained to do whatever was needed, anywhere in the world, to get the job done. They took out tangos to make the world a safer place. Michaela's work was jeopardizing that safety.

Sebastian was known as a disciplined man. He'd do what had to be done. He still had an erection. So what? He could still fire a weapon—dick be damned.

Still, killing a woman, *any* woman, in cold blood went against the grain. Killing *this* woman who'd been an integral part of his fantasy life for the past two years . . .

Stop whining and do your fucking job, Tremayne.

She'd been so damned smart and funny, quick to catch his silly jokes. She'd shared his sense of humor. . . .

Reality check. She was responsible for the arming of the nuclear bomb.

He wished he could see her. But he'd needed the element of surprise the darkness had afforded him. Now he regretted removing the lightbulb, because he wanted to see her naked. Wanted, damn it, just this once, to see each exquisite inch of the body he'd only dreamed about.

Fucking her was his job. That's all it was. *Yeah, right.*

He'd followed her from the corridor to her room and, once he'd seen the towel and kit bag in her hand when she emerged, opted to search her room while she showered. A wise move as it happened, because seeing her wet and naked would possibly have changed the course of events irrevocably.

There'd been nothing incriminating in the small, neat space. But then he hadn't expected there to be. Michaela was brilliant as well as clever. She'd leave no trace of her defection on the off chance the good guys ever searched the submarine base for clues.

She combed her fingers lightly through the mat of hair on his chest and brushed a kiss across his pec that shot like a bullet straight to his heart. "Are you sleeping?" she asked, then kissed him again.

"Just for a few minutes, then we can see if we can

do that a little slower." He kept the anger out of his voice with difficulty. "Shh. Close your eyes and rest with me for a bit."

"I have to— Sure." He felt the flutter of her long lashes against his skin as her muscles relaxed.

Damn it, Michaela—

For a year after her "death" he'd held her memory on a pedestal. A fucking high pedestal. She was everything he wanted but couldn't have. The Holy Grail who had broken his best friend's heart. For ninety days anyway. Cole had gotten over her betrayal and departure a hell of a lot faster than Sebastian.

Until intel showed she'd crashed her Cessna intentionally.

A year later, her defection had been proven by communiqués between the Chinese and Russian tangos indicating the terrorists were pleased with Dr. Michaela Giese's progress.

He'd mourned her death for a fucking year. Then spent the next year wanting to kill her.

That's why she'd broken off with Cole less than a month after their engagement. *That's* why she'd fled without telling anyone. *That's* why, without a fucking backward glance, she'd ripped out the hearts and souls of everyone who'd loved her. She sure as shit hadn't cared about the mind-blowing kiss they'd shared. Hell, no. She'd probably forgotten *that*.

And taking a stroll barefoot down the hot coals of the past was no way to do his job. He had to maintain a calm exterior and this wasn't the way to do it. Back to the matter at hand. Literally.

Sebastian trailed his fingers down the curve of her spine and up the swell of her ass. She shivered, shifting against him, her silky skin cool to the touch.

Everything primal in him screamed to protect her, draw her naked body closer to his own. But his intellect, his training, gave him a swift round kick to the head.

She's a tango. Don't trust how you feel. Trust what you know.

"Cold?" If this was the right thing to do, then why the hell did just doing his job feel like a betrayal?

"No. Yes," she said, nuzzling his chest as she shivered again. "It's always cold here. But your body is as toasty-warm as an electric blanket. This is the warmest I've been in years— No, don't move; I don't need anything covering me but you."

Damn it. She was a snuggler. Her breath was warm on his skin as she dropped small kisses wherever she could reach. In another time, another place, it would have been perfect. He would have reveled in the feeling of her curling up against him like a kitten. Now it was torture because he wasn't wishing he knew what her creamy skin or tight heat felt like; he God damn well knew.

"How did you find me?"

Like it or resist it, her kisses and petting touches had already given him a cockstand. "Intel between the Russians and Chinese," he said flatly, willing the erection away. Once was for king and country; twice was a whole other ball game. "Your name was mentioned." Seven times. In glowing terms.

"How long ago?"

How long since he'd known she'd turned was really what she was asking. "Year."

A few beats of silence echoed in the darkness as her finger traced a figure eight over his heart. "How's Cole doing?"

"Married with a kid and another on the way," he told her boldly, capturing her hand to keep it still so he could concentrate on something other than the feel of her. "I'm godfather to his daughter."

"I'm glad he's moved on."

"Are you?"

"Yes." She shook her head gently, and that silky chestnut hair teased his nipples. "I never wanted him to be unhappy."

If that were truly the case, she'd be married to the poor bastard right now. Not turned rogue and about to unleash a nuclear bomb that would flood the world and plunge it back into the Dark Ages. He couldn't help it; he had to say something.

"You not only ripped out his heart without anesthetic, you stomped on it for good measure when you walked out on m—*him* without explanation." The memory snagged in his constricted throat. Cole, on the other hand, had moved on within months. Sebastian wished *he* could have fucking done the same.

She turned her face into his chest and replied, her voice subdued, "I didn't have a choice."

Yeah? How much did they pay you? "Everyone has choices, Michaela."

"Not everyone."

Sebastian wished this interlude were over. Her rubbing her body around his like a cat in heat wasn't helping his resolve.

He gauged the time and realized that he needed to delay her at least another half hour to give Cohen time to disable the nuke. Their encounter had been too fast.

Cohen needed time. Especially if part of the nuke was Chinese and the other part Russian. Cohen could manipulate both, but he had to speak the language of the original components to get them to respond, which took time.

"They eventually found the wreckage." Her heat suddenly became like a brand to his skin. No longer sensual, but caustic. He wanted to get off the bed. He wanted to be fully dressed, armed to the teeth. He wanted, God damn it, the light on and an ocean between them.

What he really fucking wanted was a frontal lobotomy so he could forget she'd ever existed.

"Everyone presumed you were lost at sea." *Except me. No. I was idiot enough to hold out hope that you were still alive.* Picking up her hand, he kissed the center of her palm, and she sucked in a breath. "Cole and I went to your funeral, June twenty-eighth. Wasn't a dry eye in the place."

The two friends had gone to the crash site together. Been part of the search team. Her body hadn't been found. In the end, they'd buried an empty coffin.

For the first time in his life, Sebastian had drunk himself into oblivion on returning home. His binge had lasted a week. The memory far longer.

She raised her head, and the heat of her gaze bore through him even in the absolute darkness that engulfed them. "How did you get here, Sebastian— teleportation?"

"Yeah."

"You couldn't do that on your own."

She knew he wasn't part of T-FLAC's paranormal division. He had a power but not wizard-level powers.

She was working the angles. Trying to figure out how to take the money and run.

Not so fast, sweetheart. Without a submarine—and

the one at the dock was decrepit and useless; they'd checked—the only way in or out was swim or tele-port. Nobody would last ten seconds in the freezing Arctic Ocean without becoming an insta-Popsicle, not even with a full-body LockOut suit inside a dry dive suit. There wasn't anyone who would aid her when this particular shit hit the fan of her making. No one.

She lifted her head in the darkness, her body tensing. "Cole?"

The question was a gun to Sebastian's head. *Shit.* He knew she still had feelings for Cole no matter what she said. He was still a fucking idiot.

"Not the only wizard with T-FLAC. Anatoly Cohen teleported me in."

She shifted so her chin was propped on her palm, which lay uncomfortably over Sebastian's churning heart. "I have some things I have to do before we can leave."

You won't do either, Sebastian thought savagely, rolling over to cover her body and pin her where she lay. *Not "do some things" nor leave.*

Maybe, if he was very lucky, confirming her death for himself would eventually give him peace.

God, he hoped so, because living without her had been purgatory.

CHAPTER FIVE

She'd fantasized about being with Sebastian for so long she was afraid this was too good to be true. Michaela knew she only had a few more minutes to bask in the amazing postcoital glow of real sex with a very real Sebastian. A few more minutes to relish the lazy stroke of his hand caressing her skin, a few more minutes to listen to the steady beat of his heart beneath her cheek.

The others expected her. More important, she had a job to finish. No matter how much she wanted to pretend everything was normal, it wasn't.

"How did they convince you to join them?" Sebastian asked, his voice noticeably cooler than moments before. "How long before you accepted Cole's proposal did you decide you were going to screw him?"

For several erratic beats of her heart, Michaela couldn't understand his questions. The sound of her pulse was roaring too loud in her ears. Lifting her head from the warmth of his broad chest, she tried to marshal her thoughts. Anger replaced the afterglow as his words dropped onto her heart like an anvil. "What?"

Damn it to hell. Where was the light so she could see his face? She sat up, her back against the icy-cold steel wall butted up to one side of the narrow bed.

"Let me get this straight," Michaela said through clenched teeth. "Are you accusing me of *turning*?" Was her heart beating? She sure as hell couldn't feel it as her temper rose. "Of signing up with a group of known tangos? Assisting them in their attempt to melt the polar ice cap to— Do you think I came here *willingly,* you stupid son of a bitch?" Pitch-dark or not, she was seeing red.

Tight fingers manacled her wrist as she struck out. Clearly his night vision was excellent, because she couldn't see him at all. Tears of fury and hurt stung her eyes, and she curled her fingers against her palm hard enough to feel the bite of her short nails.

"Oh, I *know* so, sweetheart."

"Screw you!" she said, stung. Angry. Hurt. "Don't—" *Call me endearments with so much disdain.* She shook off the prison of his fingers. He took up the whole damn bed. To leave the room—hell, just to get to her clothes—she'd have to crawl over him.

Kicking him in the thigh, she snarled, "Get the hell out of my bed." He sat up, but she could tell he was still blocking her way intentionally. She kicked him again and he grabbed her foot. His hands were hot and hard, and he didn't let go no matter how much she fought him. Fine. She stopped struggling and remained perfectly still.

"Tell me you didn't sign up for a fat paycheck." How could he sound so . . . so *callous,* so uncaring? How could she have misread him so completely?

"I didn't sign up for *anything*." She took pride in the fact that while angry tears streamed warm and salty down her cheeks, they weren't evident in her voice. "I took a short flight out of Bozeman to clear my head. The next thing I knew, I was here."

"Except the Cessna was discovered on the rocky shores of Diomede in the middle of the fucking Bering Strait just a hop, skip, and jump from here! Explain that."

Hurt started pushing aside anger, forming a large, unswallowable lump in her throat. She liked the anger better. "Tongpan," she answered simply. "Please let me up. I'm running out of time, and I don't owe you any expla—"

"Who or what is Tongpan?"

"What the hell do you mean, who or what is Tongpan? Don't you know? Doesn't HQ know? He's the terrifying and powerful wizard responsible for kidnapping me mid-flight. The guy whose sick mind came up with this insane scheme. The guy that T-FLAC damn well should have known about ages ago. What the hell are they doing at HQ, playing tiddlywinks and taking naps?"

How was it possible that the organization that was so interconnected with the wizard world was unaware of the existence of the terrifying man who had forced her to participate in this nightmare, who'd not permitted her to take her own life rather than do what he wanted? She refused to dwell on the beatings, the starvation, the threats, and the torture endured to ensure her cooperation.

She thought grimly that if the light were on, Sebastian would see some of the scars on the skin he'd been stroking just moments before—the external scars, at least. She'd made good use of the self-hypnosis skills that T-FLAC's instructors had drilled her in so rigorously; otherwise, she'd be at the mercy of night terrors for the rest of her life.

She'd endured all that and more until she'd figured out a way to reverse everything she and the other nuclear physicists had done in two years. When they'd locked her, freshly beaten and naked, in an empty, cold room filled with harsh light to keep her from sleeping, she'd mentally turned the blank walls into whiteboards. She focused on those walls and drew schematics and formulae for hours on end, until she'd found the perfect solution, an invisible Trojan horse she could drive right through the middle of their plans.

True, it lacked an exit plan—maybe it wasn't perfect after all. But she was satisfied that she'd be able to defeat her captors. Then she'd been as docile and compliant as Tongpan and Gangjon wanted. It had been hard to convince them that her breakdown was genuine, and she felt that she deserved an Oscar. It would have to be posthumous, but still . . .

She felt the blast-furnace heat of his body as he shifted, still blocking her exit. His warmth didn't in any way mitigate her bone-deep chill. She'd never be warm again.

"Never heard of this Tongpan." Sebastian's tone was dismissive, raising her blood pressure a few more points. Great—T-FLAC didn't know about Tongpan, so Sebastian was prepared to write him off as insignificant. He deserved to be blown up, dammit. Then he could meet Tongpan in hell.

"Yeah? Well, I don't give a flying crap one way or

the other." She couldn't wrap her brain around the fact that Sebastian had made love to her. Not out of desire but to extract information. No wonder it had been fast. He wanted to get it over with as quickly as possible. She suddenly wanted a shower, and for once, she wanted it to be cold. Just as ice-cold as her insides felt at the thought of him using her like any operative would use a tango to get what they wanted.

Her throat went tight. "Did you—" *Come to extract me or neutralize me?* was the question she was too damned chicken to ask. She didn't want to know the answer. No, she knew the answer; she just didn't want to hear it, didn't want it to come from that face, in that voice.

Pressing her fist to the churning acid in her belly, Michaela faced the truth: He wasn't here as her bodyguard, her rescuer. He'd been sent as her executioner.

No time to allow the devastating hurt to consume her. As a scientist, she was nothing if not pragmatic. "I have something imperative to attend to before you ki—"

A crackle preceded an announcement on the PA: "Dr. Giese, report to the mess hall immediately."

"I have to go."

"They can wait another five minutes. Tell me what happened."

"Let me up."

He shifted to allow her to get by him. She clambered ungracefully past him and stood beside the bed, shivering, fumbling for the lamp so she could get dressed. "I was kidnapped. I've been a prisoner here for two years. I may be a mental wizard, but I don't have the luxury of just teleporting myself out of danger; I had no choice. I had to stay and *deal* with it." She bent down to grab her panties from the floor. "I consider myself deep undercover, and you're an asshole—"

The door handle jiggled seconds before the door burst open, spilling in a cone of light to illuminate her standing there bare-ass naked. "This day just gets frigging better and better," she muttered.

"Dr. Giese? Are you all ri— Oh Lord. Sorry. Sorry."

For several beats they stared at each other, before Ackart collected himself and shut the door with a thud, leaving her once again in the stygian darkness.

Oh my God. He'd seen Sebastian. Ackart couldn't have missed him lying on the bed illuminated by the hallway lights. Larger than life and naked.

"Dr. Gangjon came through on the video-conference—he says you have five minutes to present yourself." Ackart's voice sounded muffled through the heavy door.

"Be right there." Michaela raised her voice as she fumbled with her clothes. Not for the first time, she wished to hell she had a gun.

Hurry hurry hurry. If she ran like the hounds of hell were on her ass she could catch up with Ackart before he reached the others. Try to convince him not to tell anyone else about Sebastian. Using what method of persuasion? The man was afraid of his own shadow. He sure as hell wouldn't want to piss off Tongpan or Gangjon. No. Ackart wouldn't keep Sebastian's presence a secret. Especially now when all they'd been working for was about to be unleashed on the world.

Damn it. "What did you do with the lightb—" It

was placed in her hand. "About time." She fumbled for the lamp.

"What's that guy's threat level?"

"Dr. Ackart was also kidnapped. He's no threat. Unless he tells someone he saw you."

"You'd better stop him before he does so."

"Yeah. I'll be right on it as soon as I'm dressed. Are you armed?" she demanded, trying to slide her legs into her jeans at the same time she was trying to find the threads for the bulb in the ancient lamp base.

"Right now? Just my penis and my good looks."

Despite the seriousness of the situation, Michaela caught herself huffing out a laugh. "Funny." She refused to be charmed by him. The misguided moron. "Hurry up and get dressed; I have to stall Ackart before he—" She clicked the light switch, flooding the tiny room with brilliance. She heard his sharp intake of breath, then glanced at the bed for a lingering look at Sebastian Tremayne naked. The bed was rumpled but empty.

Michaela did a double take, then turned 360 to search the entire room. ". . . tells . . . Where the hell did you go?"

"Right here." Sebastian's voice indicated he was a few feet in front of her. Seconds later, his warm breath ruffled the fine hair around her face. The smell of his skin made her dizzy with lust.

Wait a minute. . . . Frowning, she put out a hand and encountered a warm, hairy chest and satiny skin. "You can't turn—"

"Invisible? No, I can only take a wizard's imprint. Imprinted Cohen. As long as I can touch him I can chameleon his powers for a whi— What the hell is *this*?"

He grabbed her upper arm; his thumb traced the row of scars on her biceps. "And this?" A finger followed the raised marks left by Gangjon's scoring a warning around her rib cage with his nails.

"Old news," Michaela snapped.

"Who," he demanded, his eyes feral, "did this to you?"

Just about anyone who felt the need for a punching bag. Just about anyone who tried to molest her or wanted to force her to work on something she abhorred. That about covered every man on base. She shook off Sebastian's hand. "I have to get out there."

"Here." She felt movement, then saw black fabric seemingly floating mid-air. "Put this on."

"Your LockOut? Won't this make it harder for you to kill me later?" The fabric was impervious to bullets, knives, and other weapons. It was not, Michaela was sure, impervious to Tremayne's accusations and erroneous suppositions.

He drew in a breath.

Frustrated, buddy? Aren't we all?

"We need to talk."

"Yeah?" She quickly kicked aside the jeans she'd been struggling one-handed to pull on and pulled the slightly loose material up over her freezing-cold legs and hips, immediately enveloped in the specially developed temperature-controlling material. It was made to be skintight and automatically contracted around her body; the difference in their sizes was a total nonissue. She muttered a quick blessing for the genius who'd pulled this one out of the hat. She finished dressing, wearing jeans and a sweater over the black LockOut. Scooping her hair back in an untidy ponytail, she secured it with one of the office-type rubber bands she kept in a tuna can by the door. "We'll take a meeting," she said sarcastically. "Have your girl call my girl and make an appointment."

"Michaela—"

"No. You don't get to say anything. We're done here. I have to disable the nuke. I've done half the process; now I have to complete what I started. You can do whatever the hell you want to me when I'm done."

"Would it help if I said—"

"*No.*"

"Better go after your weasel-faced friend before he tells everyone he saw you naked."

"The salient point is that he didn't see *you.* Naked or otherwise. Thank God."

Sebastian took her wrist, startling her a little since she couldn't see him. Tilting her watch so he could see it, he cursed under his breath. "Need to make physical contact with Cohen in the next sixteen minutes or I'll materialize."

He'd be hard to explain. "Great. Unlikely a communications device will function down here. I presume you took that into account and set up a rendezvous point and ETA? This place is twenty-five miles of crisscrossed tunnels carved into bedrock. Should take you six hours or so to search every room if you—"

Talking to the Invisible Man was damn irritating, and extremely disconcerting.

"Materialize. I want to see you."

One minute he wasn't there; then he was.

Michaela's foolish, foolish heart went into joyous overdrive seeing his beloved face. *Oh, God.* It was amazing seeing him here, in the flesh. His dark, shaggy hair was too long. His face was more craggy. But his pale blue eyes were just as piercing, just as alive and filled with mystery, and the dimple was just as she remembered it. A tidal wave of emotion filled her chest to capacity. It hurt to look at him.

He unexpectedly took her face in his warm hands, and she jumped; her heart raced like a rabbit. "I really haven't—"

"I couldn't have killed you," he whispered, kissing her temple, her cheek, brushing her mouth with his. "I would never hurt you."

Too late.

CHAPTER SIX

Being locked under ice for almost two years had taught Michaela the value of patience. If she'd been in his position, presented with the same cold, hard facts, *she* would have assumed the same thing.

Pissed her off, but she got it.

Life, especially hers, was too short to waste on anger. "You could've at least *asked* me before getting naked in my bed," she whispered as they hurried down the empty passageway to catch up with Ackart before heading to the communications room.

She had no idea what Sebastian was thinking as he walked with her. Two years of honing her listening skills allowed her to hear his small intake of breath. Being aware of nuances had saved, if not her skin, then her life on more occasions than she could count.

"This requires a longer conversation than we have time for right now," he whispered back. He was practically on top of her. She shivered as a surge of warmth flooded her body.

You think? "Convenient."

"Not so much," he muttered dryly.

"I have to go in here." Michaela indicated the

door to the comm room. "Wait out here for me. I don't want them to see or sense you."

He grabbed her upper arm. "I don't want you going anywhere alone."

"What you want is of no interest to me, Tremayne. They're expecting me. Let go."

His look spoke volumes. Braver people than herself had quailed at that dark, narrow-eyed glare. Clearly he didn't like her going in without him. Too bad. They'd both trained for situations where one had to watch a partner walk into danger.

"Time's of the essence," she said in a low, urgent whisper when his fingers tightened on her arm as if sheer brute force would prevent her from doing her job. "The longer I spend chatting out here, the less time I'll have to do what has to be done so we can get the hell out of Dodge."

After a second or two, he released her, leaving the brand of his fingers on her skin. "Watch your six." He reached out and tucked a loose strand of her hair behind her ear in a gesture at odds with his hard expression.

Even though she'd have liked nothing more than to fall into his arms and forget this whole mess, Michaela stepped out of reach. "Stop thinking of me as a woman, Tremayne. I'm an operative with an urgent directive. One I can*not* fail. Step aside."

He shifted out of the line of sight. "Be c—"

Michaela sliced a hand across her throat indicating he shut up, then reached for the door handle. Nothing and no one could be allowed to distract her.

She turned her back on him and opened the heavy door, firmly closing it behind her.

"You're late," Gangjon informed her, clearly annoyed. Hollywood handsome, with ash-blonde hair combed back off an impossibly perfect face, his dark eyes were soulless as he looked out from the monitor. "Sit."

Even though he was only present on-screen, she sat, Pavlovian-style, immediately, as if he were in the room.

Michaela had slipped into the vacant seat beside a red-faced Ackart and turned her attention to the flat screen on the far wall.

Sergei Gromyko gave her a distracted glance. He, too, had been kidnapped and brought on board for the project. In his late eighties, with thin gray hair and a prominent strawberry-like red nose, he'd admitted a week ago that he knew they were going to be killed as soon as their jobs here were done. He hadn't seemed that bothered by it.

Gangjon looked down on the three of them, sitting there on their uncomfortable, metal, straight-backed chairs. Michaela hated the man with every fiber of her being. He was completely amoral, soulless, and ruthless. As he walked them through the last hours of what was expected of them, Michaela listened for any hint of what Kang Gangjon had planned.

As far as he and his cohorts knew, there was nothing anyone could do to disarm or disrupt the nuclear bomb they'd all spent two years building. None of them knew that Michaela had programmed a new default code into the fission-bomb triggers months ago.

Inputting a fifteen-part, alphanumeric password that only she knew would compromise the nuclear bomb. Even if she were to be prevented from going back in to finish the second half of the disabling process, it would prevent the apocalyptic explosion that would destroy the modern world. The resulting explosion fissle would still create a radioactive mess of slightly activated plutonium, which would then disrupt the surroundings made of lithium tritide and uranium. Disrupt them into little bitty radioactive pieces. But buried under miles of ice, they would have less impact.

And even less than that if she managed to finish what she'd started.

It was no surprise when she came to the conclusion that the vile-tempered, sadistic megalomaniac up on the video monitor had no plans for them at all. At least none that involved any of them being alive twenty-four hours from now.

"Sir," Ackart murmured deferentially. "The sequence codes have almost all been programmed. Once the last code has been launched— How do *we* leave?"

"Let me worry about that, Doctor," Gangjon told him. "Let me worry about that. Complete your jobs in the prescribed time, and as promised, you will be free to go back to your lives." *Yeah, as radioactive, cremated remains.*

The monitor went black.

So this was it. Michaela's heart raced, and her palms felt sweaty. Less than three hours to go.

"Lying sack of shit," Ackart muttered as they filed out of the room. It was the most rebellious she'd ever seen him. "Let's go up to the dock to see if they left us a submarine."

They hadn't, but Michaela was happy for him to go in the opposite direction of where she was going.

"Excellent idea. Why don't you go with him, Dr. Gromyko? I'll go to the lab, then meet you out there."

"If there is a submarine, it'll only seat two," Ackart said practically.

"Then don't wait for me." When Gromyko tried to argue, Michaela reached over to squeeze his frail arm covered in layer upon layer of clothing. "I'll find a way out too; I promise."

Ackart held out his hand. His fingers were shaking. "It's been an honor working beside you, Dr. Giese—Michaela. Godspeed to you."

Michaela watched the two men walk away. Anger made her cheeks hot. Sebastian stepped from the doorway that had concealed him when they were out of earshot.

Michaela indicated the direction of the lab and they fell into step. "Gangjon knew from the start they were going to leave us here to die."

"There's only that wreck of a sub out there. Doesn't run. We checked."

"I know. I've jogged on that damned dock twice a day for the past year to monitor security and watched the comings and goings of the principals. They use tadpole subs. Come on. Let's do this. Think your pal, Cohen, will be capable of teleporting all of us?"

"'Course."

She felt the weight of Sebastian's hand on the small of her back before he started rubbing a circle with his thumb. Michaela wanted to be stoic enough to move out of reach, but the reality was, she craved the comfort of his touch. The caring human contact after being deprived of it for what felt like a lifetime.

"How much further?"

"About a hundred and fifty yards. There'll be at

least two security guys at the door. Maybe more now we're so close to the end game."

Michaela slowed her steps. She felt a foolish need to prepare him, even though she knew T-FLAC operatives were prepped no matter where or when. She'd been resigned to her own death, but the thought of losing Sebastian, so soon after being reunited, terrified her.

"How many on the base total?"

"There *were* thirty. Now? I'm not sure. I haven't seen any of them since last night. They're just as expendable as the others left behind, so I doubt Tongpan and the other head honchos took any of the guards out with them. They're here—*somewhere*." Michaela rubbed the goose bumps on her arms. Sebastian's LockOut kept her body climate-controlled, but this chill was bone deep.

She paused for a moment and took a deliberate, slow-paced breath, a breathing technique she'd learned for situations of high stress when it was important to be centered and in control. She glanced at Sebastian. Solid, grim. There.

"Don't underestimate them. They aren't rent-a-cops. Apparently Dr. Gangjon brought them with him at the beginning of the project. They were combat-trained in Russia or China, practically from birth."

"Worried I can't hold my own?" Sebastian's teasing voice faded slightly, and she turned to see him literally disappear, as he melted into the background.

He'd chameleoned against the dirty cream and green wall, duplicating the background exactly and blending in seamlessly.

"That's freaking creepy, but very cool." Even though his image was a very faint shimmering outline, she could still feel the comforting warmth of his large body beside her, and smell his musky scent.

"Isn't it, though," he murmured against her mouth as she turned her face up. His lips were hot, his tongue slick and cool as he slipped it into her mouth.

The kiss made her blood heat and her skin flush but by necessity was woefully brief.

Michaela wanted to melt into him. To absorb that warmth into bones she was sure would never be warm again. She'd known she'd die here. Alone and forgotten. And while she had every faith that Sebastian would attempt to extract them, Michaela wasn't positive that would even be possible. They were fathoms beneath a mile-thick ceiling of solid ice. Hundreds of miles from land. Surrounded by icy ocean.

She had a bad feeling. A very bad feeling.

Sebastian had filled her in as they walked. The rest of the T-FLAC extraction team waited for the two men to teleport to a fishing boat at an undisclosed location.

The only way out was Sebastian's partner, Cohen. If anything happened to him . . . Unless Michaela and Sebastian found the wizard within the next four hours and he could teleport them the hell out of Dodge, they'd die here.

No Cohen, no way out.

She felt the hair on her nape lift moments before Sebastian's large, warm hand brushed against her chilled skin. "I'm not going to allow anything to stop you—"

"I know. Thank you. It helps having a bodyguard." Nobody would see him. But they'd sure as hell see her, and if they suspected anything—had even a *hint* of what she planned to do—they'd kill her first and ask questions later. A full-body shudder rippled through her.

"Think of me as your personal Kevlar." Sebastian's fingers tightened around the back of her neck. Warm and solid. "Nobody will stop you. And no one, I mean no one, is going to hurt you."

"From your lips . . ."

She wished she felt a tenth of Sebastian's confidence. Up until now she'd been fine with her fate. It was a shitty, unfair fate, but it was the hand she'd been dealt. But Sebastian showing up had instantly changed all that. Suddenly she wanted more. Craved it with every cell in her body.

She wanted time to be loved. Time to share walks on a sunny fall afternoon through the colorful carpet of orange leaves with him. Time to share morning coffee and snuggle up under a blanket with him on Sunday mornings. Time to grow old together.

None of it was going to happen. She'd missed out on her chance when she'd been too confused by her own feelings to tell Sebastian exactly why she couldn't marry Cole.

No, there hadn't been a moment's regret, until now.

"This is it. No guards, which is odd." Michaela eyed the shimmering space she still hoped was Sebastian, then slid her key card through the security reader.

Usually two of Tongpan's men were stationed outside the door. Their absence made her uneasy, but it made this considerably easier. No security other than a card access. Only a dozen crucial players were still on the base. No one expected sabotage at this juncture. They'd all been working too hard for this moment, for their promised release. A promise that would never be delivered; because in three hours, everyone left behind would be dead. No loose ends.

The lighting was brilliant, and she squinted as she always did as her eyes adjusted. For the past two years she'd spent twelve hours a day in this room. But the faint electrical hum of the machinery and the shadowless surgical brilliance of the overhead lighting didn't feel in any way comforting or give off any warmth. It was cold. Endlessly and unforgivingly cold.

Sebastian shimmered back into a visible form beside her, and she had to keep herself from jumping back at his instant reappearance.

He snagged her upper arm. "How were you planning on getting out of here?" He narrowed his eyes, the planes of his face turning hard. "You weren't, were you?"

She shrugged. "I was dead either way. If they discovered what I did, or I'd refused to do what they wanted, they'd have tortured me to death, no question about it. At least this way, I'd die knowing I'd managed to save a few million other people. Fair trade, wouldn't you say? Although, I don't know if Ackart and Gromyko see it that way." She went to her usual workstation and turned on the monitor, settling into her chair for the thousandth, and maybe the last, time.

"Jesus, Michaela—"

"I was okay with it," she told him. She threw him a brief smile, then gave all her attention to the glowing screen, checking and rechecking the numbers, comparing them to the codes in her head. A weapons lab in China had done the original design, but most of the construction and precautions had been implemented by Michaela and the rest of Tongpan's team. "There wasn't multiple-choice."

"Well, while not multiple, we do have a choice. As soon as you take care of that, we locate Cohen, and we're outta here. Do what you have to do. Can you talk me through it, or would talking me through your process be distracting?"

"Considering a degree in nuclear physics?" Her eyes sparkled as she rose to cross the room to a setup that looked like something out of a 1950s, science-fiction B movie. What the hell?

"Just call it latent curiosity," Sebastian told her easily. Jesus, the equipment was as old and dilapidated-looking as everything else on the sub base. Damn place hadn't been used in more than forty years. "Just curious how this is going to go down."

"The fission-bomb triggers of most H-bombs are solid or hollow spheres of fissionable material—hollow in this case. See here?" She shoved hair out of her eyes as she indicated the silvery orb surrounded by wires running every which way. The weapon was shiny new. Top-of-the-line. Big.

Jesus.

He braced a hand on the console beside her and took a cautious look inside the belly of the beast.

"That's Uranium-235 surrounded by a sphere of explosives. Delicate choreography is required in detonating the explosive, because it must explode perfectly symmetrically on all sides so that a perfectly spherical ingoing wave of explosive force momentarily compresses the fissionable sphere to a density at which the nuclear explosion occurs. If the explosion is not sufficiently symmetrical, the explosion becomes a 'fissle,' a failed nuclear explosion."

"An excellent goal," he muttered facetiously, watching her slender fingers working with the precision of a surgeon within the tangle of wires. "What's next?"

"Cut the wires to the detonators to disable them on one side of the sphere of explosives. The explosion will be asymmetrical, and the bomb will become a fissle." Michaela straightened, a satisfied look on her face. "Done. Nothing will reverse what I've done. We have two hours, thirty-seven minutes before they expect detonation."

She didn't tell Sebastian that the explosion, given what she'd done, would still be considerable. Not large enough to melt the polar ice cap but big enough to destroy the base and anyone in it. If he got them out, great. If not, well, he wouldn't spend his last two hours worrying about being blown to hell.

"Good." He took her hand. "Let's find Cohen, and get the hel—"

Cohen strolled in. His gaze flickered from the computers to Michaela. "What the fuck is she doing here? *And* she's wearing your LockOut?" the other man muttered, clearly incredulous. "Jesus, man." Cohen caught Sebastian's eye and raised a brow. "Good times, huh?"

Sebastian tugged Michaela behind him. She resisted, but he had brute strength and a deep, sinking, oh-shit feeling as he looked at his by-the-book partner. "She's coming with us."

"Are you fucking *kidding* me?" His eyes glittered with fury. He clearly had a job to do, and now Sebastian had thrown a monkey wrench into their plans. Cohen raised his SIG Sauer, pointing straight at her forehead.

"Dr. Giese didn't come to this facility willingly," Sebastian informed him calmly, struggling to keep a wiggling, equally pissed Michaela behind him. "Nor was she a willing participant in this scheme."

"Says who? Dr. Giese? Quit thinking with your dick, Tremayne. Ever considered Stockholm syndrome? Step aside. We have our orders and very little time to implement them."

Sebastian stared Cohen down over the barrel of the loaded SIG. "Over my dead body."

"Sebastian—," Michaela whispered fiercely. He ignored her, his attention fixed on his partner.

"Whatever it takes." Cohen's finger squeezed the trigger.

The loud retort of a gunshot reverberated through the room.

CHAPTER SEVEN

Damn it! Michaela thought, freaked out. *She* was wearing Sebastian's LockOut. *He* was a sitting fricking duck and could be hit anywhere.

One thing Michaela knew for sure: the bullet hadn't gone through and through. She would be injured as well. It literally felt as though her heart had stopped beating as she managed to untangle herself and get in front of him. Using both hands as well as her eyes, she searched his chest for a large entry wound.

"Damn it, Tremayne. Don't you *dare* have a fricking-fracking hole in y—"

He grabbed both hands in one of his and yanked her behind him again. That really pissed her off. Adding annoyance to sheer terror made her light-headed. She would have made a shitty field operative. "Give me a break, damn it. Stop throwing me around, Tremayn—"

The stench hit her before she managed to peer around Sebastian's biceps. "What the—" Cohen was sprawled on the floor, assorted fluids seeping out of his body. There was a great deal of shockingly red blood where his head should've been. After several thundering heartbeats, her horrified gaze tracked upward as her brain computed the sequence of events. Someone had shot Sebastian's partner before he managed to squeeze off that fatal shot. Relief flooded her, then was just as quickly dispelled, replaced by terror.

Popov, Ling, and Malard had come back! They were accompanied by six security guys who fanned out inside the door.

All three hundred sweaty pounds of Afanasei Popov alone could block the doorway. He'd struck her so hard for some perceived infraction a few months back that he'd knocked her out cold. His expression said he was ready to do worse. Michaela shuddered.

Popov shuffled aside to allow room for tiny Bingwen Ling, who stood barely five feet tall. He was a classic example of short-man syndrome—ready to rip your head off to show that he could do it, forever compensating in all the wrong ways. He, too, was a sick son of a bitch. Intolerant of the smallest perceived infraction, he was a sarcastic, neurotic sadist specializing in martial-arts torture techniques that caused immobilizing pain without leaving a mark.

Beside him stood Malard. The pretentious dickhead was usually unobtrusive except when he was being as mean and spiteful as the snake that he was. His thin lips were drawn back in a feral smile, exposing a full set of large, bad British teeth.

The three senior scientists were sadistic bastards, but it was the beefy Russian bodyguards who held automatics. *Frick!*

Every weapon remained leveled at Sebastian's head. "Freeze," Popov said briskly. "Hands above your head. You too, Dr. Giese."

He'd watched too many American movies, Michaela thought, raising her hands as the men advanced farther into the room. Every fiber of her being was attuned to Sebastian as he subtly shifted his center of gravity.

Bad idea, bad, bad idea. Nine to one— All right, one and a quarter. Her training had been *years* ago, a formality when she'd joined T-FLAC. She was just one of many brainiacs. She hadn't been proficient at hand-to-hand even back then. She might be fit and in shape, but not remotely strong enough to take down a determined-to-kill-her man with a gun and certainly not an expertly trained tango or three. She'd fought her best with Sebastian earlier and might as well have been a gnat buzzing around him for all the damage she'd done.

She scanned the room for a weapon of some kind. Everything was bolted down, part of, attached to something immovable or out of reach. Not a crowbar or Uzi to be had. *Crap.*

The men advanced into the room, forming a semicircle ten feet in front of them.

"Higher." Popov pulled out a small black gun, adding it to the arsenal aimed at them. He waved the barrel at Sebastian's raised arms, and he obligingly lifted them another quarter of an inch. "Who sent you? The U.S.? *Rossiya?*" That Tremayne might be Russian did not please Popov any more than the other choices. Probably less.

Nerves clearly on a hair trigger, and without removing his unblinking stare, Popov addressed Michaela when she shifted her feet. "Please not to move, Dr. Giese." His accent thickened with his agitation. "Well?" he barked, almost unintelligible. "Are you military?" He paused as Ling tugged at his coat sleeve. "What is it?" Clearly annoyed at the interruption, Popov leaned over so the smaller man could whisper in his ear.

Popov's bald head shot up, and his eyes narrowed to slits. "What?! He *vozmozhno! Heyt!* That cannot be. T—" With a start, he blinked behind the smudged lenses of his glasses. "FLAC . . ." Popov trailed off, his skin pasty white and pearly with sweat as Sebastian suddenly just . . . disappeared.

Thanks for the heads-up, honey.

He'd chameleoned. Any advantage Sebastian could come up with was better than this Mexican standoff. Michaela managed to look as startled and nervous as the bad guys as she backed out of the way to give Sebastian room to maneuver.

Invisible, Sebastian assured himself that Michaela was as far away as she could get. There was nothing for her to hide behind. He had to reassure himself that she was a trained professional and that she was wearing LockOut from neck to toe.

"Bloody hell!" The English guy with bad teeth backed up. "Another *wizard* for crapsake?!"

Not quite. But close enough.

"You should have shot him on sight," the Chinese man—Ling—screamed, looking around wildly and waving his arms in front of his face as if to ward off a ghost.

Ghost Chameleon, Tremayne thought with satisfaction, advancing on the nearest security guard and ripping his weapon from his hand.

Pop. Pop. Pop.

Three guards dropped to the cement floor in quick succession.

Pop.

Four down.

For an instant, fear rounded Ling's eyes as Sebastian slammed him against the doorjamb with his fist. Ling staggered from the impact, looking around wildly, his face gray with fear. "Shoot him! Shoot him!" With each syllable his voice rose another octave. Sebastian punched him on the jaw, and the guy went down like a rock, crumpling across the doorway near Cohen.

Chaos ensued. For all his bulk, the fat guy moved fast, using the two remaining security guys and the Englishman as a barricade.

"He can't get past us," Popov shouted as Sebastian went for his weapon next. The fat guy wasn't about to give it up without a fight and gripped the SIG in a meaty fist.

Sebastian couldn't be seen, but he could be *felt*. He gave a swift deliberate kick that should have lodged Popov's gonads somewhere around the region of his ears. As the huge tango gasped, Sebastian clamped his hand down, squeezing the sausage-like fingers hard around the weapon. He kept moving, dodging out of the way as the security men tried to grab him.

A bullet missed his head by a whistling inch, then slammed into the solid metal door behind him with a high-pitched screech, missing the still-unconscious Ling by a millimeter.

The more frenzied and confused, the more *frightened* the men became, the calmer and more centered Sebastian became. He lived for shit like this. Although having Michaela in the room, exposed as she was, didn't make him happy.

A quick glance to assure himself she was okay got him a lucky punch to the shoulder from Ling, who'd come around and snuck up on him between the guards' bodies. At Ling's triumphant shriek, everyone turned. Now knowing approximately where Sebastian was, everyone converged on the spot and tried to grab him at the same time.

He was the piñata, Sebastian thought grimly, dropping to his knees and crawling between their legs to come up behind them as they uselessly swung their arms, hoping to make another lucky strike.

He squeezed off another shot, which was deflected as Popov ran into him, purely by happenstance, knocking him ass over elbow with his rotund body. Sebastian grabbed the front of Popov's heavy parka, pulling him down with him. He managed to roll out of the way seconds before the Russian hit the floor with a thud.

Popov managed to pull the trigger of the SIG he still gripped in a meaty fist. A hoarse, surprised shout indicated that someone had sustained a hit. That was confirmed by a truncated cry and a crash as the Brit went backward, crashing into a nearby table. Not fatal, but it would slow the guy down some.

The Russian rolled to his knees, then staggered to his feet. A lucky guess and he kicked Sebastian on the upper thigh. Pain shot up Sebastian's thigh, and his leg buckled.

As he went down, Popov grabbed him in a breath-stealing bear hug that expelled the breath in his lungs. "I have him! I have him!"

Behind him, Ling dug his fingers in the region of Sebastian's liver and did something internally. Oily black spots flashed and swirled in his vision. Felt like his insides were being scooped out with a claw hammer.

CHAPTER EIGHT

From the side of the room, Michaela watched what looked like a surreal Marcel Marceau routine. Popov had his meaty arms wrapped around *something* and was struggling to keep his hold. A pantomime starring one huge man and his invisible foe. Ling stood close by, his eyes hard.

She'd seen that look of pure satisfaction on Ling's face before— *Oh, God.* . . . Sebastian materialized in the middle of the mêlée, face contorted in agony.

Oh, shit, shit, shit. Michaela knew *exactly* how excruciating what Ling was doing felt. Bile rose up the back of her throat. Any moment now, Sebastian was going to black out from the intense pain radiating through him. Ling wouldn't release the organ until Sebastian regained consciousness. Then Ling would do it again. Sick to her stomach, she observed his wrist twisting against Sebastian's spine.

Face bleached of all color, Sebastian dropped to his knees, Ling, still squeezing, clearly enjoying himself.

"Excellent," Popov boomed. "Hold him there and bring me the woman." The security guy, a burly six-footer who'd almost cornered her in the shower more than once, sprinted toward her, grinning.

Unable to look away from Sebastian's torture, she had the ridiculous belief that if she took her eyes away—even for a second—Ling would kill him. Swallowing bile, her heart manic as she tried to come up with something—anything to distract Ling— Michaela saw something small and black flying toward her face at the same time. Automatically throwing up her arm to ward it off, she had a split second to recognize the projectile.

A gun.

Sebastian had thrown it unerringly as he went down.

She caught the SIG in her nondominant hand, switched it, and fired all on a single breath. Training was automatic. Too bad accuracy hadn't been her strong suit at target practice, but the guard was almost on top of her as she fired, and for once, his size was in her favor. Her ears rang and blood splattered her face as he went down. She didn't wait. Holding the gun in both hands, she switched her depth perception as she looked across the room and fired at Ling, who was hunched like a fricking carrion- eating hyena over Sebastian's writhing body.

The brilliant physicist's head exploded with the force of a watermelon under a sledgehammer. Next, she turned the gun on Malard, who'd procured a weapon from one of the dead guards. He was clearly unfamiliar with the weapon—his expertise was more in the realm of weapons of mass destruction—and he was desperately fumbling with it. His mouth moved, but she couldn't hear him. Her ears were still buzzing.

To trip the man as he ran past Sebastian's prone position, he shot out his leg. Gerald Malard screamed and crashed to the floor beside him, the gun knocked out of his hand and skittering across the floor.

Still white-faced, Sebastian had enough strength to grip the scientist's head and twist, breaking his neck. The room went silent, save for the rasp of their breathing and the ringing in their ears from the gunfire in the enclosed space. The air stank of gunpowder and blood, and the harsh light ensured that all the gory details were visible and inescapable. Sebastian had been in battle scenes before, but Michaela hadn't, and he didn't know how she'd handle it.

"You okay?" he asked, staggering to his feet, face contorted, pale eyes blazing like blue hellfire.

"Behind you."

"Got it." Sebastian spun around as Popov swung a chair at his head. He had to hand it to the son of a bitch; Popov wasn't giving up. Not that it was going to do him any good. Fisting the leg of the metal chair, Sebastian yanked it out of Popov's hand, then rammed the curved back into the Russian's massive chest, driving him back.

"You can kill me," Popov taunted. "But it does not affect what we built here." He smirked, his face oily with sweat, his lab coat spattered with Ling's blood. "In a matter of hours our demands will be met. We shall have our money *and* ruler and a new world order. Every major city will be destroyed, and we will be in control of all coastal ports." His smile was pure evil.

"You will die with the knowledge that you have

failed. Your countrymen will suffer and die by the millions, and everything you knew and loved will be destroyed. Your precious T-FLAC will show your photograph and you will forever be ridiculed. You'll die in infamy!"

Michaela didn't enlighten Popov. "Want this back?" she asked Sebastian, holding out the SIG, her attention still on Popov.

"Wanna do the honors?" Sebastian shoved the chair harder into the Russian's corpulent belly.

She shuddered. "No, thanks."

Popov was pressed against the wall. He stopped laughing and shifted gears, his voice changing from triumphant to reproachful. "You are like a daughter to me, Michaela. Did I not treat you well? Did I not give you tidbits from my own plate? Did I not protect you from the advances of Nickolas, Wilhelm, and the others?"

Being hand-fed disgusting cold leftovers from Popov's plate and receiving occasional bruising beatings were not her idea of fun. "The only reason you couldn't rape me was because you were too damn fat to crowd me in the shower stall and too slow to chase me like everyone else did, you sick son of a bitch. And you sure as hell didn't mind using me as your punching bag— Hurry up and shoot him, Sebastian. I want to get out of here." She turned on her heel, too repulsed to even look at Popov.

She heard the shot as she walked outside.

Sebastian joined her a moment later, wrapping his arms around her shoulders. He pressed her face into his chest, kissing her hair. "Let's get the hell out of Dodge."

She lifted her head. "How do you propose we do that?"

"We'll figure it out. Together. Move it."

Michaela grabbed the front of his gray sweater and reeled him in. "I'm not done with you, Tremayne." She stood on her toes to brush her lips against his.

"I sure as hell am counting on it." He crushed his mouth down on hers.

Breaking away, he took her hand. "Let's go see what we can use as transportation."

His fingers were warm and very solid between hers. They were going to die here today. They both knew that.

There *was* no way out of Decommissioned Soviet Submarine Base #15.

"I know where we can find a broom. Maybe we can fly out."

"Too bad we're not witches." He stroked her cheek with his fingers. "Come on, sweetheart; let's find a ride."

There were no "rides." Sebastian knew that Michaela knew *he* knew they were without a creek or a paddle.

The corridor was eerily empty, the only sound the compressed air being fed through the vents. "Exactly how long do we have?"

"Hour, six minutes."

"There's that Oh-ninety-four-class nuclear sub tied up at the dock," Sebastian offered.

"You think we can take a forty-year-old sub and make it run?"

No. He knew it wasn't operational, but with luck he'd be able to jury-rig the communicator he and

Cohen had left up there to contact the ship for just this eventuality. The operatives on the trawler would send in a submersible and extract them. If the comm devices worked. That was a huge fucking *if.* "Don't know unless we try."

Hand in hand, they jogged through several miles of corridor until they reached the open expanse of the docks.

Neither mentioned the cold simply because it was so cold at sea level no words were necessary. The words would have crystallized instantly on leaving their lips.

"Damn." Michaela slowed as she saw a body sprawled and surrounded by glossy red blood on the stained cement dock platform several yards away. "That's Sergei over there. Why did they kill him? He wasn't *going* anywhere."

"Yeah," Sebastian laughed, tightening his fingers in hers and starting to run. "He was. Look." Two small two-man subs floated just above the waterline, all but hidden by the gray bulk of the behemoth cigar-shaped 094-class World War Two sub. Looked like a whale and her pups.

"Oh my God. Popov and Ling. Of course." Her beautiful face filled with excitement. "Can we disable one? I don't want any nasty surprises. I don't know how many security guys were left behind. I'm not sure we got them all, but I'm sure I don't want to see any of them ever again, especially in our rearview mirror."

"Good plan." Although he'd already considered the odds himself. "Yeah. Why don't you get inside, out of the cold. It'll take me a few minutes to figure out what goes where."

He helped Michaela release the catch on the heavy hatch, and helped her board.

She reached over and flung her arms around his neck, kissing him hard and way too short before giving him a little shove. *"Hurry."*

CHAPTER NINE

It was a damn good thing Michaela wasn't claustrophobic. The interior of the 150-ton midget sub was about the size of a compact sports car. She didn't want to think about how the sub had been maintained, if it had been maintained at all. Nor did she want to contemplate how stable the nuclear reactors powering the engines might or might not be.

She shot a quick glance at her watch. The base, and anything on or near it, would be nothing but vapor in less than ninety minutes. "Hurry the hell up, Sebastian. What the frick are you *doing* out there?"

There was just enough gray light coming through the open hatch to see by, and she perused the simple control panel while she waited, committing the schematic to memory. When he got back, Sebastian was going to want to leave immediately.

Ignoring the rank odor of sweat and stinky feet, she hit the "oxygen" switch. Powered by diesel, an overhead light came on, and the faint hiss of compressed air assured her they wouldn't suffocate when the hatch closed. Next, she fiddled with the exhaust systems. Exhaled carbon dioxide, and the moisture from their breath, would pass through soda lime, a chemical "scrubber" to render the air breathable for a longer period of time. They had to put at least an hour between themselves and the base. Starting five minutes ago. *Hurry, Sebastian!*

The little sub was armed with a couple of torpedoes, mines, and timed explosive charges. When last had they been checked? Did they even function? *Frick!* She hoped like hell she and Sebastian wouldn't need them.

Conveniently, there was an "on" button. After several tries it caught, the cabin lights flickered to life, the sonar screen lit up, and the gyroscope appeared to be working. She felt the vibration of the propeller shaft starting to turn.

So far, so good.

The interior heater came next. The cold water would freeze them in a matter of minutes without it.

Ping. Ping. Ping. The sound of bullets glancing off the sub's thick metal hull brought Michaela's head up. There was no way a bullet could get through the pressure-resistant hull, but she couldn't say the same for Sebastian, who was out there sans LockOut.

"Outta the way. Coming through," he yelled as his booted feet appeared in the rounded hatch opening above her head. "We've got company." Slamming down the hatch, he gave the locking wheel a spin and practically fell into his seat.

A quick glance showed him everything was all systems go. "Good job."

Michaela glanced out of the small view portal no larger than her hand. "She's all yours, Captain. Haul ass. There're at least a dozen guys running around up there like chickens with their heads cut off."

"I noticed." The sub started moving forward at a snail's pace.

She adjusted the air vent to point away from her face. "Please tell me you disabled the other sub."

"Wasn't time. It'll take them a while before they're ready to give chase. It'll give us a good head start."

Go. Go. Go. "We need a few more feet clearance from the dock before we can submerge." She observed how much room was between them and the mother ship through the thick glass of the observation window, and she wished she could see what, if anything, the other mini-sub was doing. *Think positively,* she told herself. *Visualize them screaming in frustration because nothing works.*

To control buoyancy, the submarine had ballast tanks and auxiliaries that would fill with water so she and Sebastian could dive. And air so they could surface. She checked the indicator showing the water level as it rose in the tanks. "Starting the fill."

As the submarine dived, the ballast tanks flooded with water and the air vented until the sub's overall density became greater than that of the surrounding water. The sub began to sink under the ink-black surface. Movable sets of short hydroplanes on the stern controlled the angle of the dive.

Ping. Ping. Ping.

"Speed it up, sweetheart. Before they pop a hole in this tin can." Sebastian concentrated on the dive, aware of every breath Michaela took. God, he was proud of her. Despite what she'd endured for the last couple of years, she was calm and centered, and exactly who he needed beside him right now.

In a matter of hours . . .

First things first, however.

Bubbles, catching the meager light from above, rippled past the three small view portals as the little sub sank deeper and deeper. Eventually the bubbles disappeared in the darkness and there was nothing but blackness. Light didn't penetrate very far in the ocean, and they'd navigate from here on out virtually blind.

Successfully getting out of the sub base was only a small part of the problem. Now they had to head for open water. The ice ceiling was up to thirty feet deep, with ice stalactites hanging down like inverted mountains, some a hundred feet deep or more.

"I found some navigation charts over there; if you give me the coordinates of the trawler, I'll chart our course."

When she'd quickly sorted through the nav charts, chosen one, and unrolled it, Sebastian reeled off the coordinates. Her lips moved and her eyes had the same slightly unfocused look they'd had when she was working out how to sabotage the bomb. Sebastian knew she was doing a hell of a lot of calculating, and he waited silently, enjoying the discovery of yet another skill in this remarkable woman.

Her head came up. "At our present speed of seventeen knots our ETA is seventy-one minutes. We're in trouble."

Sebastian put everything at full throttle. The sub vibrated with the force of the engines.

"Yeah. I know." The sub had been designed to resist high pressure for deep-sea research rather than to outrace tangos or nuclear explosions. At least their human pursuers wouldn't be able to move any faster than he and Michaela could. Sebastian put everything at full throttle and prayed that it wouldn't just break down completely. The sub vibrated with the force of the engines.

They were down to thirty-some minutes before the nuke back at the base detonated. "They know approximately when we should check in and where we are. If they don't hear from us by then they'll send in the DSRV." At her blank look he clarified: "Deep-Submergence Rescue Vehicle."

For several minutes, there was nothing but the sound of the whoosh of compressed air and the steady ping of the sonar. The chance of the T-FLAC team finding them—even with knowledge of their starting point—was slim to none. The Arctic was six and a half times the size of the Mediterranean. They'd never be found.

Suddenly the sub bounced violently, then went into a downward spiral. The gyroscope and other instruments went crazy.

Torpedo.

"Shit. They're *right* behind us."

The ocean was a minefield of ice mountains that glowed eerily in the faint glow from their running lights as they dropped, diving at a steep angle impossible to sustain without landing splat on the ocean floor. "Pull up. Pull up!"

A direct hit would be disastrous, but the aftershocks rocking the tiny sub could be just as lethal. It took skill and nerves of steel to power the sub flat-out as it canted this way and that without rhyme or reason.

An enormous mass of ice floated over them, missing them, but causing a tsunami of wave action that had them fighting to hold on. Their sub wove up and over, between, and under the enormous chunks of lethal ice as they tumbled and drifted around it.

The other sub was right on Sebastian and Michaela's tail, and gaining fast. A second torpedo streaked across their port side, missing them by several yards but spinning their sub like a top for a full minute. As soon as he was able to, Sebastian made a U-turn, ducking behind a long, narrow blade of ice.

Michaela, anticipating what he needed, powered down the lights.

Silence hummed and pinged as the other sub drifted by. They sat there until the ocean was once again pitch-black.

"They know where we are. They'll be back." Michaela's voice was quiet and rock steady.

Sebastian identified the radio transponder, but communications had to wait. Alert the bad guys to their exact location too soon and they could kiss their asses good-bye. "Let's see if we can find a more secure location to wait them out."

With Michaela manipulating the intake of water, they sank deeper and deeper, their passage soundless. Icebergs that were merely tips above the water swelled to unnaturally enormous proportions below the water, forming an endless maze of smooth blue-green ice visible in the oncoming running lights.

He slowed to safely steer through the jutting points and eerie shapes of the frozen underwater mountain ranges.

Sebastian flipped on the exterior microphones. "Shit. Here they come again. Lights off. We need a safe— There." Big black gaping holes stared out from the pale ice, sightless eye sockets in a frozen face. "See that black hole over there? Ice cave. Our home away from home." He aimed the sub through the twists and turns, the space becoming tighter and more confined.

The deep rumbling of the other engine grew louder on the speakers. Michaela glanced out the portals, but there was nothing to see but black water and ghostly shadows. "They're getting closer."

A loud pop and swishing sound echoed in the confined space. "What the hell—" Sebastian didn't have time to finish his thought before a projectile zoomed past them, just a few feet from their port side, and slammed into a wall of ice, exploding in a brilliant bubble of fiery orange and red that lit the surrounding ice like Fourth of July fireworks.

"Torpedo. They've got two more."

He shoved the engine controls back on full throttle and zoomed through the ice maze before them. The sub shuddered as one fin nicked a high-rise-sized icicle plunging downward.

"Watch it!"

He banked hard to starboard. The sub hurtled forward into the darkness. Sebastian pointed to the dark holes scattered here and there in the ice. He saw an area that appeared deep enough. "We're going in. Not moving, not breathing, is the name of the game. Hang tight."

Michaela's hands flew over the switches and dials, turning off everything but the most basic of life support while they waited.

The rumble of the engines following them grew louder. A strip of light pierced the darkness, slashing briefly across the cave, then winking out of existence. Gradually, the sound of the engines began to fade, then once again got louder as the other sub started to circle.

"Now what?"

Sebastian pushed the button on his watch, illuminating his face with a bluish glow. "Now? We wait."

CHAPTER TEN

The dim green of the interior lights illuminated the soft curves of Michaela's beautiful face as she turned to him. The sonar's *blip blip blip* was in counterpoint to Sebastian's heartbeat. God, she was exquisite. Everything about this woman drew him to her in ways he couldn't explain even—*especially*—to himself.

Reaching out, he ran his fingers over the disheveled fall of her hair, dark in this lighting but thick and shiny and glorious against his fingers.

"We can't sit here fore—"

"I wasn't a tactile man until I met you. Now everything about you begs to be touched."

"But how long— Oh!"

Placing his hands under her arms, and in one swift move, he hauled her onto his lap. She let out a little gasp of surprise, and he said roughly, "Who said we were just going to sit here?"

She came willingly, if not with some difficulty. The space was incredibly small and she had to navigate more gears and controls than in a car; still she murmured a fainthearted protest. "But the LockOu—"

"Shh," he whispered low, nibbling a path up her arched throat. "Don't move," he cautioned as she wiggled, squirmed, and somehow managed to straddle him in the confined space. It took several moments of contortion, but she finally settled her spread thighs across his lap.

"Oh yeah." His breath snagged in his lungs as she pressed down on his erection. "*That* works."

"*We* work," she whispered; her fingers combing through his hair electrified him, causing goose bumps to pebble his skin. Settling her sweet ass more deeply in his lap, she licked his lower lip, then bit down not so gently. "I fell in lust with you the moment we met," she murmured, trailing her fingers around his ear. Her eyes were velvety brown, pupils huge in the subdued lighting.

Sebastian undid the complex fasteners that ran from under her left arm to her hip. "I was blown away when I got my first look at you. I felt like a fucking caveman. You in that dress? Jesus. I wanted to toss you over my shoulder and run like hell."

Blood pounded a frantic beat in his ears as he peeled her out of the top half of the black LockOut like a luscious piece of fruit. Her breasts were pale in the dim green light. Love and lust tangled in his chest as he stroked the petal-soft skin. "From that moment, nothing else mattered. I wanted you more than I've wanted anything or anybody in my life. And when you died, Jesus, I died too." His chest felt heavy at the memory, and his breath snagged in his throat.

"All around the timing sucked." Michaela leaned back a little to allow him access to her nipple, then whimpered low in her throat as he sucked the hard bud between his teeth and into the hot cavern of his mouth.

"Where was I—?" Her soft voice wobbled a little,

and her eyes were unfocused as she braced her hands on his shoulders as if anchoring herself. "Feeling guilty as hell to crave you so badly when I'd just promised to share the rest of my life with Cole— But . . . God, that feels amazing; don't stop! I didn't fall in love with you until I saw you were strong enough, *honorable* enough, not to take what I wanted to give you that night."

"I'm weak enough to take what you're offering me now."

She smiled a siren's smile. "Would that we could, but I'm . . . trussed . . . up—" He unerringly found the concealed opening between her legs. She was already dewy, her juices coating his fingers as he manually explored her sweet channel.

"Oh! The women's LockOut suits don't have that handy-dandy little feature!"

"Up," he instructed, his dick about breaking in half under her ass. She lifted up the requisite two inches needed to get to his zipper. Reluctantly, he removed one hand from its happy place around her breast and unzipped his jeans. Free, he replaced his fingers, slipping his cock into the slick, wet heat of her.

He wanted to sing Hosannas. God, she felt good. Amazing. Perfect.

"Ahhh." She started to move, slowly at first. Despite the confines of the sub, there was just enough room to move her hips, and she rocked back on him. Thank God the sub was only the size of a car and not actually one. At least they wouldn't have any law officers knocking on their steamed-up windows.

"Yeah," he panted as she picked up speed, her

rhythm exquisite—right on the nose, perfection. "*Exactly* that."

Lights cut through the darkness fifty yards from them. "Bad . . . guys . . . doing another drive-by."

Yeah. He saw their running lights as they glided by in their third lap. He didn't give a flying fuck. If he died now, he'd die happy.

"I was right."

"About what?"

He groaned, his body shaking. "You are damn near perfect. The question is, can I make you a happy woman?"

Arms cradling his head, she laughed against his throat. "Blissfully."

Still laughing, she joined him as they climaxed together. It wasn't a huge blow-one's-brains-out climax but rather a quiet thank you, Jesus, for the gift of this woman. Sebastian would remember this moment for the rest of his life.

However long that might be.

"Ready?" he asked as he started doing up the top half of her LockOut, pausing to press a lingering kiss to the rapid pulse at the base of her throat.

"I sincerely hope," Michaela said grumpily as she helped him right her clothing, "that you have better staying power when we get home. These quickies are all well and good, but I'm looking forward to a leisurely bout of lovemaking that takes *hours,* not minutes."

She all but fell back into her seat. Her hair was wild around her shoulders, and her eyes sparkled.

"Hours?" Hell's bells. They were this close to a frigid, watery grave, and Sebastian felt as light and free and goddamned *happy* as he'd ever felt in his life. He cupped her warm cheek in a hand that smelled of her. She'd imprinted herself on him. Saturated his skin.

"You got it. Somewhere hot and dry? Desert? Mountain? Beach?"

"Surprise m—"

The next torpedo came out of nowhere. Parting the blackness of the water, it picked up a lacy wake as it bulleted straight for the enormous ledge of ice above their hiding place.

A chunk of ice the size of the Empire State Building broke away and dropped in slow mo in the water right above them. There was literally nowhere to go. They'd run out of time sooner than either of them had anticipated.

CHAPTER ELEVEN

"Micha— What the fuck?!"

This was unexpected but her worst nightmare. They were back—teleported to the brightly lit lab. Michaela shuddered.

Teleporting meant Tongpan was back too. They'd discovered what she'd done. . . .

The cold kept the bodies strewn about from stinking to high heaven, but it was a grisly sight. Dark puddles of congealed blood were frozen in a stop-frame around the bodies.

The countdown clock on the far wall clicked off the minutes— Six. Six miserly little minutes before Michaela and Sebastian and everything else blew to hell.

"You have sorely tested my patience, Dr. Giese." The terrifying and sonorous voice sent shock waves down Michaela's spine. Spinning around, she saw her worst nightmare. Times two.

Oh, frick it. Tongpan and *Gangjon!*

Her heartbeat went into manic overdrive, and her mouth went bone-dry. There was every possibility she was about to pee her pants in sheer, unadulterated terror. She moved closer to Sebastian for sanity and strength. He took her hand in a punishing grip.

Kang Gangjon was the scariest man Michaela had ever encountered—unless he was in the same room as Tongpan; then all bets were off. She couldn't drag her gaze away from the wizard who stood beside the nuclear weapon's disabled detonators.

Tongpan could've teleported them anywhere on Earth, but he'd obviously returned to the base to see how badly she'd screwed with his bomb for himself. And brought her back to the scene of the crime to . . . what? Force her to fix it? Never going to happen. Even if she wanted to, which she didn't, that was now impossible.

There were worse things than death, and his black eyes telegraphed a clear, terrifying message impossible to ignore. A trickle of sweat ran down Michaela's temple, and her palm felt slick with sweat in Sebastian's hard grip.

"How dare—" his words resonated in the room, bouncing off the walls and floor loudly enough to hurt her ears—"you meddle with things which do not concern you?"

"That's rhetorical, I'm sure." She was surprised by how steady her voice was. By the fact that she could speak at all.

This whole near-death fricking experience thing was getting old. She'd been resigned to the hopelessness of the situation before Sebastian's arrival. Had a glimmer of hope and now was once again aware of the clock counting down every precious last minute. *Damn it*. She wanted time. Time to love and be loved by Sebastian. Time to breathe fresh air and feel the sun on her skin. These bastards had stolen two years of her life and were determined to steal her future as well.

"Who're these guys, sweetheart?" Sebastian asked conversationally, his fingers tightening painfully around hers. Under his breath, so low she almost didn't hear him, and without moving his lips, he whispered, "Do not let go of my hand. No matter what."

She was fine with that. "The shorter, unpleasant one on the left is Kang Gangjon. The tall one with the dandelion-fluff hair is Tong. . . ." *Oh, God, that hurt like knives of fire.*

The hair on Michaela's body rose as an electrical field surrounded them. It hurt like hell. She bit off the whimper trembling on her lips and pointed at the wizard as zaps and sparks zipped across her skin. "He's responsible for teleporting me out of my plane."

"Is that a fact. Tsk, tsk." Sebastian, Michaela in tow, strode toward the two men. It felt as though she were walking through razor blades as the electrical field ripped at her face and clothing. The slices burned and stung her exposed hands and face. Hot blood seeped from the wounds. Sebastian was worse off—he was unprotected by the LockOut that was saving her untold pain.

"Correct the error you made," Gangjon snapped, clearly furious. His creepy-handsome face contorted, purple with rage. His usual smooth, unctuous voice was filled with venom. His Hollywood good looks masked evil personified. "Immediately."

"Or what?" The disdain in Sebastian's voice came through loud and clear. He kept walking. Out of the corner of her eye, Michaela saw his clothing literally shredding off his body. Cuts—*deep* cuts—covered his face and throat. His shirt and jeans were in tatters. Blood dripped down his cheeks from a hundred razor-fine lacerations. But still he kept walking.

Was he *insane*? Michaela tried to pull him back, but Sebastian kept moving forward, never flinching, until he was just three feet from Tongpan, staring him down.

Sebastian was only human. T-FLAC trained but human. Tongpan was a wizard with untold power. Sure, together she and Sebastian could have taken on the world, but not Tongpan.

She'd survived starvation, beatings, abuse, being shot at with bullets *and* torpedoes, and even an underwater ice avalanche. All told, a good run. But she was going to die right here in the lab when Tongpan fried her and Sebastian to crispy critters. Or the bomb exploded in a fissle of nuclear particles, whichever happened first.

Either way, they were dead.

Her gaze slid to the clock: four minutes and nine—

Eight.

Seven.

Six.

CHAPTER TWELVE

"What did you *do*?! Fix it. Fix it!" Tongpan roared. The sonic boom of his voice caused Michaela's hair to blast back off her bleeding face. Her fingers clenched between Sebastian's were ice-cold. Her entire body trembled.

Three minutes, thirty-one seconds.

Sebastian kept walking, his steps measured.

He ignored the dude on the left, his entire focus on Tongpan. The powerful wizard had . . .

Two minutes, forty-eight seconds before the nuke blew them all to hell.

One shot. That's all I have, Sebastian thought grimly. *One. Fucking. Shot.*

His life. Michaela's life. Their life together.

One minute, eighteen seconds.

One chance.

Tongpan raised both arms, boney fingers curved, a raptor's talons closing in on its prey. The wizard's long white hair billowed around his head and shoulders as his clothing swirled and rippled in an unseen wind, making him look taller and wider than he really was. Illusion, Sebastian knew. Smoke and mirrors, but damned effective.

Sebastian's internal clock yelled for him to hurry.

One minutes, sixteen seconds.

Dragging Michaela with him, he charged Tong-pan full tilt, free arm extended.

One minute, fourteen seconds.

Sebastian punched his closed fist into the middle of the wizard's rock-solid chest.

His body was instantly engulfed in silver smoke and white-hot flames. Sebastian's arm burned from fingertips to shoulder as he chameleoned Tongpan's not-inconsiderable powers.

One minute.

It wasn't working!

Sebastian's last thought was, *Oh, shit!* Then everything went white.

CHAPTER THIRTEEN

"You didn't see what *I* saw," Michaela said lazily, swishing her bare feet in the clear, warm water. Sebastian enjoyed the sight of her slim, bare legs as she allowed yellow and blue tropical fish to swarm around her toes.

They were sitting, both bare-assed naked, on a sun-bleached wooden dock that stretched out into the crystal-clear, aquamarine water in an undisclosed tropical location.

Nearby, palm trees whispered in the ocean-scented breeze, and the sun picked up diamond-bright chips in the sugar-white sand of the nearby curve of beach.

T-FLAC had gifted them a week on the company's private island, appropriately called Paradise. On the other side of an emerald-green mountain range was the organization's training facility, but the north shore was completely, blissfully private. And completely off-limits except to Sebastian and Michaela for the week.

A small, well-equipped bungalow with a big bed and enough food to give them much-needed energy was all they wanted or needed.

"And what was that?" Sebastian stroked his fingers

lazily up her warm, lightly tanned hip, the late afternoon sun having baked their cold bones all afternoon.

For the first time ever, he'd experienced severe motion sickness during the teleportation and transference of Tongpan's powers. In fact, even after all this time, Sebastian still felt the faint hum of the wizard's powers deep inside his body. He hoped to hell it would eventually go away and hadn't mentioned the residual effect to anyone except Michaela.

Sebastian suspected he might end up in T-FLAC's psi division after all. He'd cross that bridge when and if he had to.

He and Michaela had spent a week in T-FLAC's Montana medical facility getting checked out before being flown on the company Bombardier Challenger to the island. The deep scratches on her skin caused by the wizard's spell were completely gone. As were Sebastian's own injuries. He had felt an overwhelming relief. Sebastian had more scars on his body than he cared to count. But he couldn't bear anything to mar Michaela's silky skin.

Crystals of powder-fine sand sprinkled across the slope of her shoulder sparkled in the afternoon sunlight, begging the brush of his lips. Her skin was hot, gritty, and tasted of salt.

"You fried Tongpan into a crispy wonton." Michaela shuddered and, as Sebastian stroked a hand down her back, turned her head and shot him a delighted and feral grin. "His skin *bubbled,* and his eyes *melted,*" she said with relish.

Sebastian laughed. "Bloodthirsty wench." With a tug, he pulled her onto her back on the warm wood dock, their feet still dangling in the water.

"You do know," Michaela managed, pretending to ignore his busy hands, "usually the honeymoon comes *after* the wedding."

"I know this is all back assward, but . . . marry me, Michaela. When I first saw you, you stole my breath. I haven't caught it since."

She stroked his cheeks. "Ditto."

He kissed her navel, his hand gliding up the smooth skin on her inner thigh. "You stopped *and* started my heart."

She wrapped her slender arms about his neck. "I couldn't stop looking at you."

"What about now?"

She gave him a lazy smile, eyes wicked. "I can't stop touching you."

"Works for me. I wanted you beyond reason two years ago. Now I have a million reasons to love you." He lifted his head to look up at her. "We have a lot to talk about. . . ." Looking into her velvety eyes, he saw they were filled with love and promises. "We've never discussed kids, but I'd like four—"

Her eyebrows went up, and her eyes sparkled. "*Two,*" she said firmly, her fingers combing through his damp hair.

Ah, man. Did he know her, or what? Two was— "Perfect." God, he loved this woman. "I want to grow old with you. What do you say?" Not giving her a chance to answer, he kissed her long and slowly, only letting her up for air when she shoved at his shoulder.

"Was there a question buried in there somewhere?"

Sebastian gathered her beneath him, the healing sun on his back and the woman he loved in his arms. With a shout of laughter, he rolled her off the dock.

They landed with a splash in the sensually warm water. With a shriek Michaela took off, arms and legs slicing through the crystalline water as she swam to shore.

With lazy strokes, Sebastian tagged behind her, knowing she'd allow him to chase her until she caught him.

TEMPTATION IN SHADOWS

Gena Showalter

CHAPTER ONE

Gabrielle Huit blinked open her heavy eyelids and moaned. Her temples throbbed as if her brain was hooked to a generator and every few seconds the switch was thrown, electric shocks traveling from one side of her skull to the other.

Moaning again, she scanned her surroundings. She could see . . . nothing. Her vision was blurred from the pain, and the shadows around her were too thick. But she wasn't home; that much she knew. The air was too dusty, too cold; she kept her place clean and warm.

She tried to shift to her side, hoping a different angle would elicit different results. Metal rattled and a hard weight pulled at her wrists, keeping her still. Metal—chains?

Don't panic. Yet. Where was she? How had she gotten here? Last thing she remembered, she'd been outside, holding a gun and fighting the urge to commit murder. Something had knocked out her targets and a second later a dark cloud had enveloped her. *Then* a sharp sting had torn through her neck, shooting fire and weakness through her entire body.

"I'm sorry," a deep voice had whispered. "So sorry."

She'd focused on that voice as if it were a lifeline—until she'd been unable to focus anymore. Though she hadn't seen anyone nearby, strong arms had banded around her, lifting her up and preventing her from falling as her trembling knees collapsed.

Now, she was trapped inside a . . . room? A cell? She still couldn't tell. Her own panting breaths filled her ears as she tugged more forcefully at the metal. Again, the links around her wrists remained steady. She really was chained. *Oh, God.* Someone had knocked her out and abducted her. Someone had freaking knocked her out and abducted her.

She'd told herself not to panic, but a knot began to grow in her throat, cutting off her air supply. Someone had managed to bypass her security, both external and internal, and overpower her completely. She was now trapped. Helpless.

Calm down. Figure this out. Yes. Yes, she could figure this out. She just had to breathe. To do so, she just had to swallow the knot. Gabby forced herself to gulp, to slowly breathe in, out. In, out. *Better,* she thought, her lungs filling. *Okay. Time to think rationally.* Who would have done this? The government, maybe?

The men she'd wanted to shoot had certainly looked the part. Dark suits, sunglasses, and shiny Glocks. More, they'd known what she was capable of and had prepared for the worst. But how had they drugged her? They'd never even approached her. Someone else was responsible, then.

So . . . who else had been there?

No one that she had seen, and that terrified her more than anything else. She barely managed to stop another knot from growing. Being taken like this— again—was what she'd feared her entire life. The first time, she had been studied, used. Hurt. She'd woken up strapped to a table, her head split open by a rogue agency scientist suddenly able to download computer files straight into her brain. If the government were responsible this time, how much worse would it be for her?

A moan suddenly echoed—and it wasn't hers.

Gabby scrambled backward until a wall stopped her. The erratic pounding of her heartbeat seemed loud, like a beckon to whoever lurked on the other side of the chamber.

"Hello," a male rasped groggily. Chains scraped the floor—but she hadn't moved. He was bound, too? "Anyone there?"

Her panic receded. Somewhat. "I'm here," she said, voice shaking.

There was a pause. Then a shocked, "Gabby? Is that you?"

Her jaw dropped as recognition took hold. "Sean?"

"Where are we? What's going on?" The more he spoke, the more substance his words had and the better she could hear the deep, sexy rumble that had fueled her fantasies the last few weeks. Best forgotten fantasies.

"I'm chained to the wall," she told him. "You?"

"Yeah. Me, too."

Why would someone take them both? And how terrible of a person was she, to be relieved that they were in this together?

"Do you know who has us?" she asked.

"No, sorry. Last thing I remember, I was walking out of my apartment and some guy was asking me for the time."

Okay. So. There went her government theory. Sean was the bodyguard of a nightclub owner—a nightclub owner she, too, worked for—but Sean was normal. Moody, yes, and hot as hell, but still normal. There was no reason for the government to abduct and study him.

Unless . . . what if they knew how much she desired him and thought to use him against her? They could threaten to hurt him if she failed to cooperate. She groaned.

"You hurt?" he demanded in a tone mixed with equal measures of concern and anger.

Not yet, she thought, but couldn't deny that his concern warmed her. "I'm fine."

His image flashed inside her mind. He was tall, lean but muscled. His skin was sun-kissed, his chopped hair dark, and his eyes so electric a blue they shocked her every time she looked into them. Even with the black, swirling tattoos that curved around his temples, he epitomized perfection.

She'd often wondered why he'd marked himself that way, what it meant to him.

"Maybe we're going to be ransomed," he said. The prospect didn't sound like it bothered him. "I mean, we work for the same wealthy man."

"They should have taken him, then, 'cause I doubt Rowan Patrick cares about getting me back." She'd met with Mr. Patrick a few weeks ago, shortly after he'd bought the club where she worked. The next day, he'd asked her out. She'd said no. She'd already been fascinated by Sean. Then, a few days later, Mr. Patrick had asked her out again. Again, she'd said no. His frustration with her had been very clear.

"True," Sean finally replied. "You aren't his favorite person."

Was Mr. Patrick coldhearted enough to have planned this out of revenge? "Would he have done this . . ."

"No. I've known him a long time and that's not his style." Sean sighed. "You wouldn't happen to be loaded, would you?"

"No." Oh, she could make money. Plenty of money. She had the means to acquire any amount of cash she desired, at any time, but she'd never done so. There was too much risk.

So what motive did that leave?

The man who'd . . . enhanced her had let her go. Could he have decided he wanted her back and then hunted her down? But again, why bring Sean into it?

"We have to get out of here," she said, pulling at her chains. Her wrists were already abraded, and she winced as metal cut past skin and warm blood beaded. "Preferably before our abductor realizes we've woken up."

"Stupid asshole didn't frisk me." There was a twinge of satisfaction in his voice. "My blade is still pressed against my ankle."

Thank God for stupid assholes. "Do you know how to pick a lock?" she asked. She did, but as dark as the room was, Sean couldn't toss her the knife without the possibility of losing it.

"Oh yeah. During my misspent youth, I learned a lot of naughty skills I shouldn't have."

She heard the rustle of clothes, the slide of chain against wood, an angered, "Shit! Cut myself," then finally the clink of metal.

"One down," he muttered.

"Hurry."

"Am." Another muttered curse, then another *clink*. "I'm going to kill whoever did this."

"Ladies first."

He chuckled. "Bloodthirsty, are you?" One moment he was across the room; the next his big, strong hands were on her, patting her down as he searched for her wrists. Despite the danger, she shivered. He was hot, callused . . . a temptation she couldn't afford.

"Okay?" he asked.

"Yeah." Barely.

"I can't see anything and might cut you. If I do—"

"I'll live. Promise. Just get these things off me." How long did they have before their abductor checked on them?

One of Sean's hands slid the length of her arm and stopped at the chain. He leaned in, warm breath trekking over her face, the scent of whiskey filling her nose. Thankfully he didn't cut her as he'd feared. He was infinitely gentle as he freed one wrist, then the other before clasping her hand and tugging her upright.

Her knees proved to be weak and buckled— damn drugs—but she never hit the ground. Sean's arm snaked around her waist and held her up.

"I've got you."

She shivered. "There's got to be an exit."

"There is. Look." He spun her around.

Gabby fought a wave of dizziness as she did as

commanded. As thick as the shadows were, she saw only darkness. "I don't—" *Wait.* There, at the floor where she'd been sitting, was a thin slit of light. Once again her heartbeat sped into a gallop, this time from excitement. "A doorway!"

"Yep. Wait here."

He released her, and she stifled a whimper, already missing his strength. At least she managed to remain upright on her own this time. A moment later, the sound of metal sinking into wood reverberated. She knew the sound all too well.

"Why aren't you jimmying the lock?" That would have been quieter.

"Blade's too big to fit inside the cylinder. I'm having to detach the hinges." As he worked, he said, "Did you get a look at the person who grabbed you?"

"No. He said he was sorry, but never showed his face."

"Damn. I didn't see him, either."

She wrapped her arms around her middle. "I'm sorry you were dragged into this. I mean, this is all my fault." It had to be.

"What do you mean?"

"I don't think we're meant to be ransomed. I think—" *God.* Should she tell him? He deserved to know. After all, if they failed to escape, he might be tortured for information about her. Or worse, experimented on. And going into that sort of situation blind was a lot worse than knowing what to expect and why. *That* she knew firsthand.

Still, years of silence, of secrets and running, of hiding to stay alive, kept the truth bottled inside her. If she told him and they got out of this, she'd have to always wonder who *he* told.

"Nothing," she said. "I think nothing."

"No. You think something, but we'll talk about it later." The door separated from the wall, and welcome light flooded the room.

Gabby blinked against the sudden brightness, her eyes filling with burning tears. To compose herself, she turned and studied her prison. It was a small bedroom, of a type probably found in every suburban neighborhood. The walls were beige, and there was a dresser pushed against the far right. A twin-sized bed rested beside it. Only, there were no pictures, no knickknacks.

Sean peeked out. "Clear," he said. "Come on." He grabbed her arm and ushered her into the hall. Like the bedroom, it was devoid of personal effects.

Again, her government theory was shaken. She would not have been locked inside a bedroom, inside a home, with no guard posted at her door. "Is there a computer in this place?"

"I don't know, and I don't want to take the time to find out." He kept his blade at his side and tugged her around a corner, stopping to glance inside the other doorways—two bedrooms—along the way. "Clear."

"You don't understand." She dug her heels into the wood planks, bringing him to a quick halt. "I might be able to learn who abducted us and why."

"There's no time."

"Please."

He faced her, expression hard as granite. "You a hacker?"

"Something like that," she said, and licked her lips nervously.

He tangled a hand through his hair. "How long do you need?"

"No more than a few minutes."

His brows furrowed together. "That quickly? How is that—"

A pained moan sounded from another room. Sean whipped around—but not before she glimpsed the murderous light in his eyes. Though she couldn't see an intruder, she prepared to attack as well. Then the shadows painted over the hallway walls seemed to suck inward, surrounding them, keeping them hidden, and she frowned. Something similar had happened a few times before. She didn't know how— unless her abilities were changing?

"This way," he whispered, and hooked her finger around his belt loop so that both of his hands could remain free. "And be quiet."

Forever they seemed to walk but she couldn't see where they were going or even what surrounded them. Odd. Still, Gabby knew how to take care of herself but couldn't deny she liked being guarded like this.

Over the years she'd taken hundreds of self-defense lessons and learned to fight as dirty as possible. She'd had to. She'd grown up on the streets, a target for every pimp in need of a fresh-faced little girl and every junkie desperate enough to steal from a starving kid.

"Bill?" Sean said, and there was a mix of confusion, anger, and upset in his voice. He crouched down.

As the shadows cleared, Gabby pulled herself from her musings and gasped. A man lay on the floor, blood pooling around him.

Sean worked frantically at the man's clothes,

revealing a gunshot wound to the stomach. "What the hell happened?" Sean demanded, pressing the heel of his hand against the hole to staunch the crimson flow.

The man—Bill—grimaced. He was average height, probably late forties, with mocha skin and dark eyes that were glazed with pain.

Intending to help, Gabby rushed to the duffel bag resting on the other side of him. If medical supplies were inside . . . *please be inside.* Her fingers shook as she unzipped it, the blood splattered across the handles smearing on her palms. This man couldn't be their abductor—could he? Sean knew him, was concerned for him. But how else would the man have known they were here?

Damn it. Only clothes rested inside the bag.

"Be . . . trayed," she heard him rasp. "Came here . . . free you . . . run." The man's head lolled to the side. His chest ceased its shallow movements as breath escaped his cut and parted lips on a final gasp.

"Motherfucker!" Sean growled.

"I'm sorry," she whispered as she faced him, and she meant it. Losing a friend was tough. Losing a friend to violence was tougher. "You can mourn him. Later." Forget the computer. "Right now, we have to get out of here."

The anger drained from Sean's expression, leaving something hard and unreadable. "This wasn't supposed to happen. Bill wasn't supposed to die."

She opened her mouth to respond. None of this was supposed to have happened. Before she could utter a single word, however, a loud crash reverberated from around the corner.

Sean jumped to his feet. Blood coated his hands and shirt as he gazed around wildly.

"Bill's tracks end here," a new voice said from another room. Male, harsh. Determined. "Check every room. If you find the other two, you know what to do."

Footsteps pounded.

Sean muttered another curse under his breath and grabbed hold of her. Shadows once again seemed to suck inward, surrounding them, as he jerked her forward, to the back door.

She couldn't see anything but Sean and gloom. But she could hear hinges squeaking, feet pounding. Gabby bit her lip to keep her cry of surprise and fear inside, when Sean suddenly yanked her against his chest and stopped. More footsteps pounded, blending with the rasp of breath. From multiple people. Still, she couldn't see them. What the hell was going on?

Without a word, Sean started forward again. He kept a tight hold on her hand, and she was glad. She was still reeling. That had to be it. She'd just watched a man die, and now her mind wouldn't let her see the men hunting her.

Outside, she thought a few seconds later. She had to be outside now. Cool, crisp air caressed her. Why couldn't she at least see sunlight? Moonlight? Something? And how was Sean navigating through this?

Gabby managed to maintain his quick pace for several miles, rocks and twigs cutting into her shoes. But by then she was sweating, fighting for every burning breath, trembling. "I . . . can't . . ."

"Just a little further." Sean didn't even seem winded, the bastard. "You can do it."

An eternity later, he stopped and the shadows disappeared completely, revealing amber moonlight, a forest bursting with thick, lush trees and a—a car? Sure enough, he removed a leafy canopy from the frame of a two-door sedan.

"How did you know—"

"Just get in," he commanded.

She obeyed as if her feet were on fire. Now wasn't the time to chat. No one had followed them—to her knowledge—but it was better to be safe than sorry. Except when she and Sean were inside the car, he pulled a key from his pocket and used it. And it worked, the engine roaring to life. A thousand questions seemed to rush through her mind. Only one continued to echo, though. *What. The. Hell?*

As he maneuvered out of the forest and onto a gravel road, she decided chatting couldn't wait. "How did you know where the car was? How did you have a key for it?"

"Lucky, I guess."

Ha! Bad was the only kind of luck the two of them had had tonight. But fine. She'd tackle this another way. "How did you know that man? Bill?"

"He was my boss."

"I thought Rowan Patrick was your boss."

Silence.

Gabby refused to let this go. "Did Bill abduct us?"

"No. He was a good man."

"Then how did he know—"

"I don't know! Okay? I don't know. You and I were supposed to be taken, but Bill wasn't supposed to be there and he sure as hell wasn't supposed to be killed."

Gabby shook her head, trying to make sense

of Sean's words. "Are you psychic?" A possibility, she supposed. After all, she was proof that people with extraordinary abilities existed. "'Cause there's no other way for you to have known what was and wasn't supposed to happen back there. There's no other way you would have known to hide a car in some random forest."

Silence slithered between them, and she thought he meant to ignore her. Then, he sighed, stopped the car at the side of the road, and pierced her with the darkest stare she'd ever seen.

"I know because I'm the one who abducted you."

CHAPTER TWO

Three weeks earlier

"This, gentlemen, is your target. Gabrielle Huit. Gabby to her friends. Twenty-seven years old, five eight, and approximately one hundred and thirty pounds."

Sean Walker studied the female's photo on the wall in front of him. Thick brown hair, straight as a pin. Big brown eyes, olive skin, no freckles that he could see. She was utterly nondescript. Totally dismissible. Unless you concentrated on those eyes.

The brown was a mix of honey and cinnamon—*I must be hungry, because damn*—and were filled with haunting pain. As a twelve-year agent for Rose Briar, an independent firm that offered a safe haven for anyone exhibiting extraordinary abilities, as well as destruction for anyone who abused those powers, Sean had seen that look enough times to know her life had not been all sunshine and candy. But she'd survived, which meant she was strong. He admired strength.

The photo disappeared, replaced by one of Gabby walking out of a redbrick apartment building. That was quickly followed by one of her strolling down a sidewalk, people and taxis meandering around her as she sipped a cup of coffee. Next she was handing a kid a few dollars. Money Gabby couldn't spare, if the report on her bank account balance—an account she kept under a false identity—could be believed. Finally, Sean saw her in a dimmed club, a tray clutched in her hands as a man reached out to pinch her ass.

"She's a technopath," Bill, his boss and the man now in charge of Rose Briar, continued.

"A what?" Sean and fellow Rose Briar agent Rowan Patrick asked at the same time. They shared an amused glance. Though they looked nothing alike, people often accused them of being twins.

"A technopath. She's a human computer." Bill's head tilted to the side. "Well, kind of." He scrubbed a hand down his face. Though his skin was the color of coffee, he somehow appeared ashen. "I'll start from the beginning. I just hope you're ready for this." He paused. "About twenty years ago, I was among a group of Rose Briar agents who raided a lab belonging to Dr. Karlis Fasset. It was my first mission, but one I'll never forget."

Bill raised a small black remote, pressed a button, and Gabrielle's face disappeared, a new one taking its place. Sean hated the loss—and that pissed him off. She was a job, not a possible date. The new mark was a studious man, probably early thirties, who was thin, almost gaunt, with pale skin and thick glasses.

"Kids were disappearing off the streets in broad daylight, yet there were no witnesses," Bill said. "We suspected we were dealing with someone who could teleport. *Then* we found one of the kids. His head had been shaved, was scabbed and scarred, and he was mentally and emotionally traumatized, but he managed to lead us to Dr. Fasset's lab. After going through the doctor's notes, we realized he had abducted ten kids in all. Kids who were homeless, parentless, and wouldn't be missed. He had implanted all kinds of shit into their brains, basically making them remote receivers."

"Bastard," Rowan said.

Rowan was a good man and an even better agent. He and Sean had done countless missions together and usually met their objective with low collateral damage. With his blond hair, green eyes, and you-can-trust-me smile, people tended to welcome Rowan into their midst, few questions asked. They couldn't help but want to befriend him. Even emulate him. Only later, when that angel face revealed a devil's intentions, did they regret their decision.

"Those kids, not that they're kids anymore, can now download files from other people's computers into their brains," Bill said, his dark eyes grim. "They don't even need to touch the damn things. If the computer is on, they can access what's inside."

Wow. "What about codes and encryptions?"

"We're not sure about that."

Still. Stomach tightening, Sean leaned back in his seat. As far as unnatural abilities went, that was a big one. The ramifications were devastating. Government secrets—theirs for the taking. *Any* secrets—theirs for the taking. If someone like that fell into the wrong hands . . .

"It gets worse," Bill said. "Dr. Fasset had already released all the kids back into the wild, so to speak, before we discovered what he'd been doing. He'd renamed them, actually numbered them in French.

Only good thing he did was put their fingerprints into both police and government databases so that they'd be traceable. Over the years, we've been hunting them and managed to find Quatre, who was the one to lead us to the doctor, as well as Six and Neuf. Four, six, and nine. And let me tell you, despite the names and the fingerprints, finding those last two wasn't easy. Some of the kids were adopted, their names again changed, and their files sealed. Some were never picked up. Gabrielle Huit, number eight, was of the never-picked-up variety."

"So how'd you finally find her?" Sean asked.

"She'd gone off the grid, but was arrested a few weeks ago for assaulting some guy at a coffee shop. Broke his nose, busted three of his teeth."

Rowan laughed. "We're talking about the mouse you just showed us, right?"

She's not a mouse. Those eyes, Sean thought again.

"Why'd she do it? Beat the coffee guy up, I mean." For the most part, people abhorred physical violence. Women especially. They went out of their way to avoid it and didn't tend to rush headlong into it.

"When questioned," Bill said, "she told cops that the man had kiddie porn on his laptop. And she was right."

Good for her, then. Sean only wished she'd removed *all* the bastard's teeth.

"Anyway, we'd already flagged the ten sets of prints, so we were notified immediately when hers were scanned. She's here in New York, a waitress at some nightclub. Eye Candy, it's called."

"You want us to kill her?" Sean asked with a tinge of . . . regret. Yes, regret. That didn't mean he'd hesitate. He might admire the woman's spirit, but he always did his job.

"No. No, no, no." Bill held up his hands, that little black remote anchored between his fingers. "We want to study her, question her, so we're sending you in to gain her trust. And if you hear nothing else I say, hear this. Gaining her trust is imperative. When we questioned Quatre, the stuff in his brain self-destructed, killing him. Six didn't want to work with us, but she didn't want her ability any longer, either, so we operated on her, hoping to deactivate what had been done. But again, the chips and wires caused some sort of self-destructive reaction and killed not only the girl but the people operating on her."

Rowan leaned forward and propped his elbows on the square tabletop in front of him. "What happened to the last? Neuf?"

Bill's shoulders slouched ever so slightly. "We made him comfortable but kept him locked up. We didn't know what to do with him, but didn't want him free, others able to use him. The continued anxiety caused a meltdown. After only fifteen days, we found him dead in his cell."

Sean and Rowan shared another look, this one pure *Oh, shit.* Sean thought, *No pressure.* Gain the girl's trust and be careful not to incite her nerves for a prolonged period of time.

He rubbed the tattoos at his temples. They were swirling Celtic designs he both loved and hated. Usually the action calmed him. Not this time. "How do you want us to do this?"

"Remember I told you she works at a nightclub?" Bill waited for their nods. "Well, the owner, Thomas

Wayland, was dealing on the side and was happy to give us the club and a smooth transition from his rule to ours in exchange for his freedom and a one-way ticket out of the country."

"Nice of him," Rowan said with a laugh.

Bill grinned. "Wasn't it, though? We've had an agent inside for two weeks, a female, but she hasn't had much luck. Gabrielle keeps to herself. We think a boyfriend can get her to open up and ease her into helping us." There at the end, his gaze had zeroed in on Rowan.

"Me? Again?" Rowan asked, pointing at his chest. He was grinning. While he wasn't attracted to Gabby, he liked variety and sex—however and whenever he could get it. "Is it Christmas already?"

Sean wasn't surprised the blond had been chosen as the romancer. Like every Rose Briar agent, Rowan possessed an unnatural ability, and it sure as hell beat the shit out of Sean's. Sean could manipulate the shadows. Rowan could read a woman's desires—and give her exactly what she craved—without her ever saying a word. Gabrielle Huit wouldn't stand a chance.

And that did not cause every muscle in Sean's body to clench with anger. It didn't. Really.

"You are to be a rich, up-and-coming entrepreneur," Bill told the agent.

"Easy. But what do you think this Gabrielle will like?" Rowan rubbed two fingers over his stubbled jaw. "Well, besides this beautiful face of mine."

Bill strode to the table against the far wall, lifted several sheets of paper, and handed them to Rowan. "Bentley, our woman on the inside, compiled a profile on what she thinks the target will prefer in a man. Gabrielle is disgusted by the club's patrons, thinks they are cheaters and liars. She enjoys lattes, but doesn't often venture into coffee shops. Too many pervs with laptops, I suppose. Therefore, you will be as un-pervy as possible. You will drink coffee and be sensitive. Maybe pretend to read poetry and that kind of shit. Oh, and if she thinks you're interested in marriage, even better. That might prove how trustworthy you are."

Rowan's grin never wavered. "I'll put love quizzes and letters to my mom on a laptop and make sure the thing is on when I call her into my office for a chat with the new boss."

"And my job?" Sean asked.

"Eyes and ears," Bill said. "To everyone else, you're the hired muscle. That way, it won't seem odd that you're always around, digging into everyone's business, while protecting Rowan and his employees. And yeah, you'll need to protect Gabrielle. We don't think anyone else knows who she is or what she can do, but secrets have a way of getting out. . . ."

* * *

Two days later, Sean finally found himself face-to-face with Gabrielle Huit. Rowan was at his desk, drinking a cup of coffee he didn't really like, with his laptop in front of him and conveniently turned on. Sean stood behind him, and Gabrielle sat in front of him, back ramrod straight, shoulders squared, and face expressionless.

In person, there was nothing mousy about her. Her brown hair was like silk, gleaming in the light.

Her eyes were honey and cinnamon, just as Sean had supposed, only he hadn't noticed the length and thickness of her lashes, framing those eyes and giving them a take-my-panties-off-with-your-teeth tilt. Her nose was small, dainty, her cheekbones just a little rounded. Her lips were lush and pink, and her skin a deep gold. And she *did* have freckles. A smattering on her nose.

Rowan would get to trace then when he bedded her.

Sean's hands fisted at his sides.

"I'm so glad to meet you, Gabrielle," Rowan said, his voice as smooth as scotch. "As I mentioned during the staff meeting, my name is Rowan Patrick and I'm the new owner of Eye Candy. The man behind me is Sean Walker, bodyguard, bouncer, and friend. Now, before we begin, can Sean get you anything? A delicious cup of coffee, perhaps?"

A moment passed. Gabrielle didn't speak or even twitch in her seat. She simply sat there, silent and still. Was she downloading the files in Rowan's computer even now?

Her brow furrowed; then a few seconds later a smile was lifting the corners of her mouth. Yep. She'd just opened the files. Question now was whether or not she liked what she'd found.

"Gabrielle," Rowan said when her expression once again cleared.

"What?" She blinked, shook her head. "Oh. Sorry. Please, call me Gabby."

Sean liked the sound of her voice. A little raspy, a lot seductive.

"Would you like that coffee, Gabby? I always have coffee around, I just love it so much," Rowan said.

"Or would you rather have something to relax you? You look nervous. Sean's happy to fetch anything you desire."

Of course he was. He was the lowly bodyguard/errand boy.

"No, thank you," she said, her gaze flicking to Sean. It didn't remain on him for more than a few seconds, but he felt the heat of it all the way to the bone. "I'm fine."

Rowan sipped from his cup. "Well, there's no reason to be nervous, I assure you. This is just an informal meeting for us to get to know each other."

She didn't shift, didn't even twitch. "I'm not nervous."

"Oh. Well, good." Rowan waited for her to say something else, but she never did. With a sigh, he ran a finger down the paper in front of him. "Your file says you've been working here for six months."

"That's right."

There was another long pause as they waited for her to elaborate. Again, she didn't.

Rowan settled back in his seat. "What'd you do before coming here?"

They already knew the answers because they'd done an extensive background check on her, *and* her aliases, but they wanted to, one, see if she'd lie and two, get her to open up.

"I waitressed for another club."

Truth. But just as before, she offered nothing extra.

Rowan ran his tongue over his teeth and laced his hands at his middle. He frowned. Was probably frustrated. Females usually offered him their panties at this point.

"So . . . do you like working here?" Rowan asked.

"Yes."

Sean's lips twitched.

Suddenly Gabby's gaze lifted and locked with his, brown against blue. He knew she saw amusement in his. He saw . . . nothing in hers. Her expression remained completely unreadable.

He wasn't disappointed. Really. At least Rowan was striking out, as well.

Hey, you're supposed to want *him to succeed.*

God, what was it about the girl that was screwing with his common sense? He didn't know her, had never spoken to her, and wasn't the one who would be sleeping with her. No, he wouldn't be the one sinking into that soft body, hearing her passion cries in his ears, and riding tide after tide of pleasure.

His hands were clenched again, he realized.

"I want you to be as happy working for me as you were with your former boss." Rowan lifted a pen and began tapping it against his knee. "If you have any problems, if anyone gives you a hard time about anything, you come to me and I'll take care of it."

"I will. Thank you." She pushed to her feet, the conversation clearly over in her mind.

Rowan didn't speak as she turned on her heel and strode to the door. Didn't speak as she opened it, exited, and shut it behind her with a gentle click. Then he swiveled in his chair and leveled Sean with a dark glare.

"What the hell just happened?"

"That's called a strikeout," Sean said with a grin. "I've never seen you crash and burn like that, my friend."

"I know. Embarrassing is what it is. I mean, really."

Rowan tangled his fingers through his hair. "You got a better response than I did."

"Please, I got nothing, same as you."

Rowan offered him a sheepish smile. "I know. But I felt the heat pulsing off you the moment she stepped into the office. *Then* I saw the fantasies you were weaving about her and decided to throw you a bone. So you want her, huh?"

Sean lost his grin but managed to shrug. "Doesn't matter. Unless you picked up on her weaving fantasies about *me*?"

A sigh. "Sorry. Her mind was a blank slate to me. I didn't pick up on a single thought, emotion, or desire. It's like she operates on a completely different frequency than the rest of the world."

She probably did, with all those wires and chips in her head.

"Still," Rowan continued, "we can call Bill and tell him you're the one who should be—"

"Nope." The word burned his tongue, and he hated himself for saying it, but he didn't take it back. Success was too important. "I don't exactly inspire trust in the women I date. The opposite, in fact. Something about me makes people distrust my every word and action." His affiliation with the shadows, with darkness, most likely. They must have sensed it on some level. "You're better at romancing and I'm better at killing."

Rowan nodded reluctantly. "I thought I had her when she downloaded my files. She cracked a little bit of a smile." He shifted thoughtfully. "Even though we're abnormal ourselves, it's so weird to think a human can do that. Act like a computer, I mean."

"Yeah." Made him wonder what else she could do. What they didn't know about.

Another sigh. "So what do we do now?"

He didn't have to think about it. "We do what we're good at. You work your way into her pants and I eliminate anyone who tries to stop you." Himself included.

CHAPTER THREE

Thursday through Sunday, Gabby worked from 7:00 P.M. to 3:00 A.M., her usual nights and hours. Only difference was, her new boss and his bodyguard. Mr. Patrick was in his office upstairs, standing at the wall of windows that overlooked the entire club, watching her. That shouldn't have bothered her. He was a handsome man, almost pretty. But bother her it did.

Why? He was the kind of man she usually preferred—on the rare occasions she allowed herself to date, that is. Clean-cut, well mannered, established. He'd had letters to his mom on his laptop, even. Sweet letters. Loving letters. Not many men were that sensitive, and she liked that about him.

But he wasn't the one who had fascinated her. The moment she'd walked into the office earlier that week, Sean Walker had consumed her attention. He was big and tattooed, his gaze unwavering, his expression etched in constant challenge. There were secrets in his eyes . . . a darkness that should have frightened her.

Unlike Rowan, Sean was the kind of man she usually avoided. Hard, rough around the edges, a fighter. The kind of man that reminded her of her past, of those nights spent on the streets, alone and scared. Of those days locked in some madman's laboratory, a lab rat whose head had been shaved, whose skull had been sawed open—whose brain had never been the same.

Hell, her *life* had never been the same. Before releasing her, the asswipe who'd operated on her had given her a warning: *Go to the authorities and spend the rest of your life in someone else's laboratory. Have your head examined and spend the rest of your life in someone else's laboratory. Tell someone what was done to you and spend the rest of your life in someone else's laboratory. But if you do the smart thing and tell no one, you'll keep your freedom.*

She hadn't realized the extent of what had been done to her until years later, when laptops and cell phones became so prevalent. She'd walked into a building and suddenly found file after file opening up in her brain. Private information, photos, password-protected documents.

For several years, she'd assumed she was going crazy and hallucinating—but she'd been too afraid to get help. As if she could ever forget the warning she'd been given. Only when she'd worked on her own computer, trying to write a résumé, had she realized the truth about her ability. Once she'd saved that résumé, it had downloaded into her mind, just as thousands of other files had done, and she'd known it wasn't a hallucination.

Secrets were hers for the taking. Secrets she didn't want. Secrets that could bring down an entire nation.

Why the man responsible had let her go, she didn't know. What he'd hoped to prove, she didn't know that, either. She only knew that it had taken nearly a decade to learn how to shield her mind from automatic downloads. Sometimes her firewalls failed her and things seeped in, but for the most part, she now controlled what entered her mind.

Like on Wednesday, when she met her new boss. Curiosity had gotten the better of her, and she'd wanted to know what kind of man she would now be working for. Thomas Wayland, former owner, had had his quirks and a violent temper, but he'd left her alone and paid her under the table.

Mr. Patrick refused to pay her in secret, but he wasn't selling drugs out the back door, either, so she could live with the change. Didn't mean she'd pay her taxes, though, and put herself on the grid.

"The new boss is *hawt,* isn't he?"

Gabby turned. Bentley, a waitress like her, pressed up against the bar, unloading the empty beer bottles from her tray. She looked to be Gabby's age, late twenties, had a short cap of black hair and pretty hazel eyes. Her skin was pale and freckled. She always had a friendly smile, and everyone seemed to like her.

"Sure," Gabby said, remaining noncommittal. That was always easiest.

"I wonder if he's available."

Thankfully, they didn't have to strain to hear each other. The band and dance floor were enclosed by glass and the bar and tables in a separate room, keeping the music and laughter muted.

"Ask him." As the bartender handed Gabby the drinks she'd requested, she loaded them onto her tray. "Maybe he'll take the hint and invite you out."

"You wouldn't mind?" Bentley asked, biting her bottom lip.

Gabby laughed. "Why would I mind?"

"Well . . . I hear he asked *you* out."

Yesterday, in fact. And the day before. Why he wanted her she hadn't yet figured out. Average-looking as she was, he might think she was desperate and easy. Not that he needed desperate and easy. The guy could get anyone he wanted, including the lovely Bentley. "Yeah, but that doesn't mean I said yes."

"So you said no? Are you crazy?"

Not Gabby's favorite question. "Yeah, I told him no."

Her irritation must have oozed through her voice, because Bentley's cheeks leached of color. "Are you interested in someone else, then?"

"No." *Yes.* Part of her wanted to confide in Bentley, to tell all. But trust did not come easily to her, no matter how benign the topic. Even the smallest details could be used against you.

Where was Sean, anyway?

She hadn't seen him all night. But sometimes she would have sworn he was watching her, his electric blues boring into her, taking her measure . . . wanting. Probably wishful thinking on her part. Men just didn't look at her like that. Not plain little Gabby who didn't have a lot of curves and was merely cute on her best days.

She sighed. She'd dreamed about him every night since meeting him. Dreamed of him walking from the shadows in her bedroom, standing over her, and reaching out, smoothing the hair from her face. His skin was always hot, like a brand, his fingers callused.

He liked to murmur to her, soft, soothing things she couldn't decipher. Once he'd even brushed his lips over hers. She'd moaned in pleasure, but he'd torn away from her rather than press his weight into her and give her what she craved. Him. Only him.

She scanned the club, through the masses and around the tables, but there was still no sign of him. Disappointment filled her. He was supposed to be guarding the place and the employees, right? Why wasn't he?

God, she had it bad.

"Something wrong?" Bentley asked. "You're frowning."

"Oh." Damn it! Caught mooning. "No, nothing's wrong."

"You sure?"

"Yep."

Bentley shook her head as if trying to dissolve a troublesome thought, then lifted her notepad. "Well, I guess I should get back to work," she said, and strode to the tables in back to take orders.

Gabby gathered up her tray and headed in the opposite direction. She stopped at one of the side tables, this one surrounded by drunk twentysomethings. One by one she placed their beers in front of them.

When she released the last one, someone grabbed her wrist and tugged her forward. Without her arms to stop her momentum, she tumbled into the lap of the man closest to her. He laughed and snaked his arms around her, holding her captive. The tray clattered to the floor.

Everyone else at the table laughed as well.

Gabby ground her teeth in annoyance. "Let me go," she said as calmly as she was able.

"But I like you where you are," her captor said. "And admit it: you want to be here. Otherwise, you wouldn't have thrown yourself at me."

That earned several more chuckles.

Just as Gabby latched onto his thumb and shoved it backward, toward his wrist, the man howling in pain, she saw Sean step to the table. He was scowling.

"There a problem here?" he demanded, his voice hard as steel.

Gabby popped to her feet, heart racing, and released the man's thumb. "No," she said, hating the way her voice shook. Sean probably thought she was scared, but she wasn't. She'd dealt with men like that her entire life and knew how to handle them. She was excited, despite the fact that she might get fired for her actions.

Finally, Sean was with her again.

To her surprise, he smelled like mint and evening primrose. The floral fragrance should have been feminine, but on him it was delectably masculine, and she found herself breathing deeply.

"Hell, yes, there's a problem," the man growled, jumping up. Though he wavered on his feet, he glared down at her. "You broke my thumb, bitch."

Gabby returned his glare with one of her own. "And you sexually harassed me, you son of a bitch." She moved to flatten her palms on his chest and shove him back into his chair, but he was already out of reach.

Sean had circled the table, come up behind her, and slammed his hands on the man's shoulders, sending him propelling into his chair. Sean leaned down, putting him nose to nose with his opponent.

Everyone at the table went silent and no one moved to help their friend. Probably because Sean looked capable of cold-blooded murder just then.

"You ever touch her like that again and I'll cut off

your hands. Ever talk to her like that again and I'll cut out your tongue. Believe me, I'm very good with knives. Do we understand each other?"

Shock overwhelmed Gabby. Sean had defended her.

The man paled, the blue veins underneath his skin now visible. He nodded. "Y-yeah, man. Yeah."

"Good." Sean patted him on his cheek and straightened. "Finish your drinks and get out. You won't like what happens if you linger."

The command was not met with any protests. In fact, everyone at the table grabbed their beers, downed them as quickly as possible—liquid even spilling out the sides of their mouths—and raced from the building.

She and Sean stood in place for several minutes, silent. His back was to her, and that was for the best. She didn't want to see that fierce, determined expression, didn't want to feel the lance of attraction that always followed the meeting of his gaze. Didn't want to like him any more than she already did.

Of course, he had to turn eventually. Thankfully, though, he didn't look down at her. He kept his attention just over her head, a muscle ticing in his jaw.

"You okay?" he asked. Still his voice was like a barely banked inferno.

Concern. For her. Wow. "I'm fine."

He arched a brow. "Stuff like that happen often?"

She shrugged, careful to keep her expression blank. Not that he was looking at her. Why wasn't he looking at her? Sure, she wanted to avoid catching his gaze and feeling that lance of attraction, but what was *his* reason? "Depends on your definition of 'often.'"

"I'll take that for a yes."

"Smart man."

His lips twitched into a smile as his gaze fell . . . only he didn't meet her eyes. Yet. First he studied her chin, then her lips, then her nose. When those electric blues finally collided with her plain browns, every muscle in her body tensed and a shiver of awareness slid the length of her spine. God, he was beautiful. And yeah, maybe his tattoo and badass demeanor reminded her of her days on the streets, but suddenly she couldn't recall why that was a bad thing.

"What time do you get off?" he asked.

Loaded question. Was he asking her out? But while the words had been sexual, his tone had been matter-of-fact. "Around three, after my area is clean. Why?"

"I'm going to walk you to your car."

That was his job, keeping everyone safe. Not special treatment. That's what she told herself, anyway, but that didn't stop her heart from skipping a beat. "Okay."

"And then, of course, I'll follow you home."

Wait. What? "Uh, no, thanks." She didn't live at the address in her personnel file. She never had. It was better that way. If anyone came for her in the dead of night, she wouldn't be where they assumed.

The thought of having Sean over, though, of getting to know him and spending the night locked in his arms, was heady. Heady enough to cause her breath to hitch.

"That's not necessary," she forced herself to add.

Once again, his brow arched. "What if those guys are waiting for you? What if they follow you home?"

More of that concern . . . it was as potent as a

caress. No one had ever concerned themselves with her safety. "I can take care of myself. I swear."

"Oh, really?" His gaze dropped to her lips and lingered this time. "Know how to lose a tail?"

To admit that yes, she did, would be to invite questions about *why* she did. Gabby simply shrugged.

Someone bumped into her, and she stumbled forward. Sean caught her by the arms to steady her. She experienced another sizzle of awareness, and maybe he did, too. Neither of them backed away.

"I want to kiss you," Sean said suddenly, gruffly, "but my boss wants you for himself."

Her eyes widened. Sean wanted to kiss her. Sean Walker actually wanted to kiss her. *You have to get away from him. You can't allow him to do what he wants—even though you want it, too.* "I don't want your boss." *Damn it.* Why had she said that?

"Why?"

Because I want you. "He's not my type."

"And what's your type?"

"Temporary." That was the truth, and that's the way it had to be. And yet even those temporary dalliances ended poorly. Every time. Someone would get too attached, usually her, but she would still have to move on when the time came because staying in one place for too long allowed a person to develop habits, and habits could make that person a target.

Sean ran his tongue over his teeth. "And you think Rowan wants more from you than a good fuck?"

Probably not. Which made him perfect for her. "You ask a lot of questions," she grumbled. Talkative men were annoying. Sometimes. God, why didn't Sean annoy her?

"I should walk away from you," he said darkly.

"Yeah, well, I should walk away from *you*."

Now his eyes narrowed. Every word out of her mouth seemed to anger him. "Do it, then. Walk away."

"Believe me. That's not a problem." Except it was. Still. She turned. She didn't handle challenges well.

His fingers curled around her shoulders, and he jerked her back around. The shadows in the club seemed to swirl around them, thick and impenetrable, chasing away the rest of the world until they were the only two people in existence. She bumped into his body and his arms banded around her. Before she could say a word, his lips smashed against hers and, rather than ease her into the kiss, he thrust his tongue past her teeth and into her mouth, conquering, demanding.

Stopping him never entered her mind. She moaned, sinking into him, tongue rolling over his. His taste was orgasmic. Mint and cherry. Heat radiated from him, such delicious heat.

One of his hands tangled in her hair, angling her head for better, deeper, wetter contact. The other hand glided down her back, gripped her thigh, and hooked it to his waist. The new position opened her up, placed her core just over *his* thigh. Another moan escaped her, this one hoarse and needy. She could feel him, his muscle against her clit.

Thank God she'd worn jeans. Had she done laundry and worn a skirt as usual—and as required— she would have been rubbing against him and he would have felt how damp she was.

She shouldn't be doing this. Not with him. Not in a crowded club. Not even in private. She'd managed to avoid male temptation for the past two years, and she preferred to keep it that way. There'd be no tears when she left. And she *would* leave; she always did. Except her solitary, nomadic lifestyle had been getting to her lately, depressing her. That was probably why she'd spent six months in New York rather than her standard four.

"I'm hard as a damn rock," Sean suddenly growled.

Oh yes, he was. That erection rode up her belly, tall and thick and teasing just right. *More, more, more,* she thought. It had been so long, and this was so freaking good. Good-bye tears be damned. "So?"

"We have to stop," he insisted. He was panting. His eyes appeared black rather than blue, shadows swirling in their depths.

"Yes, stop." Her cheeks flushed with embarrassed heat. "That's exactly what I was going to say."

"Good." His arms fell away from her, and her knees almost buckled.

She managed to remain upright as she struggled to find her breath. A girl could get used to—and addicted to—being kissed like that. Like she was the entire world. Like everything revolved around her and nothing mattered but her pleasure. Like her body was worthy of worship.

But rejected like that? No, thanks. No kiss was worth that. *Liar.*

Thankfully no one was whistling or telling them to get a room. In fact, as the shadows faded from around them, she saw that everyone was going about their business as if nothing had happened.

"Don't leave the club without me," he said. "Understand?"

"I—I won't." *Except that I will.* Clearly noncommittal evasions weren't going to work with this determined man.

"And I'm following you home."

"Sure." *Sorry. No can do.*

He crossed his arms over his chest. "You wouldn't happen to be lying, would you?"

"Of course not." *Yes.*

"Good."

"Now if you'll excuse me," she said, raising her chin, "I have to return to work."

"Not yet. We haven't discussed that kiss."

He was teasing. He had to be. "We don't need to. It's over. Done."

"Yeah, we do need to discuss it. You need to know that it won't be happening again."

"Fine," she said, hoping she sounded relieved rather than disappointed. Wishing she *felt* relieved rather than disappointed. *This is stupid.* All that darkness inside his eyes couldn't be good. He was better off as a memory.

"Believe me. It's best this way," he added, mirroring her thoughts. "I might be as temporary as Rowan, but I'm a hell of a lot more than you can handle." With that, he strode away.

CHAPTER FOUR

For two and a half weeks, Sean followed Gabby home. Well, to the address she'd given her former boss. From the very first, she had known Sean was following her—even though she'd ducked out of the club, trying not to draw his notice. But notice her he had. Every damn time. He was always hyperaware of her and knew the moment she split. He'd race out and be on her tail in seconds, not even attempting to hide.

Well, until she reached her supposed destination.

She would park, exit her car, and wave him on. Wave—aka flip him off. He would drive forward, pulling shadows around the vehicle and hiding his location. When she would lose sight of him, she would reenter her car and head home. To her real home. Again, he would follow—but those times she had no idea.

Tonight was no different.

She exited and "waved."

He waved back, fighting a grin, and eased his Tahoe forward.

The tattoos around his eyes burned as he scanned the surrounding area. No one but him probably noticed, but the plumes of darkness branching in every direction were writhing and groaning, desperate to avoid the light of the moon and street lamps.

Come to me, he beseeched them.

They didn't hesitate. As if they'd merely been waiting for the invitation, they danced toward him, flattening against his car, shielding it—and thereby him—from prying eyes.

"Freaks me out every damn time you do that," Rowan said as he crawled into the front passenger seat. For the first time, Sean's friend had accompanied him to "keep you from doing something you'll regret." Not that Gabby had known. Rowan had lain in the backseat the entire drive. "I can't see a damn thing."

"I can." Sean's gaze could cut through shadows as easily as a knife through butter.

Gabby was in the process of settling behind the wheel of her car. Though more than two weeks had passed since their kiss, they hadn't touched again. Not even a brush of fingers.

He was becoming desperate for more.

That kiss . . . it was the hottest of his life. He'd forgotten where he was, what—and who—was around him. He'd never, *never,* risked discovery like that. But that night, having Gabby so close, those lush lips of hers parted and ready, those brown eyes watching him as if he were something delicious, he'd been unable to stop himself. He'd beckoned the shadows around them, meshed their lips together, touched her in places a man should only touch a woman in private, and tasted her.

Oh, had he tasted her. Sugar and lemon. Which meant she'd been sipping lemonade during her breaks. Lemonade had never been sexy to him before. Now he was addicted to the stuff. Drank it every chance he got. Hell, he sported a hard-on if he even spotted the yellow fruit.

At night he thought about pouring lemon juice over her lean body, sprinkling that liquid with sugar, and then feasting. She'd come, he'd come, and then they could do it all over again.

Seriously. Lemonade was like his own personal brand of cocaine now—which he'd once been addicted to, had spent years in rehab combating, and had sworn never to let himself become so obsessed with a substance again. *Good luck with that.*

"I'm getting nowhere with her," Rowan said. "You, she watches. You, she kissed."

"Yeah, I've been meaning to talk to you about that." Gabby's car passed his and he accelerated, staying close enough to her that anyone trying to merge into her lane wouldn't clip his car because they couldn't see him. Not that anyone was out and about at this time of night. "She's mine. I don't want you touching her."

"Finally. The truth. Which is a good thing, because I already called Bill and told him you were gonna be the one to seduce her."

"Thanks." This was one of the reasons he and Rowan were such good friends. "But I thought you were here tonight to keep me *from* her."

"First, you're welcome. Second, I lied. Third, what about that shit about women not being able to trust you?"

"I'll deal. She'll deal." She would have to. He wanted her, had to have her. *Would* have her.

Sean had kept his distance from her these past

few weeks for the mission. Rose Briar needed her secrets, her abilities, after all, and Rowan had been their best bet of getting them. *Had been*. Not anymore. The thought of another man touching her filled Sean with rage.

A rage so dark even his precious shadows trembled in fear of him.

Gabby *would* be his. She might be a creature of secrets and gloom, hiding from the world, running from what she could do and what others would do to her if they knew, but there was a better way.

He would teach her that things could be different. He would prove she wasn't alone in this. And she would trust him, just as Bill wanted. Sean would not feel guilty about earning that trust, either. He wasn't only doing it for the job; he was doing it for Gabby. He was going to improve her life.

She merged onto the highway, accelerating. He followed.

"What's the quickest way to gain a person's trust?" he asked, thinking aloud. He'd never cared enough to try before. But with her, skittish as she was, he would have to do something. Something that would kick-start their relationship without scaring her into self-destruction.

"This a trick question?"

"No."

"Well, that would be saving their life. You do it once, and they belong to you forever." Rowan shuddered, as if he had a few clingers he now regretted saving.

Sean nodded. "That makes sense." However, he didn't have the time to wait for real danger to strike. More than that, he didn't like the thought of Gabby being in any sort of peril. A single scratch on that delectable body and he might kill someone.

"So . . . what are you thinking?" Rowan asked.

There was only one way to go about things, keeping Sean in control and Gabby safe. "We put Gabby in supposed danger, not for very long, of course, we don't want her to self-destruct, and I rescue her. We can even create a mystery she can solve, like who wanted to hurt her, forcing her to tell me what she can do with computers."

Slowly Rowan grinned. "How devious you are. Wise as a serpent, harmless as a dove. I like it."

"Call Bill. See what he thinks. At this rate, a year could pass before she opens up enough to even go on a date with me."

As they exited the highway, Rowan withdrew his cell and made the call. Sean tuned out his friend's voice, concentrating instead on Gabby's car. He wondered if she had the radio up, if she sang aloud to the songs. Her head was swaying from side to side, as if she was imagining herself dancing.

He liked the thought of her so relaxed and wished she would feel comfortable enough with him to simply enjoy herself like that. *Soon,* he thought.

"Bill's a go," Rowan said a short while later, closing his flip phone. "Says we can abduct both you and Gabby and you can whisk her to safety."

Excellent. An abduction provided everything he needed: a frightening situation that would make them a team, an opportunity for him to showcase his rescue skills, a mystery—who had abducted them and why?—and a common enemy.

"Arrange it," he said.

"Already in the works," Rowan replied with a grin. "Bill thinks I'm a genius. Because I, of course, took credit for everything."

Sean's lips quirked. "Of course."

"He thinks we'll be ready to go as soon as next week. First he wants to find a place to store the two of you. A place that looks impenetrable and menacing but one you can escape without making her suspicious."

"It should be somewhere remote, too, forcing us to spend a few nights alone as we make our way back to civilization."

Rowan laughed. "Who says you aren't a born seducer? Maybe when you guys return, she'll be so in love with you, she'll do anything you ask. Even work for Rose Briar."

Maybe. Hopefully. He saved people with abilities like his own and protected those who didn't, was well paid, and had friends who understood his differences and didn't judge him. Gabby might not admit it, but she was in need of all of those things. Except . . .

"I don't want her love," he said. Love would only complicate matters. She'd want more than he could give and then, boom, he'd do exactly what he hoped to avoid: hurt her.

"That's for the best, I suppose. Soon she'll be firmly ensconced in Rose Briar, and too busy for you to be more than an afterthought."

Sean, nothing more to Gabby than an afterthought. He liked that even less than dealing with a woman in love.

"Now, when the time comes," Rowan said, "I'll sneak into Gabby's house, knock her out, and—"

"*I'll* handle Gabby." There was no room for argument in Sean's tone.

"If she sees you—"

"She won't."

"—everything will be ruined," his friend continued anyway. "The entire plan will mean nothing. And besides, this way, you won't have to lie to her. You will have done nothing wrong."

"I'll handle Gabby," he repeated. And Gabby, well, she couldn't hold any lies he told against him. After all, she'd lied to him about allowing him to escort her home. The little pretender hadn't radiated a single pang of guilt, either. "Just so you know, if I don't want to be spotted, I won't be spotted." He didn't mention that he'd been inside Gabby's apartment every night since meeting the woman. First time, he'd snuck inside to make sure her door locks were acceptable.

They hadn't been.

Second time he'd visited her, he'd spent hours installing new locks, making sure her key still fit and that everything still *looked* the same.

Because some of the windows hadn't had locks— someone had removed them and Sean was willing to bet it had been Gabby, easy escape and all that— he'd adhered them to their seals so that she, or anyone else, wouldn't be able to open them. He'd placed a motion detector with remote access in her hallway. That way, he controlled when the device was turned on and off and knew every time someone set foot near her bedroom.

Third time, he'd told himself it was to make sure she hadn't discovered his adjustments. He'd taken one look at her, as she lay so fitfully in bed, and admitted he'd been lying to himself. He liked looking at her. He liked being close enough to touch her.

The fourth night, he *had* touched her. He'd traced his fingertip along her jaw.

Fifth night, her lips had beckoned and he'd kissed her. A soft kiss, a simple meeting of their mouths. Again he'd tasted lemon and sugar, and had instantly hardened. The erection, though, he could have handled. But then she'd moaned, a sound so laden with need he'd had to leave before pouncing on her.

Later that same night, when he'd lain in bed and thought about what had almost transpired, he'd realized that more than kissing and touching her, he wanted to know everything about her. What she liked, what she didn't like—in bed and out. If she remembered her time in captivity. What the last man in her life had been like. If she knew anything about her family, if she missed them. What snacks she preferred—after sex and before.

Maybe then, when he knew everything about her, this need he had for her, this protective, possessive obsession, would wane. He could reduce her to the same status as every other female he'd ever allowed himself: forgettable.

Temporary, as they both liked. As *he* needed.

His father was like him, a summoner of shadows, and had often warned him of the dangers of prolonged relationships. While summoners could handle the darkness, embrace it even, others could not. And the more time summoners spent with people, the more that darkness seeped into their partners, driving out their inner light. Driving them into madness.

He didn't want that for Gabby. Which meant he could enjoy her for a little while. Only a little while. Once she was ensconced in Rose Briar, however, he would have to walk away from her. If she didn't walk away from him first, that is.

A few minutes later, they reached Gabby's home. Her real home. The building was a bit run-down, the red brick crumbling, but the wood trim was freshly painted and the pavement smooth.

There were eighteen cars in the side lot, and he scanned them. One of them, a sedan, had never been there before. There was a wet spot under the exhaust, as though it had been on for a prolonged period of time. That, in itself, wasn't incriminating. But tinted as the windows were, no one but Sean would have been able to see the two men inside, one at the wheel and one in the passenger seat. See them he did. And that *was* incriminating.

It was nighttime, yet both men were wearing sunglasses. They also wore suit jackets. The kind cops wore to conceal their weapons.

"I think we've got an armed visitor," he said as he parked.

"Where?" Rowan asked, looking around.

Rowan still couldn't see past the shadows, but Sean didn't want to send them away, alerting Gabby and the men to his presence. "Three o'clock."

"Maybe their presence is unrelated to Gabby."

"Maybe not. Either way, you gotta stay here, bro. Sorry. You can't see through my shadows and we need them right now. We can't allow anyone to spot us." Amid his friend's protests, Sean emerged. He commanded the shadows around the car to remain and summoned new ones to shield his body. They happily complied, whisking to him, wrapping around him, cool fingers caressing his skin. Only places they didn't touch were his temples, where the tattoos resided.

He remained in place, enjoying their ministrations. This was where he belonged, where part of him longed to stay forever. The shadows loved him, worshiped him. He was their king, his commands their greatest pleasure.

But as he stood there, Gabby stepped from her car. The moment he spied that fall of silky brown hair, he remembered why he was here, what he needed to do. Ever watchful, she scanned the area. For a moment, their gazes locked together and his breath hitched. She couldn't possibly see him. No one could.

She turned fully, stopped, reached out, then shook her head, mumbled something to herself, and turned again. Rather than move forward, she remained in place. She stiffened, her hands clenching at her sides. What was going on?

Finally, she leapt into motion, pounding up the steps and into her apartment. The door closed with a snap, and the slide of the lock soon echoed.

Sean worked his way to the mysterious car—but paused when he heard Gabby's lock turn again, followed by the creak of her door. Footsteps rang out, and then she was barreling down the stairs. She was scowling—and she was holding a 9 mm.

Shock poured through him because she, too, was heading for the car. Armed as she was, he expected the men to speed away. That's what any sane person would have done. Instead, they opened their doors and stood, shocking him further.

He looked them over but didn't recognize them.

The driver was five nine or ten, the passenger easily six one, putting him a little under Sean's six three. And still, without the shield of metal, neither seemed fazed by Gabby's gun.

Did she know them?

"Pervert," she growled. "You should be in jail, rotting with other disgusting offenders."

With her words, understanding dawned. Sean realized what had happened—and knew what was going to happen. The men were there for Gabby. Rather than attack her, frightening her, they'd put files they knew sickened her on a laptop to draw her to them.

Clearly, Gabby's secret had been leaked.

Shit. Shit! He was on his own with this. Rowan, trapped in the car and darkness as he was, still had no idea what was going on.

"Hello, Gabrielle. I knew those files would get your attention," the driver said with a grin.

Gabby stumbled, paled. "Wh-who are you?"

The passenger lifted his arm, his own weapon suddenly gleaming in the muted light. No, not a gun, but a tranq. Sean didn't think; he simply acted. Rushing forward and withdrawing his SIG Sauer, silencer already attached, shadows holding him close, he fired.

Pop. Whiz.

The man grunted and fell as the driver whipped around. But it was too late. Sean had already adjusted his aim and fired a second round. This man fell, too, muscles spasming as his shoulder absorbed the bullet.

Still in motion, Sean sheathed his gun and grabbed the tranq that had been dropped. Gabby was rushing to the car to see what had happened and he met her halfway. A scream tore from her mouth as he jerked her into his body, and he hated himself for scaring her. Knew it was dangerous, but it couldn't be helped.

"I'm sorry," he said. "So sorry." And then he pressed the tranq into her neck and squeezed the trigger. Strong as the drugs inside were, the blood-brain barrier was immediately broken and she collapsed, sleeping deeply, and he hoped peacefully.

He swept her into his arms and held her close. Even though he knew she was safe now, his heart had yet to slow down. "Rowan," he called. "You can come out now." Mentally, Sean commanded the shadows enveloping the car to part.

Rowan jumped out, scanning, trying to take everything in at once. He sprinted over to the fallen men, both of whom were moaning and crying. "Sean? Where are you?"

Sean shooed the shadows away from him and Gabby with only a thought. "Here."

"What the hell happened?" the agent demanded, staring wide-eyed at the carnage.

"I only wounded them, so you might want to disarm them before you allow yourself to be distracted."

With a grunt, Rowan frisked them and tossed their weapons out of reach.

"They wanted Gabby," Sean explained.

"Hired hands?"

"Probably." Which meant, whoever wanted her was still out there.

"Shit," Rowan said.

Yeah. That about covered it. "Get them in the car and take them in for medical care. Just make sure they're under lock and guard at all times. I want to know what they know."

"Consider it done." Rowan scooped up one man, carried him to the Tahoe, deposited him, and then did the same to the other. Both continued moaning and crying, but only one tried to fight. Him, Rowan used the tranq on.

In the distance, Sean could hear sirens. Someone inside the building must have heard the screams or watched from their window and called the police. He settled back into the SUV, Gabby in his lap.

"Get us out of here," he told Rowan when the agent claimed the wheel, "and let Bill clean up the rest of the mess."

The Tahoe shot forward, tires squealing.

"And to hell with waiting," Sean added. He glared out the window. "The abduction happens now. When she wakes up, I want to be with her." Earning her trust and keeping her safe from attacks like this.

CHAPTER FIVE

Present day

Warm—but hardly safe—in a sedan Sean had stolen in front of a grocery store after ditching the one he'd "found" in the forest, Gabby clutched her arms around her middle and peered into the night. Where they were headed she didn't know. She didn't recognize the expanse of fenced pine or the tar-topped roads.

She had willingly stuck with him up to this point, numb from everything that had happened. Being kidnapped, watching a man die, hearing Sean's confession: *I'm the one who abducted you.* Now, her adrenaline was crashing, her mind was clearing, and a sense of dread was settling in the pit of her stomach.

"Explain what you meant back there when you said you were the one who abducted me," she demanded, finally facing him. "Why would you abduct *yourself,* too?"

His profile was carved from steel, his neck rigid, his jaw clenched, his lips pulled down. "I'll tell you only if you promise to remain calm."

"I'm not promising you a damn thing." Not until she had answers. And even then, that didn't guarantee she'd keep her promise.

"Then I'm not *telling* you a damn thing."

She gnashed her teeth together.

"You may not know this, but fear is detrimental to your health. More so than with normal people."

Normal people, he'd said, which meant he knew *she* wasn't normal. He also knew about her headaches, then. If she allowed herself to wallow in fear, or any negative emotion really, she would develop a migraine. And only when she calmed herself down did that migraine go away.

Thankfully, she hadn't reached that point. Yet.

"I'm getting more scared by the minute, so you had better tell me what the hell is going on. How do you know about me?"

There was only a moment of silence before he said, "I work for an agency called Rose Briar, and if you dare try to open that door and fling yourself out, I will follow you and you won't like what happens when I find you."

Didn't take long to read between the lines. "You're government," she gasped out, paling. She'd lusted after the man, for God's sake, and he'd been out for blood.

"No. We aren't *officially* with the government. We're . . . independent, though national security is the reason we were formed."

"Unofficial." A very dangerous word. "You think that makes you better? Well, news flash. It doesn't. It makes you worse. 'Unofficial' means there's no red tape to get in your way. You have no rules, no regulations. And you and I both know there's no such thing as independent. Someone on the inside has to have their fingers in your pie."

He flicked her a dark glance. "We do government work when asked, yes, getting into places their people can't, getting information, apprehending terrorists, but our duties do not include experimenting on people with unusual abilities. And you and I both know that's what you're thinking. We actually protect people from that."

Please. She liked to think she was too smart to believe him. At least today. No use arguing about it, though. There were other things to discuss. "What do you want with me, Sean? If that's your real name."

"It is." A sigh pushed from him, seeming to drain his tension. "Look, when you were a little girl, your parents died in the car accident and you went to live with your aunt and uncle. Six months later, you bolted."

Tiny ice crystals formed in her bloodstream, cutting at her veins. "Yes. So?"

"So you were living on the streets."

"Again, yes." She heard the unspoken question in his voice. What had happened at her aunt and uncle's house to make the hunger and unmerciful elements of the streets easier to bear?

"Tell me," he beseeched. "The truth, please."

After everything he'd done, he expected her cooperation? "Why should I?"

"Because I just got you out of that house. Without getting shot."

"Yeah, well, I could have done it on my own."

He rolled his eyes. "Because you're bored, then." He reached out and placed his hand over hers, his skin as warm and callused as she remembered. "Please, Gabby."

Maybe she still wasn't thinking straight. Or maybe the tenderness in his voice mixed with the gentleness of his touch was too much to resist. Either way, the story spilled from her before she could stop it, the details of her terrible past dragged out of the shadows and into the light.

"They couldn't have children. They were so happy to have me, made me feel so welcome. But every day he seemed to watch me more. Then, when it was just the two of us, he started touching me. Innocent touches at first, as if he was trying to console me."

Sean's hands tightened on the wheel, his knuckles bleaching white. "Shit. I hate him already."

Sean's anger on her behalf spurred her on. "I told my aunt he was creeping me out, and she told me I just misunderstood his intentions. She also told me to watch my mouth, that accusations like that ruined people's lives. She loved me, I knew that, so I believed her and felt guilty for almost getting my uncle in trouble for something he hadn't really done. After that, he was distant with me and I felt even worse about it. About how wrong I'd been. Then, I came home from school one day and he was the only one home. He'd been drinking. He barged into my room and told me I owed him. That he was the reason I had a place to stay, food, and clothes, and how could I have almost destroyed his life like that? He unfastened his pants, told me to get on my knees and kiss him all better and that he'd kill me if I told anyone."

"What happened?" Sean croaked out.

She shrugged. She'd expected this unveiling to

hurt. Strangely, it didn't. The memory was distant now, like watching an old movie unfold. "I got on my knees and bit him until I tasted blood. He had to backhand me to dislodge my teeth. While he was stuffing himself back into his pants, I bolted, as you said. Only had the clothes on my back, but I didn't care."

"If he's still alive, he'll be in custody by morning."

Sweetest. Words. Ever. "I meant to go back, to tell the police what had happened so they could stop him, but then . . ."

"You were taken."

"Yes." And those first few days, locked away by a stranger, blood taken every few hours, she'd wished to God she'd just stayed with her aunt and uncle. That thought had angered her, though, and that anger had given her the strength she'd needed to survive. "You know what happened to me there, I'm sure."

He nodded stiffly. "You were experimented on, your brain turned into a computer."

"Basically."

"A long time ago, Bill found the guy who did it, and he's been looking for you ever since."

"But how did he finally find—my arrest," she said, understanding dawning.

"Yeah."

Stupid temper. It always got the best of her. "And the doctor?"

"He escaped. No one knows where he is. I'm sorry."

So many times she'd dreamed of killing the guy. Slowly, painfully. The moment she saw him, that dream would become a reality. She knew herself well enough to know she would attack. So maybe it was best no one knew where he was. It certainly saved her from committing murder.

"You're here to what, Sean? Take me in, lock me up? Earn my trust and convince me to do something for you?" She pressed her tongue against the roof of her mouth. That's why he'd kidnapped her, she realized. To save her and earn her trust. God, she was a fool.

"No. No!" he added with more force. "We just want you to work for us. Willingly."

Willingly. Ha. She knew how these agencies worked and that's why she had ruined her life in an effort to avoid them.

"Rose Briar agents are very much like you, Gabby. They're different. We can do things other people can't."

"Oh, really. What could Bill do?"

"Photographic memory."

"That's not an ability."

"Actually, it is. But anyway, Rose Briar is the only place I've found where those like us are accepted rather than condemned."

Yeah. Right. He was just trying to relate to her, to get her to do what he wanted. He was trying to lure her into a false sense of security. Trying to get her to crave that kind of acceptance. Well, she already craved it; she just didn't believe it was out there. Some people might pretend to admire her ability, but the moment she invaded *their* space, learned *their* secrets, they would turn on her with claws and fangs bared.

"And what's your power?" she asked dryly. "Putting innocent girls in dangerous situations?"

Tensing, he rubbed at one of his tattoos. "I . . . I control the shadows."

"Oh, please," she said, but then she thought back to their kiss, there in the club. Shadows had enveloped them, blocking them from view. Then, back at that house, shadows had again enveloped them and kept them safe from prying eyes. While she was locked up in that bedroom, shadows had thickened the air, preventing her from seeing anything.

Her stomach twisted. *Dear. God.* Sean was telling the truth.

Though she hadn't asked for more proof, he said, "Come to me," in a seductive whisper. The shadows rose from the ground outside the car and floated swiftly to the windows, keeping pace.

Suddenly she couldn't see out. A gasp escaped her. "Sean!" They were going to crash!

"Go," he said.

She thought she heard a moan of disappointment as the shadows whisked away, clearing the window and allowing her to once again see the road. "You can . . . you just . . ." Her jaw dropped.

"Yeah. I did. And now that we've established that, let's get back to you. There were nine other kids taken and experimented on."

"You're changing the subject? *Seriously*?" He was the first person she'd ever met who was as different as she was. She wanted to know everything about him. Had he been teased as a child? Chased and tormented? When had he first learned of his ability, and how had he mastered it? What did he do when there were no shadows present? Could the rest of his family manipulate the darkness?

"I'll tell you about my power later. Now, did you know others had been taken?"

"No. I never saw anyone but the doctor. Never

heard anyone but the doctor. So this power of yours . . ."

"The man who operated on you guys set everyone free," Sean continued, ignoring her. "We don't know why. We found one right away, but it took a long time to find two others and when we did . . ." His shoulders slumped. "All three are dead. Extreme fear caused some kind of self-destructive reaction in their brains."

"They *died*?" The knowledge caused fear of her own to spark in her chest, and she forgot all about questioning him. If he was telling the truth, and she thought that he was since the emotion had always elicited headaches, this fear could kill her.

On cue, her temples started throbbing and she moaned.

"Stop," Sean demanded.

"Stop what?" she rasped past the sudden lump in her throat. People just like her had died. Probably painfully, horrifically.

"Don't think about the past. Think about the future."

But he'd been questioning her about the past. And . . . "Do I even have a future?"

He flicked her another glance, this one so intense she shivered. "You sure as hell do. It involves you, me, and a bed. After that, there'll be a few repeat performances. And by the way, where's the quiet, nontalkative Gabby I know and like?"

A lie. He liked her better this way. Why else would he have asked her so many questions? *Information. Duh.* Well, she could see the excitement in his eyes. Excitement she suddenly shared. Sean. Naked and in bed. With her. Touching, kissing. *Oh yes . . . kissing.* For more than a night, too. That's what "repeat performances" meant, she was sure.

But did his desire spring from his mission, or for her?

Damned common sense, not letting her enjoy a moment's reprieve. She ran her tongue over her teeth, anger sparking, growing, replacing both her excitement and fear. "If you kissed me because they told you to—"

"Stop right there. I kissed you because I wanted to. And to be honest, I wasn't supposed to do it. I just couldn't help myself."

That mollified her somewhat. She desired him more than she'd ever desired another man. If he'd merely kissed her to soften her, she'd . . . she'd . . . still want him, she realized. *Damn him.* She was drawn to him. To the contradictions of him. Darkness swirled inside his eyes and was proof of his dangerous nature, yet he'd never once hurt her. Had been nothing but gentle with her. Had protected her.

Sighing, she studied her surroundings. The vast expanse of forest had thinned, and there wasn't a soul or car in sight. Lamps were posted along the sides of the road, their light providing a pretty golden glow. She had to stop thinking about kissing him and wanting him and concentrate on answers.

"You were there, when those two men drew me out and attempted to kill me," she said.

"Yes."

"Did you kill them?"

"No. I injured them. In fact, I need to get ahold of Rowan and find out if they talked."

Rowan. She should have known he was in on this. "He's an agent, too, isn't he?"

An abrupt nod.

And she'd never suspected. Seriously. How dumb was she? "Well, that stupid love quiz now makes sense. When asked what he liked most about a woman, he said a positive outlook and an appreciation for moonlit strolls, yet he struck me as the big boobs and no underwear type. I was supposed to fall for him, wasn't I?"

Another nod.

God. The balls on these men, thinking that passing a few "Is He Worth Taking Home to Mom" quizzes and she'd melt. "So what's his ability?"

"Charm."

She snorted. She was dumb, yes, but not completely brain-dead. "You don't want to tell me the truth about your friend, fine."

Sean merely smiled.

Frustrating man. "Do you trust him? Could he—"

"I trust him with my life."

Which meant she was supposed to trust him with hers, but she wasn't sure she could. She didn't even trust Sean. Not fully. More than she should, yeah, but not fully. "So why did you kidnap me? And yourself, for that matter? I asked before, but you never answered." Yeah, she'd figured it out on her own, but she wanted to hear what kind of lies he would weave.

He flicked her another glance, this one smoldering. "I wanted to spend a little alone time with you."

Now she was the one to roll her eyes, hopefully drawing attention away from the pulse suddenly hammering away at the base of her neck. "Nice try."

"Fine. It was the easiest and fastest way to gain your trust."

The truth from him. Wow. How unexpected—and warming. "Did you think I'd just smile and thank you when I found out you'd lied to me and used me?"

"Yeah. If you hadn't noticed, lying is part of our relationship."

She couldn't refute that, so she didn't try. "So why exactly does Rose Briar want me to work for them? And who were those guys back there?"

"You're kidding, right? With the first question? You can steal information in the blink of an eye. As for the men . . . the one who'd been shot was Bill, my boss, as I told you. The others, the ones with the guns." He shrugged. "I don't know, but I plan to find out. With your help."

"And if I don't want to help? What are my options?"

"You can live your life as you are now, but someone will always be watching you because too many people know about you. If you ever tried to lose that someone, well, you would be deemed a rogue and killed."

Wonderful. He wasn't lying this time. There was too much dread in his tone.

Gabby wasn't sure what she wanted to do. She only knew she was tired of running, so tired, and that she'd been found—by two separate agencies, it seemed like—so all that running had been for nothing, anyway.

She uttered another sigh. "I'm sorry. About your boss, I mean."

"Thank you. He was a good man."

They lapsed into silence, and a short while later they reached civilization again. There was a gas station, a few drive-thrus, and two motels. Sean parked in front of the motel closer to the road.

"This where we're spending the night?" She eyed the brownstone that formed a half-moon around a crumbling parking lot.

"Nope. We're getting a room, yes. But all we're doing in it is making a call and ditching the car. *Then* we're finding someplace else to sleep."

*   *   *

Sean had chucked his cell phone the moment they reached the highway, allowing oncoming traffic to run over it. There was an activated GPS in it, so anyone at Rose Briar could access his location. Besides Rowan, he didn't know who he could trust right now, so he hadn't wanted that information so freely available.

He procured a motel room, as promised, and while Gabby sat at the edge of the bed, he called Rowan. There was no answer, which wasn't like the agent. *Shit!* Was Rowan on the run, too? Hurt?

Sean left a message, telling his friend what had happened to Bill, that he had Gabby and would call again soon. Not for a moment did he doubt his friend's loyalty. Rowan had known where he and Gabby had been "locked up"—hell, Rowan had driven Gabby there—and if Rowan had been the culprit, the man could have easily done the hit there.

So . . . who did that leave?

The scientist who'd operated on Gabby? Bill had considered that a possibility before the mission had ever begun. The government? But why wouldn't they have contacted Rose Briar directly? They always had before. A *foreign* government, perhaps?

Whatever the answer, this was a bad deal.

"All right. Let's go," he said, taking Gabby's hand and helping her to her feet.

She'd handled his admission better than he'd anticipated. He supposed to someone who'd been through as much shit as she had, being lied to and used was nothing. And that saddened him. Of course, he didn't like that sadness and squashed it quickly. It meant he was emotionally involved, and that he couldn't allow.

Gabby didn't protest as he led her back into the night, summoning shadows to hide them from view. They walked the few blocks needed to reach the other motel. He didn't release the shadows from around them as they entered the building. He didn't release the shadows as he stole a key and headed for their new room without ever signing in.

Inside, he rigged his belt to the door lock. If anyone turned the handle, his buckle would rattle. Wasn't top of the line in security, but it would have to do. His resources were limited—he hadn't given himself much to work with at the safe house, not wanting Gabby to be suspicious—but he didn't want to drag Gabby through the night, keeping her awake and nervous while he looked for the necessary tools. At least he had a gun. Finally, he shooed the shadows away.

"What do we do now?" she asked, sighing and plopping down on one of the mattresses.

If only he'd stolen a key to a room with a king, rather than two fulls, he could have suggested a snuggle. Snuggle: guy code for *I really plan to feel you up.* "Tonight, we rest. Tomorrow, we start digging for information."

"Wow. An intricate plan I never could have come up with on my own," she said dryly, massaging the back of her neck. "Only, I would have worked in a shower."

His cock instantly hardened. *Gabby, naked and wet . . . oh yeah.* "All right. Work in a shower." *Please, please, please.*

"I will." Gazing anywhere but at him, she stood.

He followed her into the bathroom. When she tried to shut the door and it banged into the toes of his boots, she whipped around and gasped.

"What are you doing?" she demanded. There was a breathless quality to her voice that she couldn't hide.

Without a word, he checked the bathroom. There was a window, big enough for her to climb through if she so desired. He frowned. Wily as she was, he didn't trust her to stay put.

He turned to her, drank in the rise and fall of her chest, the nervous swipe of her tongue over her teeth. *Oh yeah.* She planned to run. His gaze took in the rest of her. The lips he'd tasted only once but craved even now. The face he'd dreamed about for weeks now. The sweetly curved body he'd panted after, the breasts he'd longed to knead, the nipples he'd wanted to suck.

There was only one way to go about this. He stepped forward. Grinned.

She stepped backward. Gulped. "I ask again. What are you doing?"

"Looks like I'm showering with you," he said.

CHAPTER SIX

Gabby stared over at Sean. He leaned against the bathroom door, pupils blown with the force of his arousal. At just the *thought* of being with her, and the knowledge was heady. He was as beautiful as always, jaw like granite, shoulders wide. Only now he had an erection, long, thick, and hard, straining past the waist of his pants.

Despite everything, she wanted him and had trouble catching her breath. "I'm mad at you."

"I know." He didn't move from his post at the door.

"I don't trust you." He had lied to her, planned to use her, and only confessed because those plans had gone to shit.

"I know."

She licked her lips. "When the shock of what's happened wears off, I'll probably hate you."

Still he remained in place. "I know that, too."

"Having sex won't mean anything. It won't change anything between us."

"Yeah, but it'll make us feel good."

Feeling good sounded, well, too freaking good to

resist. "Well, okay then. We understand each other. Take off your clothes."

Not wanting to see his reaction to her words, she spun, bent over, and turned the faucets until water sprayed into the tub. Next she removed her boots and socks. Was she really going to do this? Be with a liar of still-questionable intentions?

Hello. You're *a liar of still-questionable intentions.*

Behind her, she heard something slap against the sink. She looked over her shoulder, saw a condom. An agent was always prepared, she supposed. Next she heard the rustle of clothes, the whoosh of fabric hitting the floor. This time she spun, heart racing in her chest. Sean was completely, unabashedly naked.

First thing she noticed, he was dark-skinned and didn't have a tan line. Second, rope after rope of muscle formed a trail down his stomach. Third, his erection was magnificent. As long and thick as she'd imagined, the head swollen and already wet. A tremor moved through her.

Yes, she was going to do this. They hadn't kissed since that time in the club, and she was desperate for another. Except they weren't lost in a passion cloud right now, so she'd never be able to blame this decision on insanity. Her hormones would have to take the blame. But she was still going to do this. She felt like she'd wanted this to happen for forever.

Sean knew who she was, what she could do, and he hadn't run screaming. Like her, he was different. And oh, God, besides feeling good, the thought of letting go, of forgetting the world for just a little while, of those strong arms wrapping around her, holding her close and tight and safe, was irresistible.

"Change your mind?" he asked roughly.

"No. But I *am* going to let you do all the work." The words were meant to taunt him, but she ended up taunting herself. "You owe me."

"I don't mind." Grinning, he closed the distance between them. "And I take it back. I like this talkative Gabby a lot." His fingers curled around the hem of her shirt and lifted. Willingly she raised her arms, and the material swept over her head.

He sucked in a breath, his gaze glued to her tattoos.

She fisted her hands at her sides to keep from covering them. Different-colored flowers were scattered over her stomach and back, leafy vines connecting them. Some were prettier than others, and some were oddly misshapen.

"I used to let new artists practice on me," she explained. "For money." It had been better than selling her body, one tattoo keeping her fed for a week.

"I like them," he said, voice thick.

A sigh of relief escaped her—which was weird since his opinion on her body didn't matter to her *at all*—and she reached up, fingertips tracing his own tattoos. She didn't have to ask. He simply told.

"My father marked me when I was fourteen. The symbols are meant to anchor me. I can control the shadows, right, drawing them in and enveloping my body with their darkness, but sometimes everything inside me wants to sink into them, to become one with them. These prevent me from doing so. Prevent the shadows from fully accepting me as one of their own."

"Why on your face, though?"

"So that it's always visible, the . . . magic of it

unfettered. Now, you're still wearing too many clothes." His fingers lowered to her pants and worked the button. *Unziiip.* He shoved the denim to the floor. "Step out of them."

Gabby obeyed, left now in her bra and panties. Plain and serviceable, but black. Steam from the shower wafted around her, leaving a sheen of dew on her skin.

"You're so beautiful," Sean said, then dropped to his knees. He kissed her navel, tongue darting out, hot and wet, and her muscles quivered. That tongue followed one of the vines, swirled around each of the flowers, then traced their petals.

Her hands tangled in his hair as her head fell back, tresses brushing the sensitive arch of her lower back. "You have my permission to keep doing that."

"I would have killed Rowan if he'd touched these," he said between licks, gripping her hips. "He was supposed to be the one to win you, you know, but I couldn't let him do it. I had to have you myself. And do you know how many times I've jerked off these past few weeks, thinking about tasting you like this? Countless." He pressed his nose against her, right between her legs, and breathed deeply. "And fuck, you even smell like lemons and sugar here."

If he let go of her, she would fall. Not just on her ass, but into a void, flailing for an anchor. Never had she felt so desired. So necessary. It was as if he needed her for his survival. That he had to have her or he would die. An illusion, definitely, but as many times as she'd been rejected throughout her life, considered nothing but a piece of garbage, forgettable, worthless, the sensation empowered her. Soothed her.

"Go on," she rasped. "Tell me more."

"I can't stop touching you," he said thickly. He continued his exploration of her tattoos. His mouth was so hot it burned, his teeth scraping and stinging lightly. When he finished with the multihued designs—God, had anyone ever paid them so much attention?—he traced the waist of her panties. Her knees weakened, and she moaned. "You know the men who prefer not to taste a woman?"

"Yes." The word emerged breathless, a wisp of smoke.

"I'm not one of them." He moved her panties aside, then his masterful tongue was delving over her clit.

Another moan wisped from her, this one broken and hoarse. Her nails sank into his scalp. Soon he was devouring her, not just licking, growling low in his throat, fingers joining in the play, stretching her, filling her up. Pleasure was shooting through her, a drug in her veins, burning, boiling, blistering.

"Sean," she said on a groan. She writhed against him, pumping back and forth. The more she moved, the louder she became, and the harder he ate at her. It was too much, not enough, consuming her, destroying her concerns, her inhibitions, leaving her weak and needy, desperate for release. In that moment, nothing mattered but Sean. He was the center of her world, the reason she lived, the reason she breathed, just as she'd wanted.

"That's right," he praised. "That's the way."

"Don't stop. Please, don't stop." Gabby didn't care that she was begging. She was so close, needed more, would do anything for completion. The weakness should have embarrassed her, but it didn't. This was *right*.

His finger sank deep, so deep, just as he sucked on her clit, and that was it. The end. Or rather, the beginning. She climaxed harder than she ever had before, shaking and moaning and gasping for breath.

As she trembled through the downfall, he said, "I'll do anything. Nothing you want is too dirty or off-limits, understand?" He stood, licked her essence off his face and fingers, eyes at half-mast. As always, shadows swirled in those eyes, a living entity, calling to her, beseeching her.

Had she once considered those shadows a deterrent? Silly, that. He was the sexiest sight ev-er. She leaned into him, wanting to sink all the way inside him. Wanting the darkness to swallow her up.

"Do you?" he demanded.

What had he asked? Oh yes. Did she understand that nothing was taboo, that he'd do anything and everything she asked? "Yes, please, and thank you." There. All the polite words she could think of in one sentence. "So let's get busy doing some dirty things."

His lips curled in approval. "Strip the rest of the way first."

She couldn't force her legs to move, they were utterly boneless, and Sean chuckled. His hands worked her quickly, unhooking her bra and slipping her panties off her legs.

"Sorry," she said.

"You did warn me I'd have to do all the work. And I did tell you I was fine with that, right?" He looked her over, gaze lingering in all the right spots, making her desperate for another touch. Finally he reached out, fingertips circling her nipples. Both were hard and aching.

When he bent his head and sucked one into his mouth, she cried out in pleasure.

"God, you're perfect."

Just like that, the fire sparked again in her blood. She wrapped her fingers around his shaft, stroking up and down, and he hissed in a breath.

"I want this in my mouth," she whispered.

Gabby didn't wait for his reply. She dropped to her knees, sucked him deep, and *his* guttural cry filled the small enclosure. When moisture coated every decadent inch of him, she backed off and licked him, savoring his heat, the male spice on his skin.

He tugged at his heavy sac before gripping the base. "More. Need more."

"Feed it to me."

He aimed the plump head between her lips and once again she sucked him deep.

When he was begging as she had been, when his words were incoherent, she scraped her teeth over the velvet-soft skin, making him even more sensitive.

"Fuck," he shouted.

Clearly he wanted to grab her head and pump hard and fast, his hands fisting her hair, but he didn't let himself. Instead he reached up and grabbed the shower rod. The tip of him hit the back of her throat and she swallowed. At the same time, she looked up at him and hummed her own pleasure, loving the look of absolute bliss that coasted over his features.

The motion and vibration had him cussing loud and long. "Stop . . . stop . . . Gabby, you have to stop or this'll be over, and I'm not ready for it to be over."

She didn't want to stop. She wanted to taste him, all of him.

Dragging her mouth off of him by force, he jerked her to her feet. "Your mouth is heaven," he panted. Sweat glistened over his skin.

"Sean?" she said, cupping his cheeks.

"Yes." He sounded weary, looked suspicious.

"You know those women who don't like to swallow a man? I'm not one of them."

He groaned as if in pain. "You're killing me. Next time, okay? This time, I want inside you and I don't want to have to wait to recover to get what I want."

Yes. Yes, yes, yes. Had someone busted into the bathroom, gun in hand and aimed at her head, she would not have been able to stop. It was like she wasn't Gabby without Sean. Like she was missing a half of herself—like she'd always been missing a part of herself but hadn't known it until now. Until Sean had touched and tasted her. Until she had tasted him. But now that she knew what her life was missing, she couldn't survive without it.

Had she known it would be this way with Sean, she might not have agreed. When they parted, and they would, because she would not allow herself to create permanent ties, she would cry harder than she'd ever cried before. But again, she was powerless to stop this from happening, from losing more of herself. Hell, from *wanting* more.

Sean grabbed the condom packet he'd tossed onto the counter and ripped it open with his teeth. Once he'd rolled the latex over his length, he snaked his arms around her and lifted her into the tub. Soon the water was beating down on them both. The heat soothed the aching need in her muscles, her bones.

She expected him to pounce. He didn't. He handed her the soap. Her hands trembled as she removed the wrapper. As she cleaned up, he leaned against the wall and watched. Then they switched. By then, her muscles and bones were no longer soothed. They were on edge, waiting, hoping.

"We're not . . . done, are we?" After all, he'd put the condom on. And he'd kept it on, thank you very much.

"Hell, no," he said. And then he was on her, mouth pressing against hers, tongue delving deep.

Passion and shadows once more swept her under, and she returned his kiss with a fervency that scared her. Taking, giving, craving, silently begging, needing, clutching, clawing at him. Their tongues were practically having sex on their own, rolling over each other, battling, thrusting deep.

"You're ruining me for everyone else," he growled.

She was glad, hated herself for feeling that way, but couldn't stop the joy. She wanted him to herself, for herself. Wanted everyone else to stay away from him. *But only for a little while,* she forced herself to add.

"Tell me you want me."

"I do. I want you. So bad I ache."

He stood before her and growled his approval, then cupped her ass, lifting. She wound her legs around him, locking her ankles at his back, just as he shoved inside her. There was no slowly sinking inside, allowing her body to grow used to him. He was in her to the hilt in seconds. Their groans of pleasure mingled, his low, hers high, and it was like music, urging them on.

"Damn. Shit." Over and over he pumped, slipping and sliding, filling her up, stretching her wide, hitting all the way to her soul. "Sorry, sorry," he said.

"Should go slow. Should savor, not fuck through your spinal cord."

That would have made her laugh if her body weren't currently on fire, her nerve endings screaming at her. "No, no. You feel so good. I can take it. Can take it hard and fast."

He took her at her word. He spun and slammed her against the tiles. The cold made her gasp, but he used the leverage to penetrate balls deep. Her nipples abraded his chest as he pressed her forward and gripped her hips, spreading her thighs as wide as they could go. Only his shaft held her up, gravity causing her to fall on him with every arch of his hips. He was a part of her, that missing part, finally making her whole. Her head thrashed from side to side, and she scratched at his back, holding on for the roughest, naughtiest, and sweetest ride of her life.

His movements became more frantic, the pumps short but deep. He was close, she knew he was, and that thrilled her. Gave her power. She had done this, pushed him to the edge.

"Hate me all you want afterward, but right now you're mine," he gritted out.

The words were as powerful as a caress and Gabby flung herself over the edge, screaming her pleasure, muscles spasming, stars winking behind her eyes. She lost her hold on reality for a few minutes—maybe hours—spinning out of control, body washed with a bliss so sublime she would never be the same.

Sean roared, loud and long, then found her mouth again, tongue thrusting home as his climax hit. Kissing him like that prolonged her own climax, taking her to yet another new height.

Finally, he collapsed against her. Finally, conscious thought returned to her. The water was cold, she realized. At least Sean's big body shielded her from the brunt of it. Her legs fell from him, but her feet were like blocks of lead and she was unable to balance her weight on them.

He reached back, leaning away from her slightly, and twisted the knobs until the water stopped cascading. Without the hum of water dancing over porcelain, the raspiness of their breaths echoed.

When he faced her, his expression was unreadable. "That ever happen to you before?"

"A . . . a million times." Her teeth chattered together, her wet skin like ice as the air brushed against her.

"Liar," he said.

Yes, she was. *Nothing* like that had happened to her before.

"You were as surprised as I was."

"Don't—don't delude yourself."

He helped her from the stall and patted her dry with a towel. He used the same towel on himself, and she liked the thought of the same cloth touching both their bodies. *Silly girl.* Repeat performances aside, this had to be a one-time thing. Couldn't be more. He was dangerous, and when all was said and done, she had to run again.

Didn't she? She'd never considered working for an agency before, government or otherwise. But as she'd thought before, not having to constantly look over her shoulder and leave the things she grew to love would be nice.

Rose Briar had lied to her, though. Not that lying was such a terrible sin, but they had thought to trick her into trusting and helping. It was proof that they were just like everyone else. Their agenda was all that mattered and they would have no problem hurting her if she ever defied them, she was sure.

Sean opened the bathroom door, and even colder air swept inside. As she glanced down at her dirty clothes, she shivered *and* shuddered, not liking the thought of putting them on again now that she was clean.

"Under the covers," he commanded. "I'll have new clothes for us by morning."

So they would sleep naked? If so, they'd have sex again. She knew it, and couldn't allow it. After the earth-shattering sex they'd just had, twice could lead to addiction. And whether she decided to work for Rose Briar or not—God, was she truly considering it?—she had to be ready to walk away from this man at a moment's notice.

Only way to stop it, really, was to make him want to keep his distance.

"Thanks. Just so you know, I prefer real cotton. Oh, and thanks for the distraction," she added as if it were an afterthought, trying for a cold tone.

"You're welcome," he gritted out.

"It was . . . pleasant. I guess." Gabby sailed past him. Or rather, tripped past him. Her legs were still weakened.

In the room, she dived for the bed and scrambled under the covers. Now that passion was no longer clouding their thoughts, she wasn't as proud of her body and knew he would not be seeing it in quite the same way.

The moment she settled, she felt the mattress dip. Her eyes widened as she swung her attention to Sean.

He was scooting in beside her. He didn't ask for permission but hauled her to his side.

"There are two beds."

"I know. Now keep me warm," he commanded.

He was already warm, his body like a furnace. That heat enveloped her, drugging, delicious. "Okay, but I'm not yours," she whispered, surprised by the sense of depression filling her. "I can't be. And you called me yours in the shower, said it didn't matter if I hated you. Which I do, by the way."

"Do you always believe a man who's fucking you? We tend to say things we don't mean." He didn't wait for her reply. "Go to sleep, Gabby. We'll figure all of this out in the morning."

CHAPTER SEVEN

Quiet as possible, Sean removed the GPS tracking chip from inside the sole of Gabby's shoe. He'd forgotten he'd placed it there before taking her to the safe house. He stuffed it in his pocket and stared down at her. She was on her stomach, face turned toward him, and sleeping peacefully. She was naked, still flushed.

If she woke up and ran . . .

I'll find her, he thought.

Walking away from her just then was difficult. But he did it. Even though every cell in his body demanded he sink back under those covers, plaster that woman's delectable curves with his weight and heat, and enjoy another taste of her. He snuck through the bathroom window, so he wouldn't disturb the belt still attached to the door.

He quickly hot-wired a car and drove to the nearest—and biggest—store, a supercenter, tossing the chip out the window along the way. Thankfully, there was a bit of a crowd and he was able to blend in. He picked up shirts, pants, underwear for a man his size and a woman Gabby's. All made of cotton.

Granola bars, bread and ham, and bottles of water. A lawn mower muffler, which he planned to use as a makeshift silencer for his gun since he'd left his with Rowan. Most important, he purchased a pre-paid phone.

Of course, the entire time his thoughts remained on Gabby and what they'd done last night. He loved sex. Since his first time at the age of fifteen, while "studying" over at a girlfriend's house, he'd loved sex. The meeting of bodies, that sense of companionship, of belonging, just for a little while. But what he and Gabby had done last night . . . it had been more than sex; it had been a possession.

What was it about her that got to him so intensely?

He'd watched her these past couple weeks. She was so wary, so secretive. Not once had she opened up to anyone. Not once had she gone on a date or talked and laughed—with anyone. She'd kept to herself, jumped at the slightest noise. Tensed when someone touched her. Except him.

Sean knew about her uncle now, and wanted to kill the fucker. More than kill, he wanted to torture. And he would. When this was over, he planned to make sure the bastard never hurt another little girl like he'd hurt Gabby. The bastard wasn't why Gabby was like she was, though. As much time as she'd spent on the streets, she had to have seen the worst humanity had to offer. She'd probably seen all kinds of depraved acts. Some might even have been done to her.

Sean's hands clenched at his sides, and he fought the urge to hunt down everyone she'd ever met and kill them all. Clearly she didn't trust anyone. And just as clearly, he'd done nothing to earn her trust. Quite the opposite. That hadn't bothered him before—much—but it bothered him now. Trust was a precious thing, and he wanted hers. As much as he wanted her body.

Want, want, want. Still he wanted more from her.

He wanted her beautiful eyes to regard him with interest—sometimes they did, but he wanted more. All the time. All *her* time. He wanted to know her secrets, to share his own. He wanted to protect her, to make sure nothing bad ever happened to her again.

He wanted to take the darkness of her past and give her light for the future. Which was stupid. Him, the king of shadows, gifting someone with light. He laughed bitterly. Light wasn't something he knew. Not well, at least. But she had opened up to him a little and shown him a dry wit that delighted him and a strength of spirit not many possessed, and he'd liked it.

She had a good and generous heart, soft when it should have been petrified into stone, and had had a tough life. She deserved peace, freedom from her demons. She deserved love.

Was Sean capable of that? He'd admired his father but hadn't wanted to spend time with the man. He'd enjoyed other family members but had easily left them when his darkness had begun to seep into their lives. He respected Rowan, and a few other agents he worked with, but again, he could walk away if necessary. But love?

What he felt for Gabby had to be something else. Obsession, maybe. He scowled. He didn't like that word, either. It implied that nothing else mattered. Still, a part of him didn't mind the thought of his darkness being part of Gabby's life. He *liked* it. Wanted to share it with her. Wanted to wrap her in his shadows and float away, just the two of them.

Want, want, want, he thought again.

Stop examining your feelings, pussy, and go save your girl. Sean tossed his packages in the car, buckled up behind the wheel, and drove. He parked at the edge of the motel, angling the car so that he had a direct view of his and Gabby's room. The sun was high and bright, chasing away most of the day's shadows, so his coverage was minimal.

He was not at his best at times like this, but he had to get Gabby out of that motel room and on the road within the hour. She had to be in different clothes—people were already looking for that black top and jeans, he was sure—and she had to cut all that silky hair.

No, he thought next. Too much did he enjoy fisting that hair. He'd get her a ball cap.

Get busy. He dug out his new cell and dialed Rowan.

The agent answered on the second ring. "Agent Patrick."

Finally. "Guess who?"

There was a beat of silent surprise. "Fuck! Sean. Thank God, man. I got your message. What the hell is going on?"

"I was hoping you could tell me."

"We found Bill's body, just as you said. Someone popped him up good. He managed to drive to the cabin and crawl his way inside. Probably trying to warn you. Whoever did it followed him. We found nine sets of footprints there. They'd disabled the security we set up, so we didn't get a look at their faces."

Shit. "Why was Bill shot, though? As many secrets as that man had, he was better off alive, you know?"

"I know, and we don't have a goddamn clue as to what's going on."

Sean stiffened. "Who's we?"

"Me, Bentley. A few others who've been pulled on the case. Look, why don't you bring the girl to Rose Briar? We'll keep her safe while we figure this out."

"No. I trust you, but no one else. Bill's death wasn't some random accident, and he wasn't followed just so some thugs could rob him. They shot him for a reason. And whoever was there knew Gabby and I were there, too. They wanted us."

"Shit."

"Yeah. My thoughts exactly."

"Think it's the scientist who messed with her brain?" Rowan asked.

"Maybe." Sean pressed his head against the back of his seat, the rough material making his skin itch. "Find out what you can about him, about the other kids he fucked with, too. Maybe Bill knew something he didn't share with us." With the words, an idea hit Sean.

As high up on the power pole as Bill had been, he would have documents. Top-secret documents only he had been privy to. They could very well be stored on any or all of his computers. At the office, at his home. He might have text messages and e-mails on his phone.

First order of business, then: getting Gabby inside Bill's house. Second . . . "Did you get Bill's personal effects?"

"Yeah," Rowan said. "Why?"

"I want his phone."

"That's already been confiscated by top brass. Standard procedure, you know that."

"Yeah, but can you get it for me?"

A pause. A sigh. "Yeah. Your message said you abandoned your own phone. How do you want me to let you know I've got it?"

As Rowan spoke, Sean's gaze scanned the lot. He was just opening his mouth to reply when he spotted two men slinking along the pavement just in front of the motel room doors. Both wore jeans and T-shirts, as well as jackets. Jackets to conceal their weapons, just like the ones who'd waited for Gabby that night at her apartment?

"Sean?" Rowan said.

"Don't worry. I'll find you," he replied, and hung up the phone. His heart drummed in his chest as he exited the car. He palmed his SIG. A gunfight would bring news stations and witnesses, and he didn't want that. He hadn't had time to rig the silencer, so if he fired, he'd have to leave the scene quickly.

The men stopped in front of Gabby's door, looked at each other, their expressions equally determined, then looked around. Sean ducked under an awning, out of sight. There were a few shadows present and he willed them around his body before surging forward again.

The men must have thought the gray cloud was odd, though, because both stared over at him, brows puckered in confusion. Confusion they soon shook off to concentrate on Gabby's door. Human minds simply couldn't process what they didn't understand.

One man gripped the knob. Sean increased his

speed, sweat already beading on his skin. Both men withdrew weapons, and *they* had silencers.

Shit! Damn! They planned to kill her.

He wasn't in range yet; frustrated, helpless, angry, he picked up speed. Only two ways he could have been found. One, his call to Rowan last night had been traced and the bad guys had been in the area. That didn't explain how the goons had known what room Sean was using, though. Or two, he'd been pegged with a tracker he didn't know about. If that was the case, why hadn't the room been invaded last night?

Too many questions, Sean thought.

Almost . . . there . . . almost . . .

Sean had crawled out the bathroom window to exit the room, leaving the buckle he'd rigged around the knob in place. He hoped the jingle of that buckle had woken Gabby and sent her into hiding. He hoped she wouldn't assume it was him.

Both men frowned when the door didn't automatically open to their ministrations. The one with his hand on the knob backed up, aimed his gun, and fired. There was a slight *whiz,* followed by an equally slight *pop.* So much for finesse.

Sean, finally within striking distance, raised his own gun and fired. There was a loud bang. A grunt. Contact. The man collapsed onto the ground, a new hole in his head. A kill shot.

Sean wasn't in the mood to play.

The other man had already stormed into the room, out of sight. Cursing under his breath, Sean grabbed the fallen man's weapon without pausing and ditched his own. He heard the clang of something hard slamming into bone, a grunt, then saw wood splinters flying in every direction.

There was Gabby, wrapped in a sheet, standing behind the door. She held the remnants of the tabletop that had once been pushed into the far corner. How she'd found the strength to lift it Sean didn't know. Adrenaline did strange things, he supposed.

The man stumbled to the side, dizzy but not subdued. He raised his gun just as Sean raised his.

"Duck!" he shouted to Gabby as he squeezed the trigger.

She obeyed without hesitation, and he fired. There was a muffled *pop, whiz;* then the man was screaming in pain, his gun blown from his fingers, his hand a bloody stump.

Sean stood in place, panting, fear and fury like a fire in his veins. So close. So close to losing her. There was a bullet hole in the wall, exactly where she'd been standing. If she hadn't ducked as quickly as she had . . .

"I'm sorry I took so long," he managed to say. "Are you hurt?"

"No. You?"

"I'm fine."

She lumbered to her feet, swayed. Her skin was pale, the few freckles she possessed stark. Her hand trembled as she smoothed the hair from her brow. "He . . . he tried to kill me," she said.

"Yeah." Had that been the man's purpose from the beginning, though? Perhaps he'd simply reacted to the threat Gabby had represented. Maybe they'd only meant to scare her into submission. Truly, there was no reason to kill her and every reason to use her.

They would soon find out.

"He freaking tried to kill me." Each word was

stronger than the last as the shock left her. Growling, she kicked the writhing body. "You bastard!"

"Move away from him," Sean commanded. Reluctantly she obeyed, and he frisked the guy before taking aim. No other weapons. "You've got one chance to answer me before you lose the other hand. Who sent you? And what do you want with the girl?"

"Fuck you," the man snarled.

"I warned you." Sean pulled the trigger, and bye-bye other hand. That earned another scream. "Who sent you and what do you want with the girl? Answer or lose a foot."

"Sean," Gabby said, suddenly nervous. "We have to go."

Beyond the door, he could hear people coming out of their rooms, wanting to discover what had happened. Someone had most assuredly called the police already. "You lucked out," Sean told the still-crying man. To Gabby he said, "Come on."

"Wait. Not like this." Blood splattered the sheet still cinched around her breasts, obscene with its vividness. "I need clothes."

"Shit. Okay. Wait here. I'll be right back."

"No! Sean, I—"

Didn't want to be left alone again, he realized. He pressed a swift kiss to her lips and handed her the gun. "It'll be okay. Shoot him if he tries anything."

"Yeah. Yeah, okay," she said after gulping.

"I'll just be a minute. I left our new clothes in the car." Sean jogged outside, pushing through the growing crowd, and grabbed the bags from the car. No one tried to stop him.

When he returned, Gabby was standing exactly

as he'd left her. Gun pointed shakily toward the man. Sean claimed the weapon and handed her pants and a top.

"Dress." He shut the door behind him and kicked off his shoes, then tugged on his new clothes, and Gabby did the same. There wasn't time to appreciate the perfection that was her body or how cute she looked in her new gray sweat suit. "Let's go."

"What about . . ." She gestured to the man writhing on the floor.

"We leave him." Sean wanted to take him, though, and question him. He just couldn't manage it. Not without notice, since the guy was bleeding and would have to be carried. "If necessary, we'll either sneak into the hospital and question him there, or maybe download his file." He hated to ask her to do that, though. Didn't want all that medical jargon floating around in her head, never to be forgotten. Answers, though, would be nice.

She nodded reluctantly, and they exited the room hand in hand. His feet were bare. Just in case. He wasn't taking any chances with GPS.

Everyone was congregated around the man Sean had shot in the head, blood pooling around the body.

"What happened?" Sean asked a random stranger, as if he didn't know and was just part of the horrified crowd. All those people created shadows. There weren't enough to cover both him and Gabby, but there was enough to cover her. Which he did.

Protect her, he projected.

They responded immediately, dancing toward him. They didn't wrap around Gabby as he'd commanded but slid around him.

Her, he mentally projected, an edge to the command this time.

There were several whines, but then they obeyed, swirling around her and blocking her from view.

"Sean," she said nervously.

"I'll guide you," he replied, knowing she couldn't see.

Someone said, "I don't know what happened. I just heard this loud explosion."

"I left my room and saw . . . I think I'm gonna vomit."

Sean kept a steady hold on Gabby and ushered her away. No one seemed to pay them any heed, lost in the chaos as they were. Still. He wasn't convinced the two men had been the only perpetrators and that someone else hadn't been waiting nearby in a car, ready to speed away with Gabby's body.

Sean's gaze swept the parking lot and landed on a man standing beside a Cadillac sedan. That man was youngish, probably late twenties, Sean's age. Not bad looking, tall with blond hair. His eyes were covered by shades, shielding their color. One of his arms was draped over the open door, and the other was splayed over the hood. He hadn't been there a moment ago.

He was like everyone else, taking in the scene, curious, but there was an intensity to him that the others lacked. He didn't seem upset. There was no frown pulling at his lips. More than that, his head followed *Sean.*

Could be an average citizen who suspected—or had even seen—Sean's part in all of this. If the man didn't know Sean was an agent and had only been doing his job, he would view Sean as a murderer. But the man didn't call out, didn't try to chase Sean down. Just continued to watch him, studying, gauging.

Sean snaked Gabby around a corner, out of view. In the background, sirens wailed. "Did you recognize either of those men?" he asked.

"No."

Too bad. "If I get you into my boss's—Bill, the man who died—house, will you take a look at his computer files? He might have stored information about the doctor who messed with your head. Information he didn't give me."

Her eyes widened. "You think the doctor's responsible for the men who showed up at our door? After all this time?"

"Maybe. Right now, that's the only lead I have."

"But why would he want to kill me now?"

"Several reasons." None of which he should probably tell her. Fear wasn't her friend. But the fear of not knowing, he was sure, would be worse. "His name is Dr. Fasset and now people know about you and he might want to hide the evidence of what he's done. Or maybe wants to finish his experiment; he's a doctor after all. Or maybe he just wants to keep you out of our hands. Anything we can learn about him will help us figure this out."

She licked her lips and clutched her stomach. "All this time, I've feared being captured, tortured. Used. But I never thought someone would want me dead."

"Maybe it's not Dr. Fasset. Maybe whoever is hunting you doesn't want you dead. You nailed that guy pretty hard with the tabletop. Shooting you might have been a simple reaction," he said, voicing his earlier thoughts.

She nodded, but she didn't look convinced.

They hit another parking lot, and he picked up the pace. He wanted out of this area ASAP. Away from the strange man by the Cadillac. Until he was better armed. Then, all bets were off.

CHAPTER EIGHT

What seemed endless hours later, Gabby perched inside Sean's newest stolen vehicle, circling the dead Bill's house. Sean was casing it, she knew, as well as waiting until the sun dimmed. Time ticked by slowly, dread filling her, until finally, he parked at the far end of the street. Shadows were thickest there, lying patiently under a grove of oak trees. Plus, they could still see the house and those around it. All remained calm in the affluent suburb, most of the home owners still at work. But they could return at any moment.

"You ready for this?" Sean asked, glancing over at her.

She nodded unenthusiastically. Her years on the streets, B and E had been her specialty. No home had been safe. She'd learned the best times to snatch and grab, the best times to go in easy and linger. She'd learned the signs of a nosey neighbor and what to avoid. Usually she'd just stolen food and clothing, knowing she couldn't live with the guilt of taking something that held sentimental value. But sometimes, when things were particularly tough, she would take something easy to pawn.

Not that she'd broken into someone's home in years. The day she'd been deemed old enough to waitress had been a relief.

"Hey. You okay?" Sean asked.

You're not stealing anything this time. Just gathering information. You can do this. "Yes," she said. "Just . . . bad memories sneaking up on me."

A slow grin lifted Sean's lips.

"What?" Her reply hadn't been funny. Had it?

"It's just, the first time I met you, getting any answer besides 'yes' or 'no' from you was impossible. Now you explained something and I didn't have to beg for it. Could it be you're starting to, I don't know, like me?" His grin became megawatt.

Though she was panicking inside—she couldn't like him—she rolled her eyes. "Don't flatter yourself."

"So what bad memories were troubling you?"

"Do you really want to talk about that now?" There. He hadn't gotten any information out of her.

"Why not? I want to wait at least an hour before going in the house."

An hour? Alone with Sean? The man she'd slept with last night? The man she'd snuggled with and breathed in and dreamed about and still craved this morning when she'd woken up, upset to find herself alone?

"Why? Was he married? Is his wife still in the house?"

"Nah. Nothing like that. The longer we wait, the darker it will be. Besides, Bill was as single as the rest of us. The job kind of does that to you, keeps you from forming anything lasting. I mean, it's not like we can tell a date what we do."

"Well, you can tell other agents."

"But they work the same insane hours, leaving hardly any time for play."

"And you expect me to sign on happily for the same kind of life?"

"Like your life is any different now," he said dryly. "Aren't you the one who told me you like temporary men?"

Good point.

"So . . . have you ever wanted anything more?" he asked.

Yes. "No." *Maybe. With him.* Stupid.

There was a long pause. Whether he believed her, she didn't know.

"Have you?" she asked, and damn, she'd sounded almost . . . jealous.

He leaned against his headrest and stared up at the roof. "A few weeks ago, I would have said no. Then, I met you. Does that mean I want something permanent? No. But more than temporary? Hell, yes."

"You don't know me," she said, because she didn't want to believe him. Didn't want to soften even more toward him than she already had.

"I know more than you think, Gabby."

"Oh, really?" Her palms began to sweat. If any man could see into the heart of her, she feared it was this one. "Prove it."

Only the barest pause. "You like kids and give what little money you have to any you encounter. You probably see yourself in them. You guard your thoughts and your feelings, because you've learned you can only rely on yourself. You don't dream anymore or expect more for yourself because you don't think dreams can come true and you've had enough disappointment in your life already. But sometimes . . . sometimes you can't help yourself. Sometimes you want; you hunger."

Her mouth fell open, snapped closed.

His gaze met hers, hard, determined. "I will win your trust, Gabby. Whatever it takes."

A lump formed in her throat, and she swallowed. "Good luck with that."

"We'll see. Anyway, to change the subject, if we had a tracker, we've ditched it," he said, his tone now unreadable. He acted as if he hadn't just rocked her entire world off its axis. "I made sure we weren't followed. But I told Rowan what I planned to do— that's what I was doing when you were attacked— and I don't know if anyone was listening in and now thinks to ambush me."

This was good. This was business. *This* she could handle without wanting to throw herself into his arms, bury her head into his neck, and cling. "I've asked before and you assured me he wasn't, but I think you need to consider the possibility that Rowan—"

"No." Sean gave an emphatic shake of his head. "I trust him completely."

Wow. To trust someone like that, without any hesitation, without any doubt, would be . . . wonderful, she realized. Foolish, but wonderful. She'd never relied on anyone like that. Well, not true. Her parents. She'd trusted and loved them—and they'd died and left her to her aunt and uncle when they would have been better off leaving her to the state.

If her parents had really loved her, they would have made sure she was properly taken care of in case the worst happened. Which it had. Right? That's what love was. Taking care of someone, no matter what.

The way Sean's taking care of you now?

No, she almost said aloud. He was taking care of her, yes, but it wasn't because he loved her and wanted the best for her. *Does that mean I want something permanent? No,* he'd said. He was doing his job. Still, a shiver left a trail of goose bumps all over her body. To be loved by him . . .

Stupid, she thought again. She shouldn't want him like this. She'd had him. His taste and feel were no longer a mystery. She should be able to shove him to the back of her mind, use him to stay alive as he'd planned to use her, and then forget about him. Instead, she only wanted him more. Wanted more of that heated touch. More of that hot, wet tongue. More of that raspy voice telling her how beautiful she was, how sweet she tasted, how anything she wanted done to her would be done.

"You like me; admit it," he said, turning in his seat to stare out at the homes. His intense gaze missed nothing, she was sure.

"Your subject change didn't last long. And anyway, *I* don't know anything about *you*. Anything true, that is. You told me Sean is your real name, but I don't see how it can be. You're an undercover agent."

"There's no record of me anywhere, so I can use my real name with no worry of exposure. You can even shout it out in pleasure. Oh, wait. You've already done that. As for getting to know me, I'm—"

"I never said I *wanted* to know you," she said, cutting him off. The more she knew, the harder it would be to distance herself from him.

"I'm thirty-five years old," he said anyway. "I've

never been married, I have a secret obsession for Twix candy bars, not that I've let myself indulge lately, and my favorite color is now brown. Gold, really, or maybe you call your eyes amber."

She gulped. *Damn him.* He kept doing that, and men just didn't say things like that to her. Not usually. Especially men who'd already gotten her into bed. Not that there'd been legions. Those she *had* allowed in her bed she'd wanted more for companionship and warmth than anything else. To feel normal, for once. To pretend they were happy and had forever. Not all of them had been concerned with her pleasure. And yet leaving each one of them had been tough.

How much tougher would it be with Sean?

"Your eyes," Sean prompted.

"I call them brown." It was the only thing she could think to say. And had her voice really been that breathless?

"As for the more meaningful stuff," he continued, "I was raised by my dad. My mom was never part of my life. Dad was very strict, very demanding, and very intolerant. He had to be, I guess, or I might have given over to my dark side."

"The shadows?" *You don't want to know, remember?*

He nodded.

"Do they want you to do bad things or something?" *There you go again.*

Oh, shut up, she told herself.

"Nothing like that. They just want me with them. Always. And sometimes I want to be with them. The only problem is, shadows are naturally hungry. Because they are cold, they crave people, body heat. They want to wrap around those near them so inexorably, light can never enter, and that tends to drive people insane."

He'd said the last with a quick peek in her direction. To judge her reaction? Did he hope to frighten her? "I've lived my entire life in the dark. That doesn't scare me." And, too, being lost in the dark with Sean didn't seem like such a bad thing. The things they could do to each other . . .

Stupid, she thought. Yet again.

He grinned. "Good to know."

"That doesn't mean I like you," she rushed out.

His grin didn't waver as the garage door to the house next to Bill's suddenly opened. Out came a black Lexus. The driver, a man who looked to be in his late forties, with round cheeks and a shadow of beard stubble, was at the wheel. He held a cell phone in one hand and worked the steering wheel with the other.

Silence reigned until the car disappeared down the street. Gabby realized her heart had sped up and was slamming against her ribs, about to crack them. He'd been there all along. What if she and Sean hadn't waited? What if they'd been spotted?

"So we know no one was inside his house, holding a gun to his head and peeking out the windows," Sean said. Then, without giving her time to reply, he resumed their previous conversation. "So what did little Gabby want to be when she grew up?"

Not what she'd become, that was for sure. "A stripper. Aren't you concerned about the guy?"

"No. And the truth, please. I've realized I like it."

And what Sean liked . . . "Fine. I wanted to be a ballet dancer. I'd taken lessons and everything." Those lessons had stopped after her parents died, of course. Her uncle had deemed the expense frivolous.

"That explains the way you move," Sean said huskily. "Graceful, as if you're walking on clouds."

"Thank you." Her skin heated with pleasure, and she frowned. The man was good, seducing her without touching her. "Now shut up. I need some me time."

He laughed. "Whatever you say, sweetheart."

Sweetheart. God, she loved that. They sat in silence for an eternity, both of them watching the neighborhood for any sign of activity. Nothing changed. Everything remained calm. Finally, Sean was satisfied that they were safe and happy with the dimming light.

"Let's do this," he said, and exited the car.

Now trembling, she followed suit. Part of her expected to be shot without the car to shield her. As if someone had been lying in wait for this very moment. She stood very still, limbs heavy, nibbling on her bottom lip. Soon a throb began in her temples, and she grimaced.

"None of that," Sean said, and shadows danced their way toward her. Enveloped her, cool and welcome, but cutting her off from the rest of the world. "I don't want you scared."

Because of the others, she recalled. The ones like her—the ones who had self-destructed and died. Again, that only increased her fear.

"I'll take care of you, Midnight Lynn. That's your new stripper name, by the way." He stepped into the darkness, becoming her everything. "Come on. We're safe. No one can see us." Down the sidewalk and around cars they maneuvered.

Gabby relaxed a bit and maintained a firm grip on the waist of his jeans, careful not to touch the gun he had stored there. "Do people not notice the big black blob floating along the street?"

"To them, it's like a cloud. A gloomy mist or fog. The human eye is funny that way. It sees what it wants, what it understands."

They must have reached Bill's house, because Sean stopped. He withdrew a black velvet pouch from his back pocket, unrolled it, and pinched a silver pin. He worked the knob for several minutes.

"Might be easier to unlatch the back door," she said. "Those locks are never as good."

He chuckled. "Done this before, I take it?"

Because there was no judgment in his voice, she answered honestly. "A few times."

"An agent's home is a little different from the average American's. Guess we're just more paranoid. Every door and window is hooked to an alarm. The one on the front door is less sensitive because it's used the most and even agents like to have people over. Guaranteed there's a trap set at the back door and all the windows."

"Oh." Thank God she'd never tried to break into an agent's home, then. She would have been toast.

"We'll only have a few minutes once I open the door, so be ready to download."

"Okay."

A moment later, hinges squeaked as the door swung open. Sean already had his gun palmed and pointed ahead. "Damn," he said. "The alarm should have gone off. They've already been here, then."

"The bad guys?"

"Rose Briar." He moved inside, dragging her with

him, and shut the door behind her. Only then did the shadows around her dissipate.

The home was empty, not a single piece of furniture remaining.

"Wow. They work fast." The man had only died last night.

"They have to," Sean said darkly. "I was just hoping we'd beat them to it."

"Maybe Rowan can get—"

Sean was shaking his head. "Nope. He isn't high enough up to confiscate Bill's computers."

"Let's at least look around." Wasted trips, how she hated them.

Sighing, she strolled through the house. The ceilings were vaulted, the floor comprised of polished wood. The walls were differing shades of beige, a few places scuffed where movers had hastily carted everything away.

There was a fireplace in the living room, the kind she'd always wanted for herself. So many times she'd imagined owning a place like this, curling in front of the crackling hearth with a blanket and a book, nothing to worry about as she sipped hot cocoa.

"So what do you want—" Gabby pressed her lips together as a low-watt vibe drifted through her mind, waking up nerve endings she usually hated. "There's a computer somewhere in the house."

"They wouldn't have left something like that behind."

Not purposefully, but there *was* a computer here. Determined, Gabby marched forward. The farther away she was from the living room, the less she felt the vibe. So she turned and marched the other way, out of the living room and down another hall. The vibe grew stronger.

Sean stayed close to her heels. When she attempted to enter a bedroom, he grabbed her by the waist and stopped her, then swept ahead of her to look things over.

"Clear," he said, and she entered.

It was as empty as the rest of the house, but she closed her eyes, stream after stream of information pouring through her head. "It's here," she said, closing her eyes. "I'm linked."

At first, absorbing files like this had hurt. Maybe because she'd resisted. Now it merely tickled. She knew to open her mind, to allow the documents, or whatever they were, to fill the chip (or whatever) that was inside her brain.

How much time passed as the information flowed inside her head she didn't know. She only knew that when one hard drive emptied itself another demanded her attention. Then another. And when she finally opened her eyes, the sync complete, the bedroom was no longer as bright and the moon was high, muted golden rays seeping past the burgundy curtains over the windows.

She was panting, sweating, her limbs weak. Downloading hadn't had this intense of an effect on her in a long time, but then these were the biggest files she'd ever downloaded.

Sean, she saw, was crouched at the far wall, facing the door and Gabby, his gun pointed straight ahead in case anyone tried to enter. He was covered by thick, white film. Clearly he'd beat at the plaster until he'd found a doorway.

"Thank God," Sean muttered as he stood. "I thought I'd lost you."

"Sorry."

"Bill had a secret office down there. Computers, notebooks, but nothing I found pertained to you or those like you. You?"

"I don't know. I have to open the files and sort through them. Which I shouldn't do until we have a few uninterrupted hours of safety."

"How does that work? Never mind. Tell me, but not here." He strode to her and wrapped his strong arm around her waist. Just then, he was her anchor and she couldn't have turned away from him even upon threat of death. "I have a lot of questions for you, but first I want to get to a safe place."

CHAPTER NINE

Sean stole yet another car, a minivan this time, and drove into the pulsing heart of the city. There he bought another prepaid phone, then placed a call to Rowan and set up a time to meet him. In case anyone had been listening, they'd used code.

"I have two ideas about what's going on" meant they'd meet at two.

"Come into headquarters; we'll share a cup of the world's greatest coffee" meant they'd meet at a local coffee shop they'd gone to once, hated, but joked sarcastically about ever since.

Having a history together helped in situations like this.

He picked a random motel and had to carry Gabby to their room. As he eased her onto the lumpy mattress, she moaned. And not the good kind of moaning. She'd begun opening Bill's files and clearly they were paining her.

Sean settled beside her and placed a wet rag over her forehead.

She didn't open her eyes, and her lips pulled into a tight grimace.

Hours passed with no change. He hated seeing

her like this and worried about what she was doing to herself. If she pushed herself too hard . . . Damn it! He wasn't sure how much more he could take.

"Gabby," he said. "Break time, sweetheart."

"I can't do it. Hurts so bad every time I try," she gritted out. "They're encrypted or something. More so than anything I've ever seen."

His concern intensified. "Stop trying for a minute and look at me."

Slowly her eyelids cracked. Beautiful brown irises, glazed and slightly unfocused, soon met his stare.

"Have you ever opened encrypted files before?"

"Yes. Once. But it took a while. I was curious, you know, so I kept poking at it until something clicked in my brain and the gibberish made sense. There's just so much here, and more than gibberish, it's protected by a firewall."

"Firewall?"

"It may not be actual fire in a computer, but it feels that way inside my head. Like flames are licking at my brain."

Shit. He removed the cloth and traced his fingertips over her now-damp hairline, her temples and cheekbones. If he'd known this would happen, he never would have taken her to Bill's. *Distract her.* "How do you get the files out of your head? Or do they stay there forever?" As he spoke, he stretched out beside her. To his surprise, she didn't protest when he drew her into the line of his body but snuggled closer, her head resting on his shoulder, his arm wrapped around her back, wrist resting on her ribs.

The scent of soap drifted from her, filling his nose, reminding him of the shower they'd shared, and he breathed deeply, savoring. His cock hardened, straining against the fly of his jeans. *Bad timing, buddy.*

Controlling his physical needs had never been a problem for him before. Especially in dangerous situations. But then, he'd never wanted a woman the way he wanted Gabby.

"Took me forever to learn how to get rid of them," she said. "By the time I did, my brain was so full I couldn't process *anything*. I didn't want to leave bed, just wanted to sleep all the time. And it made me sick, some of the stuff in there. Pictures I had no right seeing, plans I hope no one meant to actually see through."

Poor thing, he thought. Young as she was, she'd been through so much. His hand glided up and down her spine, offering comfort. He wished to God he could do more for her. "So what do you have to do to get rid of them?"

"I put them in the trash."

Literally? "I don't understand."

"Every computer has a trash receptacle. I had to learn to drag the files to *my* trash."

The scientist who'd messed with her belonged underground, worms eating at his flesh. Not because he'd given her a way to free her brain of the shit it sucked inside—that had been a kindness—but because he'd done this to her at all.

Then you wouldn't have met her. She wouldn't be with you right now. Sean cupped the side of her head, angling her, and kissed the corner of her lip. "I'm sorry you're forced to go through this."

"Why would someone do this to another human being?" she whispered brokenly.

Sean's hold tightened. "He's sadistic, sweetheart. He wanted to see how much he could change you, what abilities he could give you. He probably thought to use you for his own gain."

"Why not watch me, then? Why let me go about my life?"

Had he? Sean suddenly wondered. Maybe the scientist had let her and the others go but had somehow watched them, all these years. Because really, that's what scientists did. Watched and observed. Tested.

How would he have watched Gabby, though?

With . . . a tracker, of course. Inside her brain. Sean's eyes widened. That made sense. And also scared the shit out of him. It meant the crazy bastard would be able to find Gabby anywhere, anytime.

Sean could imagine the sick fuck sitting in a room, making notes, detached, clinical, sweet Gabby nothing more than a mouse in a wheel to him. But why come after her now? To keep her away from Rose Briar? He'd wondered before, but there were still holes in the theory.

The shithead hadn't sent anyone after the other three Bill had found. The three who had died. Did Dr. Fasset think *Sean* planned to hurt Gabby and was therefore desperate to get her away from him? Did the doctor mean to save her, and thereby his experiment? But by saving her wouldn't he be *interfering* with his experiment?

Too many questions. Sean hoped there was some type of answer in the files Gabby now had in her brain. He hoped Bill had known more about the doctor and situation than he'd shared. To be honest, though, Sean would rather wallow in confusion than watch Gabby hurt herself again.

She moaned, and he knew she was working again. He needed a better distraction. There was only one he could think of . . . *You're up, buddy.* Kind of. "Let me take care of you," he rasped to Gabby.

"Wh-what do you mean?"

Right now, she didn't know people were capable of giving. Giving and expecting nothing in return. He wanted to give her something. *I want to give her my heart,* he thought. *I love her.*

He did, he realized. He loved her. There was no denying that now. He was putting her safety above his own. He was putting her well-being above that of a case. He was putting her emotional happiness above his physical satisfaction.

How could he not love her? She was smart, resourceful, witty, sarcastic, and brave. She was everything his life needed. Everything he'd never known he was missing.

To his surprise, knowing he loved her didn't upset or scare him. It . . . calmed him. Calmed him even though he knew he couldn't keep her much longer. He wouldn't risk her sanity. Wouldn't snuff out her bright light.

Yeah, she'd told him she wasn't afraid of the darkness inside him, but fear had nothing to do with it. Eventually, his shadows would push her too far. But he had her now and he would savor every moment.

"Sean," she said, his silence and stillness probably unnerving her. "What did you mean?"

"Here. I'll show you." He rolled, pinning her underneath him.

A gasp slipped from her, and then she was licking her lips. He leaned down and captured her tongue.

Warm, hot, flavored with toothpaste. His cock hardened even more. But whatever he had to do to keep his own body under control he would. He would prove to her that a man—him—could be trusted to put her first, to expect nothing from her. He would prove that she could trust him. 'Cause God knew, if a woman could trust a man to walk away with a hard-on, without complaint, a woman could trust that man in *all* things.

Not that this would be totally for Gabby's benefit. He'd be lying if he said he wasn't going to enjoy himself.

As Sean continued to kiss her, tongue plundering, feeding from her, he moved one of his hands to her breast. Plump, soft. Her nipple was already hard. He plucked it between his fingers, and her legs parted, allowing him a deeper cradle against her. Automatically, his hips arched and his erection rubbed against her sweet spot. She released another gasp.

He pulled from her lips and mouthed that nipple through her clothes, kneading that delectable mound as he did so. Soon she was writhing against him, her hands tangled in his hair, her leg sliding up and down his side. Another thing he loved about her: the absolutely hedonistic way she gave herself to him.

Her features were softened with her pleasure, her eyelids at half-mast, beautiful shadows fanning over her cheeks. Her lips were parted, red and dewy, shallow breath after shallow breath sawing in and out.

He traced a finger between her breasts, over her stomach, and played at her navel. Her belly quivered. Quivered again when he mapped the waist of her sweats, teasing.

"I love the feel of your skin," he said. "Soft and smooth, like silk."

"Of—of course you do. I'm amazing."

He also loved that smart mouth. "I love the *taste* of your skin." He licked her neck, felt her pulse jump up to meet him, fluttering wildly. "Like sugar."

She moaned. In pleasure this time.

He sank his hand under her pants, dabbled between her legs, her panties blocking him from full-on contact.

Another moan.

"I love your heat, how wet you are."

Her knees fell all the wider, giving him all the access he needed. He reached under the panties and sank a finger inside her, her inner walls closing around him, holding him tight.

"I love . . . I love when you do that," she panted.

He moved that finger in and out of her, allowed a second to join the fun, and leaned down, fitting his lips over hers once more. Arousal beat through him, strong and sure, making him shake and ache and yearn. He wanted the same to be true for her and brushed his thumb over her clit.

"Sean," she shouted. "Yes, right there. Again."

He didn't give it to her. Not yet. She was so close, and he wasn't yet ready for her to come. Wanted to prolong the moment, cause her enjoyment to soar to new heights.

"Inside me," she said. "Now."

"Am." A third finger slipped inside her, stretching her.

"No. You."

"No." In, out he moved them, faster and faster. She was arching into the inward glide, nails digging into his scalp. "Sean," she said. "Please. I want it. Want your cock."

Killing . . . him . . . because he wanted to give it to her. God, did he want to give it to her. To sink balls deep inside this woman he yearned so badly to cherish, to be a part of her. But this was for her, he reminded himself.

Sweat beaded over his skin and dripped onto her, his blood on fire, burning his veins, his organs, leaving piles of ash before re-forming, stronger than before because Gabby was a part of them.

The shadows were swirling around him, thicker than they'd ever been. Thicker than even *he* could deal with. Just then, Gabby was his only light, his very salvation. There couldn't have been a Sean without a Gabby. She owned him, was fused with him.

"Keep your eyes closed," he told her. He didn't want the darkness to scare her.

"Yes. Just . . . touch me. Kiss me."

He meshed their lips together, teeth banging, and swallowed her gasp, her moan, her very breath before giving her his own.

"Sean," she shouted again, inner walls locking down on his fingers. She clawed at his back, pulled on his hair, even bit him.

He stayed with her through it all, not disengaging from her until she collapsed against the mattress boneless, panting. Sated.

"Let me . . ." Eyes still closed, she fished for his fly with a trembling hand.

He rolled away from her and perched at the edge of the bed. He had to look away from her. She was a feast for his gaze, splayed out, flushed, sweat gleaming on her skin like diamonds and dark hair spilled over the pillows.

"We need to head out to meet Rowan." Sean had thought about leaving her behind. For about two seconds. But he didn't like the thought of Gabby being out of his sight and reach.

Especially now that he suspected she had a tracker in her brain.

"But—"

"That was for you, sweetheart. I didn't want anything but your enjoyment." He twisted, swiftly and roughly kissed her on the lips, and then stood. *Leave us,* he told the shadows. *Now.*

They hesitated a long while before obeying, and finally, the room's lamp was visible. His legs shook, and he had to adjust his pants to keep from cutting off circulation in his still-swollen dick.

"I don't understand this, Sean."

"I want to earn your trust. Like I said, I *will* earn it."

The mattress creaked and he knew without looking that she'd just sat up. If it took the rest of his life, he'd prove to her that her needs came before his own. Always. No matter what those needs were and even though they couldn't be together.

*   *   *

Gabby might not ever understand men. Sean in particular. He'd pleasured her—and then walked away from her. Had claimed it was for her and he'd take nothing for himself. Part of her believed him, even.

But men just didn't do that. Didn't give something and expect nothing in return. Not in her experience, at least. Yet he wanted her to trust him. Was determined to earn that trust. And God help her, she was beginning to. Sean did everything in his power to keep her safe. He saw to her needs. Held her, comforted her.

God, she was falling for him. He needed the information in her head, yet he hadn't liked that she was hurting so hadn't wanted her to probe further. It was new to her, this depth of concern from another. New and wonderful.

Could be a trick, the suspicious part of her nature insisted.

Could be the real thing, the other part of her replied.

How would she know?

"Almost there," Sean said.

They were hand in hand and strolling down the sidewalk of a busy shopping area. She wanted to run, to hide in the shadows, but he wouldn't let her. They needed to blend, to watch and study. To Gabby, *everyone* did something suspicious. Looked at her oddly, watched her a little too long. Followed her around a corner. It was her overactive mind, she knew, but she couldn't stop the fear. Or the headache that followed it.

At the end of the street, Sean tugged her inside a coffee shop. Only took her a second to spot Rowan. He was in a booth at the far end of the building, able to scan the entire vicinity without moving an inch.

Sean helped her into the opposite side of the booth before sliding in next to her.

Rowan slid a BlackBerry across the tabletop. "If you knew what I had to do to get this . . ." He shuddered.

"I won't ask her name," Sean muttered, stuffing the phone in his pocket. "But thank you."

Rowan grinned. "Funny. And correct. So anyway, I think I figured out how you're being tracked."

Sean gave an almost imperceptible shake of his head, and Rowan pressed his lips together. Had she not been so focused, Gabby would have missed the exchange. "What?" she asked.

Rowan arched a brow, as if he had no idea what she wanted. "Excuse me?"

"You expect me to trust you?" she gritted out at Sean. "Tell me your suspicions."

"I don't want you scared," he shot back. "And if you had known you're the reason we've been found, the reason we might be found again, you would have been scared."

"I haven't told anyone where we are or what we're doing!" So. He expected her to trust him but wouldn't extend her the same courtesy? Figured.

He just looked over at her pointedly.

How dare he expect her to simply accept this as . . . as . . . he trusted her enough to take her to Rowan. Therefore, he couldn't think that she was tattling. So what—her brain, she suddenly realized. Someone was tracking her through the wires and chips or whatever had been implanted. *Of course.* Her shoulders slumped and she did indeed battle a wave of fear. She could never hide, she realized. Would never be safe. Which meant as long as Sean was with her, *he* wouldn't be safe.

"I hate this."

"I know." He squeezed her hand, offering what comfort he could.

"But why am I being chased now, after all these

years?" she asked for what had to be the thousandth time.

"We'll find out."

Maybe the answer was in the files currently resting inside her. Maybe they were in the phone Sean had just confiscated. Or maybe she was wrong and answers were nowhere. Didn't matter. Determination filled her. Whatever she had to do, whatever she had to endure, she would break the encryption and find out.

The waitress arrived and each of them ordered coffee. Gabby doubted anyone would actually drink it, though. They were too on edge.

"Listen," Rowan said when they were once again alone. "A new boss has already been appointed to Rose Briar, and it wasn't me or you."

Sean frowned. "It damn well should have been you. You've been there the longest, and you're the best agent. Well, besides me, but right now, the powers that be can't be too happy with me. So . . . Who?"

"Bentley."

Gabby's jaw dropped. "*Bentley* is an agent, too?"

Sean gave a stiff nod. "She has an affinity for engines and things like that."

Gabby thought back to the night, not so long ago, when her car had refused to start. Bentley had soon exited the club and taken a look under the hood. *I'm not sure what's wrong,* the girl had said. *Why don't you ride with me?* Bentley had been so nice during that ride, trying so hard to draw Gabby out so they could share about their lives.

All for the job, she realized, teeth grinding together. Would no one seek her out, want to know about her, without some kind of ulterior motive?

After all, she wouldn't have even met Sean had she not possessed her ability.

She found that she didn't regret that, though.

"Bentley wants Gabby brought in," Rowan continued. "But I, of course, have no idea where she is."

She experienced a jolt of surprise. Rowan was actually helping her. Maybe Sean *could* trust this man. Maybe that trust was warranted rather than foolish.

"Got anything else for me?" Sean asked, as if he'd had no doubts of his friend's loyalty.

"I wish."

"Too bad. Keep them busy," Sean said, and stood.

"Wait. We're leaving so soon?" Gabby quickly stood as well, unable to stop her gaze from scanning the restaurant. Was everyone staring at her? "Why?"

"We have to stay on the move. If we learn anything new," he said to Rowan, "we'll call."

Rowan nodded. "I'll do what I can from my end."

The waitress arrived with the coffees and frowned when she realized two of the occupants were leaving.

"He's paying," Sean said, motioning to Rowan.

"Thanks a lot," the agent muttered, but he was grinning.

Gabby and Sean left the coffee shop the same way they'd entered, hand in hand. This time, hers was shaking and sweating. What, she wondered, were they going to do now?

CHAPTER TEN

Sean took Gabby to his house. A house that Rose Briar didn't know about. He knew his other residence was under surveillance. After all, he was currently missing and harboring a target.

He wanted Gabby safe, but she wouldn't be safe as long as someone was chasing her and had access to her every move. Someone Sean hadn't yet pegged. Only thing he could think to do was draw the bastard out, on Sean's turf, where the doors were wired to alarms and he could battle an army—and win—on his own.

"Are you going to get in trouble?" Gabby asked. "I mean, you're supposed to turn me in."

He shrugged. Yeah, he'd probably get shit for this, but in the end they would thank him. He doubted the higher-ups wanted Rose Briar's location broadcast to every scientist or criminal with a hard-on for PSAs. People with Supernatural Abilities.

She spun in a circle, eyeing everything, most likely missing nothing. "You live here?"

"When I have to." It was his safe space, his harbor away from the world.

He looked around, trying to see the place as she

was seeing it. The walls, windows, and concrete floor were painted black, better to encourage darkness. There was no furniture, but there were wooden planks nailed strategically across the ground. While Sean knew where those planks were by heart and could navigate the room with his eyes closed, anyone sneaking inside would trip constantly, their vision compromised by the gloom.

"There's a bed in the far bedroom," Sean said, handing her the phone Rowan had given him. "Why don't you go lie down? Maybe download what you can from this. See if you learn anything. If it pains you, stop. Got me?"

Other than clasping the phone to her chest, she didn't move. "And what will you be doing?"

"Arming up." He knelt down, withdrawing a knife from his back pocket.

*   *   *

Gabby watched as he inserted the sharp tip of that blade into a crack in the floor. White teeth bit into his lower lip as he pried and worked that crack until an entire block of concrete popped up.

Underneath was an arsenal. Guns, knives, grenades, and all kinds of equipment she couldn't identify.

"Paranoid much?"

He chuckled, and oh, it was a sexy sound. "I've learned to be prepared for anything."

She ran her thumb over the buttons on the phone until a light popped on. "Well, I want a gun."

"You know how to shoot? Last time I handed you one, you couldn't stop shaking."

"I wasn't scared of the gun, moron; I was scared of the man trying to kill me. But yeah. I taught myself to shoot when I was eighteen. A birthday present, you could say."

"Okay, then. Take what you want. And speaking of guns, I want you to wear this," he added, arm dipping into the hole and withdrawing a Kevlar vest. He tossed it at her.

The material slapped against her stomach as the phone beeped, signaling it was now turned on and ready to use. Her mind instantly opened up and linked.

There were a few e-mails that hadn't yet been read, others that had, but nothing that pertained to her—until a photograph flashed. It was of her—Gabby—as a little girl, head shaved, a white shirt and pants bagging on her tiny body, a thin, thirtysomething man behind her.

He had a serious, no-nonsense expression. Hers was dead. No fear, no resolve. As if she'd known the worst had already been done to her and nothing else would compare.

"Huit. French for eight," was written across the photo.

Next was a current photo of her—her mug shot, actually—from the same sender. "Your Huit" was written across this one.

There was a file accompanying it, and this one wasn't encrypted. Maybe because the sender, Sweetie-McLovin, hadn't written anything truly incriminating. It read: "Took me a while, and I doubt anyone else will have any luck 'cause damn, I'm good, but I finally deciphered it. Bastard liked his numbers. I'll send each separately. This has to be your girl. Dude fucked her up good, that's for sure. She knew shit that was in a computer she'd never touched."

There were more photos, each numbered in French. Of her, of the other children the bastard doctor had stolen off the streets. Five girls, five boys. There were even pictures of three that Rose Briar had found. They were inside a laboratory, clearly dead, blood leaking from their eyes, ears, and noses. She gagged. Was that the fate that awaited her? Number eight?

Wait. Huit. Her name. French. A number, like the others. *Of course,* she thought, eyes widening as the new files in her head began buzzing. The doctor had liked numbers, had wanted everything in its place. Sean's boss wouldn't have reworked the doctor's system when he'd confiscated the doctor's documents because he would have been too afraid to mess anything up. Which meant the former Rose Briar boss would have left everything as it was.

Numbers . . . numbers . . . her brain worked at the files once more, replacing numbers with letters, each using a point-by-point scale. There was no pain this time, and she wanted to laugh. She'd gotten it right!

Rather than open them one at a time—the cipher was as long as the encryption itself, the longest she'd ever seen, and she knew reading even a single file would have taken hours—Gabby simply decoded the file names. Anything that didn't seem to pertain to her or the others like her she pushed aside. Didn't trash, not yet, but moved out of the way.

And God, there were a lot of files. Some dating back thirty years.

"Gabby."

The deep voice called to her, demanding her attention. She blinked, trying to reach out, clasp onto that voice with a mental hand, and drag herself to it. But then a file moved front and center, as if the voice had been a key, a trigger, and opened up.

There were photos of Sean, younger than when she'd met him. Late teens or early twenties. Same eye color, but those irises were almost dead. No emotion in them, much as there'd been no emotion in hers.

Next to the photos, page after page of notes appeared. "Subject has suffered abuse. Beaten by father. Possesses a temper of his own. Perhaps uncontrollable. Recently in bar fight. Witnesses claimed he disappeared in the shadows before beating opponent senseless and—"

"Gabby!"

Her entire body shook; there were iron-hot brands on her upper arms, and they were responsible, she realized, but didn't care.

She read another page of notes. A psych report. "Sean keeps himself emotionally distant. He believes the darkness inside him deprives those around him of light. He believes their minds cannot cope with this. His father warned him of this, and therefore he expects it to happen, perhaps even creating signs of it. Signs of his own making."

Yes, he'd told her that before. Told her the darkness often drove people insane.

"Gabby, sweetheart, it's Sean." Another shake, this one harder. "Can you hear me?"

Sean. Sean was holding her. Once again she blinked and this time the world slowly came into focus. He was indeed in front of her, tall and strong and beautiful, those electric blues bright with concern. His lips were pulled down in a tight frown.

Before she realized what she was doing, she lifted her hand and traced her finger over those lips. Soft . . . naughty . . . How much had he suffered as a child? How many people had he pushed out of his life because he'd feared hurting them?

He nipped at her fingertip, creating a delicious sting. A sting he then licked away. "Where'd you go, baby?"

"Files," she managed to croak past the sudden lump in her throat. "Was able to open a few. Who's Sweetie McLovin?"

"He's a smart-ass kid who works for Rose Briar. He's wicked smart with computers."

"Well, he knows about me and the others. If anyone finds out about him, he's dead."

Sean released her, flipped open his phone, and called Rowan. The conversation was short: "Sweetie needs a pickup. He's a possible target." Then the phone was back in Sean's pocket and he was holding her again. "Anything else?"

"I'm still sifting through the information. Found some things about . . . you," she admitted softly, fully expecting him to erupt. To hate her, now that she knew some of his secrets.

"Like?" he asked, utterly calm.

The calm before the storm? "You were different. Before joining the agency, I mean. Your father . . ." *Shut up, shut up, shut up. You're just digging the hole deeper.* She didn't want Sean to hate her for her ability. Wasn't sure how she'd react if he pushed her away.

"Yeah. He was a bastard. But he wanted me

strong, able to withstand anything that was thrown at me." He grinned, and there was no edge to it. "Not sure Rose Briar would like you having access to so much information. Yeah, they want to use you, but this . . . I don't think they fully realize the extent of what you can learn."

Gabby flattened her palms against his chest, and she told herself she did it to hold herself up. Her legs were weak and shaky, after all, but deep down she knew the truth. She craved contact with this man, any type of contact. His heartbeat was fast, a little unsteady.

"So don't tell them."

He captured one of those hands, brought it to his lips, and kissed it. "Believe me. I won't."

It's what they wanted her for, though. Her ability. And they couldn't have it both ways. Couldn't have her only import the files they wanted but keep her in the dark about their own activities.

Soon, she thought, they would consider her a danger. To them, to the world. How long would they use her before discarding her? And how long before Sean grew tired of her and ratted her out?

There you go again. Not trusting. Believing the worst. He deserved better. "You really don't mind that I can learn everything about you so easily?"

"As I don't plan to keep secrets from you again, no, I really don't mind. But I would appreciate it if you promised to come to me, talk to me, if anything you learn about me disturbs you."

A promise like that implied she would be around for a while. Though she knew she shouldn't, she said, "I promise." And she meant it. Starting now.

"Your psychiatrist believes you are wrong to push people out of your life."

A muscle ticced below his eye and a rosy flush overtook his cheeks. "Every agent has to see a shrink periodically."

"Well, you're not going to drive me insane with your darkness. I told you. I like it."

"That doesn't mean—"

"Your father was wrong, Sean. Not once have I thought I was losing my mind."

"But it has happened to others," he insisted harshly.

"I'm different. Remember? My brain operates on a different wavelength."

They stared at each other as he considered her words. Then, slowly, a smile curved his lips, and the clouds cleared from his eyes. "Then I won't hold anything back from you. I won't push you away," he said. "God help you, I'll only draw you closer. I didn't have much fight left in me anyway. I want you too damn bad. Now, enough of that. For now. Or I'll forget what we're here for. Did you find anything about the man who screwed with your head? What he's like, if he's tracked others like you? If he caught them, what he did to them?"

"Not yet."

"Damn."

She pulled her gaze from Sean's—it was either that or sink into him and kiss the breath out of him. The more time she spent with him, the more she learned about him, the more she liked him and the more she wanted to make something work between them. Was that possible, though? He seemed to think so, but doubts still filled her. About his job, about her situation, her future.

"What do we do now?" she asked, not knowing if she meant physically or emotionally. He wasn't going to hold anything back now. Why had she pressed for such a thing? If she'd thought resisting him before had been difficult . . .

"Put this on," he said, holding out a Kevlar vest.

Looking around, she did as commanded. He'd replaced the concrete block, turned off all the lights but a single lamp. He'd hooked guns to the wall and aimed them in different directions.

"What about my face and lower body? Not like the vest can protect those."

"But it can protect you from kill shots to your vitals."

True. "What about you?"

"I can see in the dark and know how to duck."

But he didn't have superhuman speed. "You expect me to sleep in this?"

"Yeah."

Figured. "You gonna hold me?" She meant the question to emerge as sarcasm. It emerged as need.

"Absolutely." He bent down and scooped her up into his arms.

Gabby didn't protest. Actually, she rested her cheek against his shoulder. Those files were still opening up in her mind, bogging her down, making her drag. Gently Sean laid her against the mattress and stretched out beside her. He was fully clothed, they both were, but his body was bumpy with the weapons now strapped to him.

Earlier he'd pleasured her, sinking those big fingers deep, but he'd taken no relief for himself. Right now, he was hard. She could feel his erection against her thigh, and her mouth watered for it.

She'd never felt for anyone what she felt for this man, and she had to please him. Had to give him something of herself and not expect anything in return. Like he'd done for her.

But as she reached for him, he stiffened, cursed under his breath. He popped up. "Someone's here. Hide under the bed," he commanded quietly, fiercely. "There's a tunnel under it. Lock yourself in, understand?"

Shadows enveloped her before she could question him, blocking the room from her view. Fear blasted her, making her temples throb. She didn't have the gun he'd promised her, and couldn't see to help him.

Footsteps pounded. A lot of footsteps. There were rustles of clothing. Pops and whizzes, grunts and groans, and then golden light was shining brightly, filling the hallway and illuminating the bedroom, casting those shadows away. Why so bright? Was Sean . . . could he have been . . . Gabby jumped up.

"Sean, run!" someone shouted. Rowan. She recognized his voice and was both relieved and scared. If he was telling Sean to run, that mean Sean was alive but in danger.

She rushed forward, the light intensifying . . . stretching toward her. Sweat beaded over her skin. She found several bodies littering the hall, blood spilling from them. Clearly Sean had shot them. But where was he now?

"Let him go," she heard Sean demand, his voice rough with fury.

Gabby slowed, stepping over the bodies quietly. When she reached the corner, she stopped and peeked around the wall. There Sean was, on his knees, his face cut and bleeding, an oozing wound in his shoulder, just above his heart.

She stifled a horrified gasp.

Someone had a gun to Rowan's head. That's how they had subdued Sean, she realized. They'd threatened his friend. She also knew Sean would have continued to fight if he hadn't thought she was in that tunnel, safe from detection. He placed her welfare first in everything, she was coming to learn.

"This one," the guy with the gun said, smashing it harder into Rowan's temple, "isn't necessary. You and the girl, however, have powers I'm very interested in. So. If you want your friend to live, you'll do what I say."

That voice . . . she recognized it and scowled. Thomas, her former boss at Eye Candy. He had his back to her, was facing Sean, but she knew it was him. There were four men with him, other dead bodies lying around them. They'd brought lights, so many halogens, and were shining them directly at Sean, preventing him from summoning his shadows.

"Tell me where the girl is."

Thomas wanted her? Why?

"Like hell," Sean said. "I'd rather die."

"You might. Or little Gabby might. To save each other, I think you'll do whatever I tell you to do, though."

Sean's only reaction was a sneer. "Who says she's still alive?"

He was engaging them, she knew he was, holding their attention to allow her time to sneak away. Like she'd really leave him here to die. He'd come to mean too much to her.

There, she'd admitted it. She wasn't leaving this room without him. Because if they thought he'd killed her, they might kill *him*.

"I'm here," she said, stepping forward. "And as you can see, I'm very much alive."

CHAPTER ELEVEN

"Motherfucker!" Sean paced from one corner of his cell to another. The moment Gabby had stepped into the light, he'd reacted. He'd gone ballistic, attacking everyone around him. They'd had to tranq him, but still he'd fought, managing to take two down with him. Never had he been more determined to save someone.

The drugs had eventually zapped him, though, and he'd fallen. Why they hadn't killed him as the guy had threatened, Sean hadn't known. Still didn't. About an hour ago, he'd woken up here. Inside a four-by-four prison, Rowan sleeping on the other side in a prison of his own.

The floors were dirt, the walls stone and covered with chalk drawings. Meaning they weren't the first prisoners. Meaning the guy holding them knew what he was doing—and how to get away with it.

Both of their wounds had been bandaged, at least. But fuck, he hurt! His entire body ached and his limbs were trembling from blood loss. Clearly, he and Rowan were to be kept alive. The same was true for Gabby. Sean knew that. But that didn't lessen his fear. They could beat her . . . rape her.

They were drug dealers, after all. It had taken him a while, since Thomas had clearly disguised his features, but Sean had finally recognized Thomas as Gabby's former boss—and the man who'd watched him outside the motel.

Damn this! He wanted out of here. But unlike the time he'd abducted her himself, he had no weapons hidden on his body. They'd been confiscated.

Where the hell was Gabby? Where had they taken her?

There was an armed guard in front of the cages, watching Sean through narrowed eyes. He had already tried to engage the guard in conversation and gotten nowhere.

Rowan moaned. It was the first sound the man had made since Sean had awakened, and he raced to that side of the cell. "Rowan."

Gingerly Sean's friend sat up and rubbed the sleep from his eyes.

"Hey," Sean said, and Rowan turned toward him. "How were you captured?"

"Quiet," the guard snapped.

With a grimace, Rowan rose and approached Sean. He said softly, "Fucker attacked me right after you left the coffee shop. I like to think I'm a pretty aware guy, but damn. I didn't stand a chance. One minute I was standing, the next a sharp pain was exploding through my neck, and the next I was cuffed in their car."

So they'd known where Gabby was, just as Sean had feared. How? They didn't have access to Dr. Fasset's files. Or even Bill's. They shouldn't have been able to track her.

"Her brain, as we suspected," Rowan said, answering Sean's unspoken questions. "The smug shit couldn't stop bragging about himself and his plans. Anyway, Gabby isn't the only one good with computers. This Thomas guy has some pretty smart badasses on his payroll and they were able to hack into Rose Briar's system and learn what we'd learned."

"But *we* weren't able to track her. They were."

"That I can only guess about. They must have found a way to access Dr. Fasset's GPS, or whatever the bastard put inside her head. But the worst part is, they didn't want her." Rowan's voice was grave.

"Well, they do. But not as much as they want you."

Wait. What? "I don't understand."

"After Bill approached Thomas, the owner of Eye Candy, and told him to get lost, Thomas followed Bill, found out who we are and what we do. He wanted Gabby because she can do what his hackers can't, working quickly, getting into impossible places. Then he saw you manipulate the shadows and decided you were the better prospective employee."

Him? Sean shook his head, sure he'd misheard again. That couldn't be right.

"Think about it. With you, he can commit crimes anytime, anywhere, and never be seen."

Now that made sense. "Gabby," Sean said, rubbing at his suddenly raw throat. *He'd* placed her in danger. He was the reason she was here. They'd want to know what she knew about him; since they didn't feel they needed her ability as much as his, they wouldn't mind roughing her up.

Shit!

Rowan's expression darkened. "We've got to kill him, Sean. He wants money, power, and doesn't care what he has to do to get it. Sell our secrets, even. Which means we need to ki—neutralize Gabby, too.

She's just too dangerous in the wrong hands, and as trackable as she now is . . . Thomas may not want her quite so desperately anymore, but others will."

"Hell, no. We're not hurting her."

"I know you like her. I know—"

"No!" Gabby was a part of him now. He couldn't imagine his life without her. Didn't want to imagine his life without her. She was more important than his job. Hell, more important than his own life. Besides that, he'd told her he wouldn't push her away, that he'd give her everything, and he meant to keep his word. He'd run with her if he had to, and that was all there was to that.

"Fine. She's yours. I won't touch her."

"Good." Sean's gaze flicked to the guard. "Now, let's find a way out of here," he whispered fiercely. As powerful as Rose Briar was, as many agents with unusual gifts as there were, he knew it would be just the two of them now. Thomas was too good to have let anyone discover their whereabouts.

Rowan nodded, straightened, and squared his shoulders. Determination radiated from him. "I'll take care of it."

Thomas and crew had underestimated him, Sean knew. Most people did. They didn't understand the depths of Rowan's charm or that it was far more dangerous than Sean's own power.

With a few words, Rowan could make you blow your own brains out.

And that was exactly what was going to happen, Sean thought, as he watched Rowan turn his killer grin on the guard.

*   *   *

"You will tell me what you know about Sean Walker, Gabrielle, or I will put a bullet in your chest while he watches."

Gabby glared up at Thomas, not even trying to hide her hatred. He was blond with green eyes and very tanned skin. His features were different than she remembered, leaner, his jaw dusted with stubble. But he was still a bastard.

He'd tied her to a chair, the bonds so tight she might never feel her hands again.

"Well?"

"I told you. I don't know anything."

Slap.

Her head whipped to the side. This time—how many times had he already hit her? She'd lost count—her teeth cut into her gums and blood trickled onto her tongue. Pretty soon, he was going to close his fist and start pounding. The determination in his eyes told her that.

"And I thought you were such a smart girl. You're really starting to piss me off, Gabrielle." He uttered a long-suffering sigh. "I'm not a bad guy. I'm really not. I have a family I love, a family I want to support. Your continued defiance is the problem here. Not me. Do you think I enjoy hurting you?"

Hell, yes, he did. "How do you know I even like Sean? I might hate his guts." Her gaze circled the room. They were in a warehouse of some sort, sectioned off by thick, steel walls. This section was spacious, with a long table piled with bags of cocaine and weapons. Some of those weapons were already bloody. Besides Thomas, there was a handful of guards. Each had a gun in hand and each was watching her, waiting for the word to plug her full of holes.

Some looked bored; some looked eager for a turn. Some were simply enjoying the show. She was sweaty, dirty, shaking, and scared. For herself, yes. Pain was not fun. But mostly she feared for Sean. Fear she couldn't allow herself to feel full measure without a terrible ache in her temples. An ache that would fog her mind and make her weak.

For her own sake, she kept her breathing even, her heart rate slow.

What did they want from Sean? What did they plan to do to him? If they hurt him . . . she'd what? Want to die herself, she thought—after she killed them all, slowly and painfully. She'd do to them what she'd always wanted to do to the doctor who'd screwed with her. She loved Sean. With all of her heart, all of her soul, she loved him. She knew that now.

"Give me some credit," Thomas said. "I let Rose Briar, or whatever they call themselves, think I left the country as they'd commanded, but I remained here and watched the club instead. Waiting. I knew Agent Walker had an unusual ability, but I just couldn't find out *what* he could do. Him or the other, Rowan. Until he escorted you from that motel and he treated those shadows like his pets. The things he'll do for me . . ." Thomas laughed, a little giddy, as if he was flying high on his drugs.

"So what do you want to know from me?" she asked as if she finally meant to play ball.

His expression was almost fond as he regarded her. "That's better. *How* does he control the shadows? Tell me."

She'd expected the question but couldn't think of a believable lie. "Why not ask him?"

Frowning, Thomas leaned down and planted his

hands on the arms of her chair, placing them nose to nose. "Because I'm asking you."

"Why?" she insisted. "Maybe he didn't tell me anything. Maybe he'll be willing to talk to you."

"He's an agent. Used to this kind of thing. He'll tell me a little, omit a lot. He'll lie. Pain and threats won't bother him. And yeah, he talked to you. Otherwise, you'd be crying right now, begging for your life. But you're not. You're trying to protect him. You, who *will* buckle under the pressure. Start. Talking. *Now.*"

People like this needed to be stopped. Sean had offered her the chance to help do that. At the time, she hadn't had an answer for him. Now she did. Hell, yes. She would help. She would work for Rose Briar.

Slap.

Her brain rattled against her skull and for a moment she saw stars, her heart thundering against her ribs. *Do not fear. Do not freaking fear.* "I'm trying to remember," she said. "Give me a minute."

Slap.

Do not fear! "Let me see him and I'll tell you everything I know."

Punch. "Why do you make me hurt you like this?"

A grunt of pain gusted from her split lips. The adrenaline rushing through her helped dull the pain in her face and head, but oh, was she going to feel it tomorrow. If she was still alive. *You will get out of this. You have to.*

At least when Dr. Fasset had abducted her, he hadn't abused her like this. He'd simply locked her away, taken some blood, given her some drugs, and sawed off half her skull while she slept. When she'd woken up, he'd kept her sedated until she healed and then finally let her go.

"I just want to know that he's alive." The words scraped against her throbbing lip. "I just want to know I'm not spilling his secrets for nothing."

Thomas popped his jaw, silent for a moment. "Bring Agent Walker in here. And make sure to keep the lights on him at all times."

Two of the guards strode silently from the room.

"See. I can be accommodating." Thomas rubbed his jaw. "But you know, Gabrielle, I'm not sure you realize just how precarious your predicament is." He walked leisurely to the table and lifted one of the knives. One of the larger knives with a curved blade stained crimson.

The scent of dried blood hit her nose, and she gagged. "You might have bruised my brain a bit, but I think I'm smart enough to figure out my predicament. Being held by a huge asswad was a big clue."

He tapped the tip against the table. *Tick, tick, tick.* "You shouldn't have insisted Sean be brought to you, because now I want to give him a show. I want him to see what will happen to you if he disobeys me. I want him to know what I'm capable of." Thomas closed the distance between them.

Gabby shrank back. Didn't matter, though. She had nowhere to go.

The blade hooked to the collar of her shirt. She was gasping at the touch of cool metal, then unable to breathe as Thomas ran the tip down her top, slicing the material in two. Interest filled his eyes as he took in her lacy black bra. A bra Sean had purchased for her.

"Pretty," Thomas said, "and unexpected. Did you wear that for Sean?"

He didn't wait for her response; he didn't need to. He'd already gotten what he wanted. Terror. Her temples were on fire.

Thomas grinned, but his amusement didn't last long. Impatient, he whipped toward the open door. "What's taking them so long?"

Could Sean have escaped? Could the men be searching for him? "Yes, he picked it for me," she said to distract Thomas. "It has a front clasp and was easy for him to work on and off me."

Thomas swung back around, facing her. His eyes narrowed. "I'm not stupid. I'll fuck you if I want to fuck you, but don't think you'll be winning me over with your body. You've never been my type."

Meaning he liked big boobs and blondes. He'd paraded his flavors of the week through the club constantly, going through women like they were Kleenex and he had a cold. Yeah, he was a fabulous "family man."

"Give me a chance," she practically purred. "I can become your type." Just then, a dark cloud swept into the room and Gabby almost cried with relief. "Or not, since you're about to die."

"What do you—" Thomas paled, and it was the last thing she saw, her entire world going black.

She was blind but not deaf and could hear gunshots, grunting, bodies falling.

"What the hell?" someone shouted.

"Stop; please stop," another begged.

"No!" Thomas shouted. "No, don't—" His voice gurgled to quiet after a loud *pop*.

Then, there was only silence.

"Sean!" Gabby called. "I want to see you."

Warm fingers brushed the back of her neck, but he didn't appear and the cloud didn't dissipate. "Not yet."

Did he think she'd meant what she'd said to Thomas? "I was just trying to distract him. I didn't—"

Sean chuckled, but it was a harsh sound. "I know, baby. I know. I just don't want you to see the . . . bodies. Are you okay?" His voice had thickened, there at the end.

Her shoulders sagged with relief. "Now I am." It was over. Really over. Sean was alive, safe. Right? She stiffened again, concern beating at her much harder than Thomas had. "Are you?"

"I'm fine."

"You were shot earlier. You—"

"I'll be fine. Swear." Pause. Then, a gasp. "Oh, baby. Your pretty face." Those strong fingers gently caressed her cheek, her jaw, her swollen lips.

"I'm fine."

He sliced her bonds. "I want to kill the fucker all over again."

Hands free now, she rubbed at her wrists. Sean's shadow form gently clasped her arm and helped her stand. She swayed, and he dragged her into the shadows with him, into his embrace, holding her tight.

"I knew you'd come," she said.

"You trusted me?"

"Yes."

His arms tightened even more. She couldn't breathe, but that hardly seemed to matter. She was exactly where she wanted to be, doing exactly what she wanted to do.

"Bentley and team are on their way," Rowan said from the doorway.

"Come on," Sean said against Gabby's temple. He ushered her from the room and building, not removing the shadows until they'd stepped outside.

The sun was setting, but still she had to blink against its brightness. When she focused, Sean's beautiful, tattooed face came into view and white-hot tears filled her eyes, even as her heart swelled with love for him.

"Sean," she said, but he shook his head.

"We have some things to discuss, you and I," he said, wiping those tears gently from her face. "But not here and not now."

As he'd spoken, cars had sped from the surrounding forest and toward the building. Rose Briar had arrived, she supposed. No wonder Sean wanted to wait. What these agents would want to do with her she could only guess. And none of her guesses ended well for her.

CHAPTER TWELVE

The next fifteen minutes of Gabby's life were surreal. One minute she was alone with Sean, breathing him in, happy to be alive and hopeful for the future; the next they were surrounded by agents of every age, size, and ethnicity. Some rushed inside the building. To clean up, she supposed. Some searched under every rock, every wood plank, tearing the building up piece by piece. For Thomas's secrets, she was sure. His home would probably receive the same treatment. Someone even approached her and gave her a bag of ice.

Gabby stood in place, one hand holding that bag and pressing it into her cheek and the other fisting her side. She wanted to be back in Sean's embrace. He was next to her, but that wasn't close enough. Not anymore. No longer would she hold him at a distance. Look how close she'd come to losing him. Like him, she was going to stop pushing. She was going to give everything.

She sighed. She knew what she wanted to tell him during their discussion—*I love you*—and wondered if he planned to do the same. She trusted him not to hurt her. She did. Not emotionally and not physically. So she knew he wasn't going to drop her now that the mission was over. But still, she couldn't guess what he wanted to say.

Offering someone blind trust was . . . nice. She didn't feel like a fool, like she'd always assumed she would. She felt relieved, empowered, important.

Bentley emerged from one of the cars and strode to them, drawing Gabby's attention. The agent was frowning.

"Good job," she said with a nod. Her gaze remained glued to Sean. "But you should have come in. You should have brought her in, and you should have kept our lines of communication open."

He nodded but didn't back down. "I didn't know who I could trust."

Her expression hardened. "You trusted Rowan."

"Yeah, but I've worked with him before."

"And I just happen to be made of awesome," Rowan said, coming up behind them.

Everyone chuckled, the tension somehow broken.

A charmer, Sean had called Rowan, and Gabby realized he'd been telling the truth, even in that.

"You trusted the girl," Bentley said without rancor this time.

He flicked Gabby a white-hot glance. She gave him a half smile of encouragement, then grimaced. *Ouch.*

"Poor baby." He reached over and linked their hands. Finally. Connected again. The heat of him nearly undid her, but she remained in place rather than do what she really wanted: launch herself at him. Reluctantly, he turned back to Bentley. "We're together. Of course I trusted her."

Despite the pain, Gabby offered him another smile. Yes, they were indeed together. Now. Always, she hoped. But exactly what did he have in mind? Because she was ready to move in with him, sleep with him every night, wake up with him every morning. Maybe he just wanted to date first. After all, they'd only known each other a few weeks and men liked to take things slow. Well, everything but sex.

Bentley's eyes widened, and finally she faced Gabby. "That true?"

Gabby removed the ice and nodded.

Sean squeezed her hand in approval.

"I need to take you in, ask you some questions," the agent told her firmly. "Alone."

Before she could reply, Sean, like a storm cloud of rage, got in Bentley's face. "Don't even think of hurting her."

Bentley held up her hands, all innocence. "Never even crossed my mind."

"Uh, Bent," Rowan said, making a cutting motion over his throat. "He knows all about Operation, uh, Elimination."

"Fine. It crossed my mind," she admitted sheepishly. "Best friends shouldn't be allowed on the same team."

"What's Operation Elimination?" Gabby asked, though she thought she knew the answer.

Sean kissed her temple. "It doesn't matter anymore. Does it, Bentley?"

Bentley crossed her arms over her middle. "She can be tracked."

"But we'll have Thomas's records soon, which means we'll find out how he was able to track her. Then, we can stop it from happening again. And besides that, she'll be more valuable to us than dangerous."

Yep. She had been the target of OE. She almost pulled from Sean's grip, almost ran for the trees. However, the thought of leaving was more painful than the thought of living without Sean, so she just continued to stand there, sweating, wondering how to handle this.

"Sean," Bentley said, unwilling to give up.

How could the woman sound so calm while talking about someone else's death? That had to be why she'd been chosen to take Bill's place rather than Sean or Rowan. Gabby, of course, would have chosen Sean.

"I work with her or not at all," he said flatly.

"He means it," Rowan said. "I know because I work with *him* or not at all."

Gabby's mouth fell open. They were standing up for her, protecting her yet again. In fact, Sean was willing to give up his life's work for her and Rowan was willing to give his up for his friend. Now *that* was love.

As much hurt and rejection as she'd endured as a child, she'd never thought to find this kind of acceptance. That she had, and with such a great man . . . tears once again filled her eyes, stinging.

Sean misunderstood, bless him, and tugged her all the way into his body. She burrowed her head in the hollow of his neck. "We're done with this conversation," he said, his tone flat again. "Gabby and I are leaving. Don't try to stop—"

"I'll go with her," she said, the words muffled from his shirt. She placed a quick kiss just above his heart. "I'll talk to her."

Tenderly he cupped Gabby's cheeks, forced her to look up at him. "You don't have to."

"I want to." *For you. For us.*

"Liar," he said, but nodded stiffly. "She's taking you to headquarters. I'll follow. I'll be in the building the entire time. You have nothing to fear."

"I don't." Not anymore. And if she knew Sean, and she was beginning to think that she did, he would find a way to be in the room—though no one would know it, the shadows his refuge.

He grinned down at her, and she knew they were thinking the same thing.

*   *   *

Gabby's talk with Bentley lasted over four hours. Four hours of answering questions about Gabby's personal life, her emotions, her intentions, all while hooked to a lie detector. It was embarrassing, strangely exhausting, and in no way enlightening.

What made her maddest was that the woman had tried to get her to betray Sean. What could he do? Who had he talked to while they'd been together? Where had he taken her? Those were the only questions she'd refused to answer.

When Bentley finished with her, she sent Gabby on her way without telling her what she meant to do with her. Hire her, forget her, or kill her.

Sean was waiting in the hallway, hands shoved into his pockets. He'd showered, and his hair was damp, slicked back. He wore a black cashmere sweater and black slacks and God, he looked edible.

He straightened when he spotted her, though he didn't say a word. Just took her hand in his and led her underground to a parking lot. There he helped her inside a bright red Scorpion HX that had her drooling.

"Yours?" she asked after he had maneuvered out of the lot, down a congested road, and then onto the highway. The moon was out, a tiny golden sliver in the sky, the night dark and quiet.

"Yes."

So he clearly had money. At one time, she might have worried about that, thinking he deserved better than streetwise, poor her. Now, she just thought they belonged together. No matter what. And yeah, he would be buying her a Scorpion HX in yellow.

"Where are you taking me?" she asked.

"Home."

Okay, his short and sweet answers were unnerving her. What was wrong with him? "To mine or yours?"

No reply.

She sighed. "Bentley didn't tell me what she has planned for me. And you should know, she wanted to know all about you."

He surprised her by nodding. "That's standard. She was testing your loyalty. And you should know the results in a few days. The waiting is another test, by the way. Rose Briar wants to see what you'll do when you aren't sure what they'll do."

"So if I stick around, they'll hire me?"

"Not always. But you, yes, they'll hire. They wouldn't have gone to all the trouble to get you if they didn't want you."

"Even though I'm apparently dangerous."

"Like I said, we'll take care of that," he said confidently.

At least he was talking to her, really talking to her now.

Sean pulled off the highway, took a few corners as if they were braced on rails despite the still-thick throng of traffic, and finally parked in front of a house in the middle of suburban paradise.

He led her inside. A large home, like the one she'd once shared with her parents, only this one had dark leather furniture and there weren't any photos on the walls or sitting on the mantel of the fireplace.

"Yours?" she found herself asking again.

He turned to her, expression unreadable. "I stay here when I need peace and quiet."

She scrubbed her hands against her thighs, nervous. "Are you ready to talk to me, then?"

He nodded, crossed his arms over his chest. "First, ask me again if this house is mine."

Gabby still didn't know what was going on, what he was leading up to, and her nervousness increased. "Is it?" She licked her lips. "Yours?"

He shook his head.

She blinked in confusion. "Whose is it, then?"

"Ours."

Ours. The word echoed through her mind, and she almost jumped up and down. "You—you want to live with me?"

"Yes."

"Here?"

"Here. Anywhere."

She covered her mouth with her hands to stifle her cry of happiness. Tears were once again pooling in her eyes. Was this really happening?

"What's mine is now yours. I mean, really. It should be. You have my heart, and everything else is just bonus. You told me the shadows don't bother you, and I'm trusting you. I want to marry you, Gabby. I want to live with you. I want to hold on to you and never let you go. I love you. If you don't want any of that, I'll understand. I won't like it, but I'll understand. Only, you should know that I won't give up. I'll romance the hell out of you until you finally cave."

Her legs almost gave out. This was everything she'd ever secretly dreamed. "I love you, too. I love you and I want to marry you, live with you, be with you forever. You have my heart. Why not my life, too? But if you think that means you don't have to romance me, you are in for a rude awakening."

"Thank God." He strode to her, grabbed her up, and carried her upstairs. "I was prepared to get on my knees and beg if necessary."

She grinned. She just couldn't help herself. "Don't let me stop you."

He chuckled, and the beautiful sound washed over her. "Oh, I'll get on my knees soon enough; don't worry."

When they reached the bedroom, he tossed her on the mattress. They were too frantic with their desires to go slowly and ended up ripping each other's clothes in their bid for skin-to-skin contact.

They arched and strained together, hands everywhere, mouths devouring, tasting. Through it all, he was infinitely tender with her, careful of her wounds. She, too, avoided his bandages, but everywhere else was fair game. And when they came together, it was a promise, a homecoming. A prelude. He kissed every inch of her, telling her what he loved about her all the while.

It was the sexiest, sweetest experience of her life.

Afterward, panting and sweaty, they lay together. Holding each other, basking in the moment, the first real love either had ever known. This was unconditional, she knew. This was forever.

"You were really going to give up your job for me," she said, still awed by that fact.

"Hell, yes. You're the most important thing in my life."

A cell phone suddenly rang, echoing off the walls. Sean cursed under his breath, planted a kiss on the base of her throat, and rose to dig the phone from his pants pocket. "Sorry, but I have to take this. It's the agency's ringtone." He pressed the device to his ear and settled back into the bed. "Agent Walker."

Gabby curled into his side, more content than she'd ever been.

Frowning, he said, "Just a moment," and handed the phone to her. She didn't have to place it to her ear because he'd pressed "speaker."

"Yes?" she asked, confused.

"We'll see you at oh-eight-hundred hours tomorrow morning, Miss Huit," Bentley said, "when you'll begin training for your first mission." *Click.*

She and Sean stared at each other for a moment, and then he began to smile.

"You're in," he said.

"Wow. That was fast."

"Well, like me, they obviously know a good thing when they see it."

Holy hell. They really were going to work together. Be together. Did life get any better than that?

"Getting the job's a treat, but I'd rather talk about something else." She traced her fingertip around one of his nipples, then the other, before sliding her hand down and gripping his cock. "It's my turn to tell you everything I love about you. So settle in, because this is going to take a while."

HUNTING TEMPTATION

Lorie O'Clare

CHAPTER ONE

Seth Gere walked around a tree and paused, refusing to show his surprise. "Why don't you agree to meet in a bar like normal people?"

Jeremy Drury had appeared out of the shadows. Seth was sure of it. He'd agreed to meet his friend here, in the woods north of town. Call it his ego in full force, but he wouldn't let Jeremy see how this place gave him the creeps.

"I'm not normal people." Jeremy didn't give any indication he was joking.

Jeremy was a character, possibly a street person, not that Seth would ever ask. Jeremy was one hell of a contact. And Seth needed answers.

He gave a tight laugh, not willing to insult the man but unable to argue his statement, either. "So what can you tell me about Tray Long?"

"He's an asshole." Jeremy stood in the shadows, making it hard to see his expression, but his growl proved he was being polite.

"I already know he's a waste of flesh." Seth glanced around them, getting the oddest sensation they were being watched, although why anyone else would be in these woods on a moonless night beat the hell out of him. "He killed three people, did his time, and is out on parole. Now he's skipped out and we've got two murders with no leads and his signature all over them. We'll have DNA matches here in a day or so."

"You know he killed them." Jeremy's dark expression became visible in the shadows. His thick, almost black hair hung straight to his shoulders, but he didn't look unkempt. If he did live on the streets, he had access to a shower. Jeremy rubbed his unshaven face and stared at Seth with steel-blue eyes. "Be at the Golden Grill tomorrow night around ten."

Seth glanced around him again, the uncanny feeling someone watched him making the back of his neck itch. "What's happening tomorrow night at ten?" he asked.

Jeremy was gone.

"What the . . ." Seth looked around him, not even hearing a branch crack. "How the hell does he do that?" he grumbled under his breath, turning and heading out of the woods and back to his bike.

No matter his efforts, walking around the trees was impossible to do without dead leaves crunching under his boots. Seth slowed, standing still, and strained against the darkness as he listened. There was someone watching him. He'd bet his next paycheck on it. He continued focusing on the darkness, willing something to move. The only satisfaction he had as he continued standing in dark, damp woods was that whoever watched him couldn't see him any better than he saw them at the moment. His eyes were almost useless.

"This is ridiculous," he growled, breaking the silence around him and stalking back to his hog. It wasn't exactly a lead, but he'd be at the Golden Grill tomorrow night, although he'd be damned if he knew why he was supposed to be there.

He straddled his Harley, staring at the wet, gray cement in the small parking lot off the state park entrance, then raised his attention to the row of foreboding trees lining the edge of the parking lot. Paying attention to his gut feeling about things helped him in his line of work. Too often, following a hunch to where someone he'd been hired to find might be hiding out paid off more than pursuing a tangible lead from a reputable source. Seth wouldn't go as far to say he was tuned into his senses. He wasn't the sissy type. Seth had his reputation to uphold. And although women said they loved a man in tune with his inner self, they didn't really. They sure as hell didn't like a guy who admitted to such a thing.

Not that Seth cared what women thought of him. At least he didn't care what they thought of his mind. All he needed was the physical attraction. A good lay every now and life was good. The first sign he saw of a woman trying to figure him out, get under his skin, and he was gone.

There wasn't anyone around to see him stare at what appeared to be nothing more than cement and the edge of the forest. He didn't hear or see anything other than the dark woods and an empty parking lot. Jeremy had called Seth earlier, told him to meet out. Seth wasn't sure what he expected when he arrived. It was always a hard call with Jeremy. The man had helped him crack more than one case in the past, though. Apparently Jeremy wasn't coming back. Seth sat alone on his bike, still listening. He didn't have a clue how to fine-tune his senses. What a hell of a trick, though, if he were ever to pull it off.

I would see whoever is out there hiding and watching me.

As he dug his gloves out of his leather coat and put them on, the prickling under the back of his collar intensified. *Damn it.* Was Jeremy watching him? And if so, what the fuck? Jeremy wasn't nuts. The guy was different, but not in a "whacked in the head" way. Whoever it was, they weren't coming forward, and Seth had shit to do. Kicking his bike into neutral, he roared it to life and pulled out from the edge of the small parking lot, then headed back into town.

* * *

Jenna Drury lay with her tummy flat against the cold, damp ground. The chill of the earth helped soothe the heat burning inside her. Her brother had met with this human in the woods more than once now. If she came out and asked Jeremy why he was talking to the human male, Jeremy would lie to her, indifferent of how the lie would stink.

Jeremy wasn't a werewolf to mess with, but his preoccupation with the human worked to her advantage. She'd followed Jeremy this time and listened. Did he think Tray Long would be at the Golden Grill tomorrow night? And if so, why not kill the rogue werewolf and be done with it? The longer Tray Long hunted humans, the worse off he would make it for all of her kind.

Jenna shifted her attention back to the human when his motorcycle roared to life and he drove out of the parking lot. He was tall for a human and muscular, too, built almost like her brother. She'd never thought she would find herself sniffing after a human, but this one had her intrigued. He looked rough with his black leather and his sandy curly hair falling past his collar. The leather coat he wore made his shoulders look even broader, and roped muscle bulged under his blue jeans. He was dangerous-looking, forbidden, and a mystery. Add good looks to that and Jenna lay with her body pressed to the forest floor, damn near drooling.

When she couldn't hear the rumble of his motorcycle anymore, she stood, sniffing the air to make sure she was alone. Jeremy had already headed back, so distracted with his reasons for being out here that he didn't notice her. Damn good thing. Maybe she'd confront him about the human, but only after she figured out why they were meeting. Better she sniff her brother out than he sniff her out. Jeremy could be annoyingly unreasonable at times, even now that Jenna was grown. Sometimes her brother forgot she was twenty-three years old and treated her as if she were still a cub.

Jenna didn't smell anyone around her, but she shook her coat out silently, wagged her tail slowly, and perked her ears up, twitching them to hear all sounds around her. Then taking off, she trotted through the forest, heading the opposite direction from where the human had gone, toward the land on the other side of the state park her pack owned.

The moonless night created a setting for a good, hard run. She picked up pace, tearing at the earth with her claws as she raced across the land. The trees grew sparse and the open space around her stretched on for miles. Night dew clung to her coat, but her insides simmered with a growing heat she doubted would subside. Images of the human, Seth Gere, talking to her brother, lifting his long, muscular leg over that loud, large bike of his, and his searching gaze, when he sensed her watching him, continued playing in her mind.

She slowed when her den came into view. Jenna's clothes were where she had left them, under a rock next to a group of trees near her backyard. The den she and her brother lived in and the few dens stretching along the highway as far as she could see, as well as on the other side, were all occupied by werewolves. Her pack. The chill in the air conflicted with the burning desire growing inside her, an ache to chase down the forbidden. Even with her pack in their dens nearby, the comfort and security of being near those who cared about her didn't offer the usual solace. Tonight she'd made a decision. If her brother found out, or anyone else in the pack, they would throw a fit.

Her brother's bedroom light flashed on. A minute later her cell phone started ringing. Like she would rush through the change and endure the pain just to answer it before it went to voice mail. She didn't need to dig the phone out from her clothes to know it was her brother demanding to know where the hell she was. As open-minded and respected as he was among her pack, one word of her out running unescorted and suddenly he turned into a barbaric, overbearing pain in the ass.

She straightened to two feet, her human flesh soaked in sweat and a cruel chill making her shiver uncontrollably. Jenna struggled into her jeans and then fought with her sweatshirt, turning it right side out before pulling it over her head.

"Is there a reason you didn't answer my call?" Jeremy growled.

"Crap!" Jenna yanked her sweatshirt over her head, glaring at her older brother when he stared at her, his expression hard and his muscular arms crossed over his chest. "You scared the hell out of me."

"You must have been mighty distracted not to smell me approaching." He didn't appear sympathetic. "Who have you been out with all night?"

"Damn it, Jeremy." She bent over to put her shoes on, then clipped her phone to her jeans. "I'm not a cub. I don't ask you where you've been, or who you've been with." She yanked her hair out from under her sweatshirt and marched past him to their den. "Should I be concerned about where you've been all night?"

Jeremy howled to all who would listen that he was a progressive werewolf, determined to take their pack into the twenty-first century with a modern outlook. He followed her to their den, not saying a word. Jenna didn't press the matter, knowing in spite of her brother claiming males and females were equal, he didn't necessarily hold those views when it came to her. As stubborn and relentless as he could be, Jeremy drove her nuts out of love.

Jenna entered through her back door, leaving it open for Jeremy to follow. She headed to her bedroom, hearing the lock click into place when he secured their den. They were both fully capable of protecting themselves and each other, and their pack lived in peace, but that didn't mean challenges didn't exist. And even though she wasn't supposed to know about it, if Jeremy was helping the human sniff out a rogue werewolf, tough times might be around the corner for all of them.

One thing she knew: tomorrow night she'd be at the Golden Grill. It might take some planning, but the human, Seth Gere, intrigued her. There was something about him she wanted to check out further. Jenna collapsed on her bed, grabbing a strand of hair and twisting it around her fingers as she stared at her ceiling. Were humans into rough and wild sex the way werewolves were?

CHAPTER TWO

Seth entered Payton Investigative Services late the next morning. He nodded at the receptionist, Hannah McDowell. "Is John in there?"

"Well, if it isn't the prodigal son," she teased, then nodded to the closed door. "He's been on the phone most of the morning."

If that was a hint for him to leave John Payton alone, Seth ignored it. "Sounds like he needs a break." Seth winked at Hannah, then entered John's office before she could stop him. He closed Payton's office door behind him, nodding when the older man held up a finger and continued with his phone call.

"Mrs. Shore, if you want me to follow your husband, my fee is the same as it always is." Payton dragged his fingers through his silver hair, lowering his head and leaning against his hand as he stared at his desk. "You bring in the check and when it clears, I'll get started." He let out a silent breath, picking up his ballpoint and scribbling in the corner of his notepad. "Yes. Yes, cash is fine. Drop it off here at the office. . . . Thank you, Mrs. Shore. If he's cheating on you again, I'll find out for you."

Seth couldn't do what John did for a living. Being a private dick was a grossly misconceived line of work. So many thought it glorious and Hollywood glamorized it, but truth be told, it sucked. The lines engraved deeply on John Payton's forehead and dark circles under his eyes were proof of the stress and long hours.

John hung up the phone and reached for his coffee cup, realized it was empty, and stood.

"How close are you to bringing in Tray Long?" John asked, heading for the coffee pot in the corner of his office.

Seth wouldn't mention the Golden Grill. Maybe it was superstition, but talking about a lead might fuck it up. "Shouldn't be long now," he grumbled, moving in to pour himself a cup.

"Good. I got a phone call first thing this morning. Came in before I got here. Hannah took the message." John ran his hand over the papers scattered on the desk, found what he wanted and handed it to Seth. "There's an APB out on this one and word on the streets is the FBI is interested as well."

Seth stared at the handwritten message. "Elaine Gold. Why does her name ring a bell?" He snapped his fingers, pointing at John before the older man could answer. "That's right. There was a special on the Golds. Robbed a handful of banks. Harry Gold was arrested, but his wife went MIA."

"Rumor has it she's here in Omaha. Slap Happy sent word about a hot number staying over at the Motel 6. This one has your name all over it."

Seth didn't want to guess why John might think that. John didn't usually take high-profile jobs. He stuck to bad checks and cheating spouses and made a show about complaining that Seth had all the fun. Truth be told, John didn't have the balls to do the serious undercover work. Seth knew John hadn't always been like this. Either age was catching up with the sixty-year-old, or something along the way in his career had made him gun-shy. Seth didn't ask questions. He appreciated John setting him up with cases he didn't want. It paid the rent. And beat the hell out of Seth having to find work himself.

"I'll talk to Happy." Seth stuffed the message into his jeans pocket and drank the semi-hot coffee. "Anything else for me?"

"Huh?" John looked up from the papers on his desk. "Umm, no." He slumped into his office chair, staring at whatever he'd just been looking at. Then clearing his throat, he picked up what looked like a fax, crumpled it, and threw it in his trash. "Let me know when you're close to nailing Long."

"Will do." Seth downed his coffee, left his cup next to the coffeepot, and let himself out of John's office, closing the door behind him.

Hannah was typing at her computer but stopped when Seth headed out of her office. "Seth?" she asked, glancing at him over her small reading glasses. "You got a minute?"

Hannah was a pretty woman, petite, with straight brown hair that curved around her face and fell to her shoulders. Seth didn't really go after older women, but if he did, Hannah would be a perfect candidate. The low-cut sweater she wore with jeans that hugged her slender legs and showed off her narrow waist probably caught the attention of any man who walked into this office. Hannah looked like the kind of woman who needed protection, not the kind of woman who could protect a PI's office if some derelict started giving her grief. The kind of people who entered this office weren't the best, or the safest, to be around. She also did a lot of John's fieldwork.

"Sure. What's up?" Seth asked when she stood and walked around her desk.

Hannah leaned against the front of it, studying him with her pretty green eyes. "It's John," she said, lowering her voice to a near whisper. "I'm worried about him."

"Oh yeah?" Seth didn't mention that he'd noticed John looked distracted just now. "Why are you worried?"

"I think something is going on with him, but he tells me he's fine."

"Then he's probably fine."

She shook her head slowly. "He's lying to me."

"Then what's wrong?" Seth had learned a long time ago not to try to understand women's logic. Straight, cut-and-dry questioning was the best.

"I don't know. I just told you that," she said. "Do me a favor, please. Will you find out what cases he's working on without letting him know you're trying to find out?"

"Don't you know all of his cases?"

"I always have. But he's working on something he isn't telling me about and you know as well as me that isn't safe. I know he's hard-pressed for money sometimes, but he needs to tell me where he is for his own protection."

It wouldn't surprise Seth if Hannah's concerns for John were a bit more personal than she let on. John would need to be hit over the head with a brick to notice if any woman was interested. Which might not be a bad idea where Hannah was concerned. She was pretty, hardworking, and loyal. John couldn't do much better than landing a girlfriend like Hannah.

Seth nodded, reaching for the door handle, and winked at Hannah. "I'll see what I can find out. In the meantime, put a GPS in his cell phone. More than likely he's just getting forgetful and doesn't mean to not keep you posted."

Hannah didn't react to Seth casually flirting with her. "I like the GPS idea if I can get him to remember to carry his phone with him."

"He's a tough man, but if anyone can train him, you can." Seth headed out the door, raising his hand and waving good-bye before letting the office door close behind him. He doubted he needed to track John. More than likely, Hannah would be able to do the work herself. There wasn't time to question why she had sought Seth out about it. He had a killer and a missing bank robber to find.

Slap Happy was a small man, not even five and a half feet tall. One leg was shorter than the other, so he walked with a limp. Add thick, bushy fiery red hair to that and the man was as unique as his name. Happy worked as a custodian downtown in one of the larger office buildings and kept his ears and eyes to the ground. For years he'd been a solid informant for the police department as well as for John. When Happy saw Seth approach him just outside the main set of bathrooms off the lobby, he straightened. Happy was scared of Seth, always had been. But there wasn't any running away, since Seth had cornered him and his mop bucket.

After hanging out in the guys' john for almost half an hour while Happy explained the word on the

street, Seth headed across town to the Motel 6. There
wasn't an Elaine Gold registered, so Seth camped out
in the coffee shop across the street, watching the
parking lot and waiting for her to show up until it got
dark. Stakeouts weren't exactly his cup of tea. It was
boring as hell. Once it got dark it was too hard to tell
who came and went from the motel. Besides, he
needed to head home and get ready to go out tonight.
He would have to find Elaine Gold tomorrow.

By ten, Seth pulled in to the large shopping center parking lot where the Golden Grill was. The bar
and grill had been around for years and not too long
ago switched ownership. The new clientele seemed
a bit darker, more his age, and the place was known
for its occasional bar fight. Seth parked his Harley,
taking in the fairly crowded parking lot.

A woman grabbed Seth's attention. She appeared
from around the corner, as if she'd walked there, and
started across the lot, weaving slowly through the
parked cars. He'd always had a fondness for long hair
on women, and this lady's dark hair flowed to her ass.
The breeze lifted it, making it flow around and behind her as she moved with a quiet air of confidence
that made her appear to almost float. When the street-
light caught her in its circular glow over the asphalt,
he got a better view of her facial features. Within the
next moment she was enveloped in darkness. Seth
swore she looked directly at him. But he knew too
well that the night was good at making things appear
as they weren't.

The lady shifted her attention to the Golden Grill,
which meant she'd at least been looking his way, if
not at him. And she was alone. If she spotted him, it
didn't make her leery. She continued with her slow,

confident pace, her arms relaxed at her sides and the snug, sleeveless shirt and skirt she wore hugging and showing off one hell of a hot body.

Seth climbed off his bike and headed across the lot. He picked up his pace, reaching the door to the Golden Grill at the same time she did. She smelled good. Her hair was thick and shiny under the awning lights.

"Allow me," he offered, reaching over her head and pulling open the door to the Golden Grill.

Immediately the noise from inside made it hard to hear her response. Seth swore she said, "I planned on it."

He didn't recognize either man standing just inside the door, who were checking ID, and possibly assuring the clientele allowed into the establishment met with their approval. The pretty lady disappeared into the crowd and the tall, muscular men at the door then turned their hardened stares on him.

"Three-dollar cover," the one to his right informed him.

"Do either of you know that woman?" Seth asked, pulling out his wallet.

"Ladies are in free," the guy on the left growled.

That didn't answer Seth's question, and he had a feeling by the way both of their gazes burned into his back after he'd entered the bar, they both knew that. It didn't matter. He had a job to do. Unfortunately, the sexy long-haired vixen would have to wait.

Seth took his time walking from one end of the Golden Grill to the other. Twelve huge TV screens hung from the wall, arranged so no matter where someone sat, they could see the screen. On nights when there was a basketball game, this place was insane. Tonight wasn't one of those nights. The crowd was fairly thick, though. Quite a few leaned against the bar and he didn't notice any free tables or booths. Both pool tables in the back of the room were being used, and a couple played darts along the far wall.

When he noticed a vacant bar stool at the bar, Seth moved in and ordered a beer. Then leaning against the counter, he turned to give himself a view of the place and the people moving around him.

Tray Long—the thief and killer he was after—was a big man, his brown hair once long but now trimmed close to his head, the prison cut. Seth couldn't imagine the prick showing his ugly mug in this establishment. If there was another murderer running around town, they were damned smart and clever. Tray was suspect number one based on his M.O. His profile fit.

The bartender brought Seth his beer and he pulled out his wallet and tossed a couple bills on the bar. The bartender picked up the money, then slapped a bar rag over the smooth, highly polished, wooden counter. He gave Seth the same hard look the bouncers at the door did.

He wasn't here to make friends. Sipping his beer, he turned his back to the bar and leaned against the counter, taking in the crowd. Seth pulled out his cell phone and glanced at the time. Ten thirty on the spot. Jeremy didn't say what would happen here, but Seth prayed Tray Long would be here. Seth needed the money, and taking that bastard off the streets once and for all would be doing everyone a favor. The asshole was one sick motherfucker.

The woman with the long, dark hair appeared through the crowd, standing on a ledge across the room, which served as a small balcony. There were tables behind her filled with people as well as others standing around her. It appeared she was alone, though. She didn't talk to anyone. As she sipped at a mixed drink, she turned her attention to Seth. He swore she stared directly at him, watching him from across the room as he stared back. What was it she said to him when they entered this place?

She brought her cup to her lips, sipping her drink and continuing to watch him over the rim. Seth loved how her long, thick hair fell over one shoulder, parting around her breast and curling in soft waves at her narrow waist. The shirt she wore hugged her figure, and damn, she was hot. Hot to the point of distraction. Seth forced his gaze away first, scanning the crowd. He wouldn't let some hot temptress distract him from the reason he was here.

Tray Long was a big motherfucker. As crowded as the Golden Grill was tonight, he wouldn't be hard to spot if he was here. Seth also searched for Jeremy. Maybe the guy just wanted to meet him here. Possibly he had taken Seth's comment about normal people meeting in bars to heart.

Unable to keep his attention off the hot lady across the bar, he glanced back her way. She stood there, resting her cup against the balcony ledge, her expression somber. Apparently she had figured out she no longer had him as an audience.

Large hands snaked around her from behind and Seth stiffened. A predatory instinct jumped to life inside him. Putting his beer on the bar, he turned toward her, convinced she didn't appear happy with the intrusion. Seth couldn't see the bastard who grabbed her, his head nestled against her neck, buried in her hair. Seth wasn't the jealous type, but damn, what he wouldn't do to have his head where that guy's was.

The guy dragged her away from the balcony. But when she grabbed the ledge and spilled her drink, Seth lunged away from the bar. Whoever the guy was, the lady didn't want to be with him.

CHAPTER THREE

Jenna damn near gagged on the stench from the male who wrapped his greasy hand around her face. He was a large werewolf and a hell of a lot stronger than she was. Her fingernails dug into the wooden balcony ledge, scraping the wood, as he forcibly dragged her back through the crowd.

Stupid fucking humans. Someone could be killed in front of them and they would stifle the smell of their fear and pretend they didn't see it. Allowing a bit of muscle to come forth on her own, Jenna felt the pinch as her teeth grew in her mouth. Then she opened her mouth and got a rancid taste in her mouth from the male's flesh; Jenna's eyes watered as she bit into his flesh.

"Fucking bitch," the male howled behind her, yanking his hand from her mouth and holding it with his other hand.

Jenna didn't wait to see how upset he was. Darting around the humans who now appeared mildly interested, she headed for the small flight of stairs and toward the main part of the club.

"I don't think so," the male growled, reaching her on the stairs and grabbing her hair.

Jenna growled fiercely as she fell backward, the small stairwell creating a private area where no one else would see her attack with the strength she possessed.

"Someone should have taught you manners," she hissed, using the wall as leverage as she turned and smacked the male in the face, her claws extended. Her words were garbled with her teeth pressing against her lips as she spoke. Allowing her stronger half to come forth also heightened her senses.

Jenna stared into the fury-laden, pale blue eyes of her attacker. She didn't recognize the male, but as she made contact, scratching his face and watching red lines appear down his cheek, she did recognize the unleashed rage filling him. He had a lot of nerve getting pissed at her for defending herself.

"They've tried teaching me to behave," he grumbled through clenched teeth. "And all have failed. Now they think they can have another shot, but you, little female, are my meal ticket out of here. Don't think I won't kill you if you keep fighting me, though."

As nonsensical as his words were, she believed him. He smelled disgusting, but she didn't smell a lie. At the same time, Jenna didn't belly-up for any male, sane or insane.

"I'm not your meal ticket for shit!" she roared, bounding down the stairs, ready to run through the crowd and use every human in there, if needed, as a block against this insane werewolf.

The male behind her wrapped his hand through her hair, yanking her backward when she would have lunged out of the stairwell. Jenna cried out, feeling the pain in her scalp. At the same time, the human male who had spoken with her brother the night before in the woods stepped into the stairwell.

"Let her go, Tray." The deadly calm in his tone was uncanny coming out of a human, and it seemed to still everything around them.

The human male wouldn't smell the slight change in her attacker's scent. Jenna banked on it, though. Tray, whoever the hell he was, suddenly smelled hesitant. And she swore there was the slightest tinge of fear. Already she'd guessed this wasn't an ordinary human male, especially if her brother was meeting with him. Apparently Tray knew that, too. It took a moment before he regained his insane, cocky attitude, and Jenna took advantage of that moment.

She lunged at the human, praying his strength was as strong as his self-confidence. Tray's hand slipped out of her hair as she practically tumbled down the stairs and into the arms of the human.

Instead of taking her in his arms or pulling the two of them out of the stairwell as Jenna had guessed the human would do, he shoved her behind him and bounded up the stairs toward the insane werewolf.

Tray retreated, which shocked her even more. What werewolf would run from a human?

"I can smell the little bitch on my hands. She'll be easy enough to hunt later," Tray snarled, flying into the unsuspecting crowd of humans on the landing upstairs.

"Hunt me and you'll die!" she yelled up the stairwell.

Jenna couldn't see the male who had attacked her anymore. But she got an eyeful of muscular ass and long, powerful-looking legs as she stood at the bottom of the stairs. Then suddenly she stood alone, the noise of so many people partying around her irritating. She'd come here tonight after hearing her brother tell this human to be here. Already the male intrigued her. He wasn't a werewolf, yet he was strong enough to make a lunatic werewolf bolt at the sight of him. Jenna needed to know more.

Charging up the stairs, she searched the humans sitting at tables, or standing in small groups chatting and laughing, oblivious to the two males who had just raced past them. Jenna couldn't sniff either of them out, not with so much activity swarming around her. She cursed under her breath when she realized there was another flight of stairs on the other side of the landing. The werewolf male was gone and her human was rushing out the main door.

By the time Jenna reached outside, the human and the werewolf were already across the parking lot. And the human was still chasing Tray.

"Damn," she muttered, the entire scene so incredibly insane she couldn't blow it off and return inside.

"Are you heading home?" Bruno, one of the bouncers at the Golden Grill, stepped outside.

Jenna offered him a limp wave over her shoulder. "No one in there appealed to me."

"I'll let your brother know to expect you soon."

Jenna growled under her breath, itching to race across the parking lot and not interested in overprotective single males. "Don't bother. He's not at our den," she offered lightly, then walked quickly, aching to break into a sprint, but sensing Bruno watching her as she headed across the parking lot.

Jenna waited for the annoying comment to ransack her brain that good little females didn't wander alone at night without an escort. Bruno knew humans might be in hearing distance, though, and fortunately had enough sense not to howl after her. She hated hearing that. Good little females could do whatever the fuck they wanted to do. Including ignoring good little males.

Insanity had a really odd smell to it. Jenna tried figuring it out as she followed the scent past the parking lot and around the corner. The moment she was out of sight of the Golden Grill, she broke into a hefty jog, wishing she'd opted for something other than her lace underwire bra and short skirt. Better yet, she prayed the scent would carry her out of the city so she could change and run with some speed that would allow her to catch up to the human. As powerful as the warped smell of hostility, egotistical confidence, and fear was, the smell of her human male was just as strong.

Putting some muscle into it, and probably running faster than most humans would dub as "normal," Jenna spotted the human male trucking ahead of her. She paced herself, staying less than a block's distance behind him. There wasn't any harm in letting him know she tracked him. She was curious. The man he chased had attacked her. Different lines pranced through her head that she might use if he turned on her. Which she really wanted him to do. It was one thing for him to save her honor, and she was appreciative. But the human was more intent on chasing down a rabid werewolf than he was in her. Jenna wouldn't let that get to her.

After running a few blocks, they came back around to the back side of the shopping center where the Golden Grill was. The werewolf, Tray, was a few blocks ahead of the human. In spite of his well-built body and his apparent aggressive nature, the human male wasn't a match for a werewolf. Jenna watched Tray jump up against a wooden privacy fence and clear it. But the human slowed in the middle of the street, fisting his hands at his waist and breathing heavily as he studied the darkness.

Jenna slowed to a walk before coming up behind him. When the human turned around, beautiful gray eyes pierced her, an array of emotions washing off of him as he swallowed a couple times.

"Were you following me?" he asked, sounding surprised and out of breath. His sandy blond hair was curlier than it was in the club, and its tousled look made him even sexier.

Jenna was surprised at herself. Humans didn't turn her on. They never had. Whatever it was about this particular male screamed caution. She made a show of sounding out of breath, too.

"Men don't assault me in bars." She straightened, sticking out her chin. "I wanted to watch you take him down."

"Tray Long is not a man," he growled.

She thought of telling him which way Tray went, but then froze. "Tray Long?" she said, and dropped her attention to the sidewalk between them. "I know that name," she said more to herself than to him.

"Then you should know to stay the fuck away from him." The harshness in his tone wasn't missed.

Jenna's attention shot to his face, smelling his irritation. "He tried grabbing me, not the other way around," she snapped.

He searched her face with those distracting eyes of his. They were an odd color, especially for a human. And he was definitely pure-blooded human. The rich, dark color of them reminded her of a stormy sky, right before all hell broke loose. When his gaze dropped lower, heat washed over her.

"I'll walk you to your car," he decided, as if this whole time he was contemplating what best to do with her.

He held his hand out, turning, implying she should walk alongside him back around the shopping center.

Jenna started toward the building with him, glancing at his profile as he in turn looked at her. "I don't have a car," she told him.

"Husband?"

"No."

"Boyfriend?"

"No."

"How are you getting home?"

Apparently the species of male didn't matter. They all thought females incapable of going anywhere by themselves.

"The same way I got to the club," she told him derisively. "Walk."

He stared straight ahead, staying in pace with her, their arms brushing once while their shoes created a mutual rhythm against the black asphalt.

"I'll take you home," he said after a moment.

"Don't worry about it." The last thing she needed was her brother actually being at her den, then having to listen to him rant and rave about a human bringing her home. Although this human was her brother's friend. "I don't mind walking."

"I mind. You're not walking alone tonight."

Jenna sighed, which he apparently didn't appreciate. Before they reached the corner of the building he grabbed her arm, turning her to face him. "I realize you don't know me. But you were just grabbed by a killer. I tried apprehending him and I *will* catch him. Until then, I either take you home or stay with you until you find someone you trust to take you."

"Tray Long." She said his name, not surprised at how it changed the expression on the male's face. His frustration and determination didn't sway, and although his nature frustrated her, she had to admit the strong emotions mixed well on him, giving him an appealing aroma she didn't mind breathing deep into her lungs. "That's who tried grabbing me?" She shook her head. "I'd forgotten about the rumors spreading about him until you said his name."

"If you heard he's killed several people, done time for it, is out on parole and now suspected of killing again, then you heard right."

Jenna nodded. She hadn't given it much thought when the werewolf said he could sniff her out later, but if humans were hunting him and the rumors about him were true—that no pack would have him—then he might have sought her out intentionally. What better way to get at their pack leader than to take his younger littermate?

She shivered at the thought. Her companion touched her arm, his warm, callused fingers creating a much different sensation than what she'd experienced a moment before.

"I'll wait with you until you find a ride," he said, his baritone deeper than it was before, the tone soothing as he rubbed his fingers down her arm. "I'm Seth Gere. And you are?"

"Jenna," she offered, and wondered if she should

give him her last name. If he knew her litter, it might not go well for her.

"Jenna?" He tilted one eyebrow, obviously not liking the informal introduction.

"Yes." She lifted her gaze when she realized she stared at his broad chest and stared into those incredible dark gray eyes. "Jenna Drury," she added, watching him.

Seth cocked an eyebrow, then pursed his lips as if he knew already why she had held out on giving him her last name. "How related are you to Jeremy Drury?"

"Pretty related."

"Did you know already that he's a friend of mine?"

She shifted her weight, turning and staring at the end of the building and parking lot, which was filling up with even more cars than when she'd left. Seth considered her littermate a friend. Possibly Jeremy met him in the woods so no one would smell a human coming around their den. Jeremy didn't explain his life to her, which never bothered her because she didn't tell him everything, either. Although now she needed to figure out a way to keep Seth from telling Jeremy she was here, alone, almost abducted by a rogue werewolf, then helped chase him around town. She wasn't sure asking Seth to keep quiet would work. He'd known Jeremy long enough to call him friend and only known her a few minutes. Seth's loyalty would lie with her brother.

Apparently she hesitated long enough to give Seth the answer to his question. "So when you made your comment at the door when we entered, then watched me while we were inside the club, all of that was intentional?"

Jenna took her time returning her attention to him. She hadn't had an agenda. Not really. Other than her curiosity being piqued. But now so was Seth's. And she needed to say something or he'd think she was trying to pick him up. That wasn't her intention, was it?

"I was teasing at the door and I wouldn't say I was watching you. I noticed you and didn't know anyone else there tonight."

He nodded once, although his hard features gave her the impression he didn't feel she was out of the water yet. Jenna sighed, not liking someone who was a stranger treating her the way her brother did, as if she needed to justify her actions.

"I think it would be smart from now on not to flirt with men you don't know."

"And I think I can take care of myself." Under different circumstances she might find it cute that this human, of a species possessing half her strength, tried protecting her.

Jenna started toward the parking lot, but Seth grabbed her arm, catching her off guard when he spun her around. She slapped her hand against his chest, immediately aware of the warm, solid muscle flexing under his shirt.

"You are not walking away from here alone," he growled, his menacing tone causing her insides to flip-flop. He reached into his pocket with his free hand, pulling out a cell phone. "If you aren't going to call for someone to get you, I will."

"Who are you calling?"

"You said you were related to—"

"You're not calling my brother!" she snapped, yanking free of his grasp and feeling the sting on her skin when his fingers scraped over her arm.

"I should have guessed Jeremy was your brother." Seth walked around her, his back to the parking lot, and blocked her way. "And why don't you want me calling him?"

"There's no reason to interrupt his evening." She tried to make light of it but didn't bother searching Seth's face this time to see if he bought it.

Seth's scent told her enough. He had an unusually strong, protective, dominating aroma about him.

"Then it's decided." He took her arm again, this time not as roughly, and placed his hand on her back as he guided them into the parking lot. "I'm taking you home."

CHAPTER FOUR

Seth wasn't sure calling Jeremy about his sister was a good idea. At least not at the moment with the thoughts Seth had running through his head. She didn't argue but walked silently next to him as they neared his Harley. Seth kept his hand on her back, enjoying the narrow curve of it and how her hips swayed while she remained at his side.

"I didn't bring two helmets, so you can wear mine." He hated taking his hand off her, and shot her a side glance when he took the helmet from his bike.

She hesitated only a moment before accepting the helmet, then twisted her hair behind her head and slid it on. Seth straddled his bike and held it when she climbed on behind him, gripping his shoulder, then pressing her legs against his body as she slid up against his backside.

Jenna put her hands on either side of his waist. Seth took her wrists, pulling her hands to his stomach, then held them both in his hand, keeping her pinned against him. When the bike rumbled to life, Jenna slid closer, resting her chin against his shoulder. Seth was acutely aware of everywhere she touched him and took a moment fighting to concentrate before making an ass out of himself and tipping his bike.

"Where to, my lady?" he asked, and rubbed his finger over the smooth, silky back side of her hand.

"Do you know where the entrance to the woods is just north of town? Where all the trails start?"

"Yes," he said slowly, having been there just last night when he met Jeremy.

"Go there."

"You don't live there." He released the clutch, accelerating and letting the bike crawl out of the parking lot.

"Close enough. I can walk from there."

They'd been through this before and he seriously doubted Jenna believed he would just let her walk into the dark alone, especially in the woods at night. Seth left the parking lot, taking it easy on the speed limit, primarily because he was enjoying the hell out of Jenna's hot little body wrapped around his but also because he kept a shrewd eye on his surroundings, looking for anything that might suggest Tray Long was nearby.

"Why did you chase after Tray?" she asked, her jaw rubbing Seth's shoulder when she spoke.

"It's my job."

"Your job?"

"I'm a bounty hunter. He skipped out on his parole officer."

"So someone is paying you to hunt him?"

"Yup."

"Then me being seen with you could set him off and he might try capturing me again to piss you off."

Seth had thought of that. "It's hard saying what that motherfucker would do. He's not right in the head. You aren't going to walk home alone though."

"He's insane. I could smell it . . . I mean, I could tell by the look in his eye."

"Insanity has a smell?" Seth had never heard anyone say it like that before.

"All emotions have a smell."

"Oh yeah? What do I smell like?"

"You smell turned on," she said quietly.

Seth smiled. He could play her game, too. "Personally I like the way your lust smells," he growled, giving her hands a squeeze but then tightening his grip when she tried moving them. "It's damn near the best thing I've ever smelled."

Jenna got quiet, possibly trying to figure him out. They rode in silence until they reached the small parking lot where he'd been the night before. Seth pulled in but, instead of parking, circled it once.

"Time to tell me where you live, sweetheart."

"I really can't do that. But it's not far. You don't have to worry at all. I grew up in those woods and know each tree very well. I'm safer there than on any street block."

"Jeremy would really throw that big of a fit if he saw you with me?"

"You have no idea."

Seth wasn't sure how Jeremy would act. He stopped the bike, parking it sideways across the faded yellow line of two stalls. Jeremy was a bit different, but apparently so was his sister.

Seth climbed off his bike just in time to catch Jenna pull off her helmet, and her dark, thick hair come tumbling over her shoulders and down her back. God, he loved all that hair. It was an incredible view that he was sure for a moment left his jaw sagging. Something moved out of the corner of his eye, though, and he looked in that direction before catching hell about how he smelled like he wanted to fuck her or something.

Jenna stiffened and leaned forward, looking for a moment as if she'd climb his handlebars. "You saw it, too?" she whispered.

"I don't think we're alone," he told her, taking her arm as he studied the ominous dark trees around them.

"Don't you want to go get him?"

"Who?" Seth asked, holding her back when she tried getting off his bike.

"Tray," she said, searching Seth's face as she frowned. "I thought you said you'd get money if you caught him. He's right over there. We can catch him," she whispered, her tone urgent.

"We are not going anywhere," he growled, keeping his eye on the dark trees but not seeing anyone anywhere.

"You don't think I could keep up and help you catch him?" Her whispered tone rose slightly.

"Put your helmet back on." Seth climbed back onto his bike, furious as he guessed Tray's game plan. "Is this the way you came when you walked to the Golden Grill?"

"What?" She struggled behind Seth but then grabbed his waist when he took off out of the parking lot. "I don't get you!" she snapped. "Why would you turn down a hunt?"

"I'm not going to take him down with you by my side when he's trying to stalk you," Seth explained.

"I don't get you at all," she complained, her arms tight around his waist and her chin once again resting on his shoulder.

Seth wasn't so outraged that he wasn't aware of her large breasts pressing against his back. They'd been a distraction coming here, but Jenna breathed harder now, obviously upset, although Seth doubted she saw the big picture. He'd call Jeremy when he reached his house and pray the man wasn't too narrow-minded to understand why Seth took his sister home. Granted, Jenna wasn't a girl and definitely was all woman, but some people were overly protective of their single sisters no matter how old they were. And in Jenna's case, when it was obvious she was a bit on the wild side and had no clue when, or how, to submit to a man, it might be understandable why her brother was so much a part of her life.

"What kind of man passes up a good hunt?" Jenna didn't focus on the house when Seth parked and got off his bike but instead searched Seth's face with vibrant blue eyes that almost appeared to glow in the darkness. "I would love to hear the thinking behind this ludicrous behavior."

Her dark hair flowed down her back, swaying to the side when she yanked off her helmet and placed it on the seat of the bike. Seth picked it up and pulled out his keys, glancing up and down his quiet street before leading the way from his driveway to his front door. He had no intentions of discussing anything with her outside when it was apparent the threat Tray had made against Jenna at the bar weren't idle words.

"I don't know anything about ludicrous behavior," Seth told her, closing the door behind them and flipping on his living room light. His gaze dropped to that tight, nicely curved ass of hers before she turned around. "But it exists. Tray Long obviously has an agenda with you in it."

Jenna was checking out Seth's home, taking slow, deep breaths that filled her lungs and pressed her breasts against her shirt. The view was incredible and his body immediately reacted, blood draining from his brain and straight to his cock. Seth forced himself to focus when she gave him a shrewd look.

"I meant your behavior. Why didn't you go after him?"

"Because you were with me."

"And you think because it appears he was lying in wait for me that I wouldn't be able to defend myself?" The way she pressed her fists against her hips and glared at him made it clear she believed she could defend herself.

"I'm glad we didn't have to find out." He wasn't going to battle a female ego. He loved her fiery spirit, but it was unleashed. Whatever man decided to take on Jenna would need patience and some careful strategic tactics. Taking out his phone, he made sure his blinds were closed. Too bad he didn't have time to tame this onyx-colored hair beauty.

Jenna came up around him, grabbing his wrist and showing she did have more strength than it appeared by her small stature when she pressed down on his arm to prevent him from calling anyone.

"What are you doing?" she asked, thick lashes fluttering over her bright blue eyes.

"Calling Jeremy." Seth glanced at her small hand and fingers attempting to wrap around his wrist.

"You can't do that," she hissed.

"Sweetheart. You're in danger."

Jenna's next move surprised him and threw him off guard. She moved to face him and then wrapped her arms around his neck, not hesitating once as she pressed her body against his and tilted her head to kiss him. He blinked when her soft lips pressed against his. At the same time, blood roared through his veins, creating a rushing sound in his brain that made it damn near impossible to think straight.

She tasted good. Her lips parted and her small tongue pressed between his lips, as if she were asking for permission before deepening the kiss. It was all he could do not to growl, drop his phone, and press that soft, perfectly curved body harder against his. She'd gone up on her tiptoes to reach his mouth and when she stepped back, ending the kiss as mysteriously as she started it, her hands grazed over his chest. Her cheeks were flushed, making her eyes look like beautiful sapphires. Her dark hair streamed past her shoulders. Jenna was a sensual creature, seductive and enticing. He would love time to explore every inch of her, physically as well as her mind.

"Do you kiss any man who tells you you're in danger?"

"Nope." She took a step backward, creating space between them, and touched her lips with her fingers. "But you aren't going to call my brother, and if you do, you'll have to explain why you kissed me after bringing me to your home."

Seth raised one eyebrow. "Why I kissed you?"

She was sexy as hell with her face flushed and her lips full and moist. But damn if she'd make a liar out of him. And it was her idea. Seth moved just as quickly as she had. Clearing the distance between them, he lifted her off the ground, pressing her back against the wall with enough force she gasped. When he seared his mouth to hers, the moan that escaped her made it impossible for him not to turn hard as stone.

Seth impaled her mouth with his tongue. Where a moment ago he was offered a sample, he now took all there was. Pressing his hips against her, letting her feel how hard she made him, he kept her pinned against the wall while dragging one hand through her thick hair and tilting her head to deepen the kiss.

Jenna gripped his neck, dragging her nails down his flesh with enough pressure to scrape the skin. The sting fed his craving for her and he growled, barely hearing the small voice in the back of his head that told him to slow down. At this rate he'd rip her clothes off her and bury himself deep inside her. They could get to know each other later. She started this and he had no problem finishing it.

Seth hated the nagging voice that persisted in his brain, working its way through the fog of lust. Jenna kissed him with ulterior motives. Granted, she wasn't exactly fighting him off now, but he needed to regain his thought process and maintain control of this situation.

"Damn it," Jenna hissed when he released her, allowing her to slide down the wall.

"Now I've kissed you," he grumbled, tasting her on his lips.

Seth stepped backward, but her flushed face and now-tousled hair made such a hot fucking picture that he forced himself to create more distance, walking across his living room in spite of the pain in his groin. Ordering his cock to calm down wasn't easy, but calling her brother would do the trick.

"Seth. No!" Jenna tried jumping at him.

He held her back with one arm, placing the call and hearing it ring in his ear. When she heard her brother pick up, Jenna retreated, almost running to the couch and planting herself there, her legs pressed together and her head in her hands.

"Jeremy, we've got a situation," Seth began.

"Did you catch Tray Long?" Jeremy asked, his voice muffled as if he'd been sleeping.

"Nope. But I ran into him. I also ran into Jenna."

"Jenna?" Jeremy demanded, his voice suddenly a lot clearer than it was a moment ago.

Seth turned to face her and she stared at him, her expression blank.

"Yup. I've met your sister."

There was silence on the other end and something prickled down Seth's spine. He wouldn't jeopardize his friendship with Jeremy, albeit a working relationship. Jeremy was a good man.

"Tray Long tried taking her twice. I intervened both times and now have her here at my house."

Again silence. Seth waited it out.

"Give me your address," Jeremy finally said.

CHAPTER FIVE

Jenna leaned against the counter, breathing in the smell of the coffee she'd made when she first woke up. Jeremy was in the living room, and from the sound of it so were Bruno and Haze. Not that Jeremy would have much to say to her anyway. No matter how appreciative Jeremy had been to Seth, not once commenting on the fresh scratch marks going down his neck, the moment he'd had her alone, Jeremy had chewed her ass out.

She wasn't sure what was worse, her brother yelling or the silent treatment. Not that he had a right to yell, or ignore her. And she shouldn't let his temper get to her. She was twenty-three years old, a grown female, with the right to decide who she spent her time with and what she did while she was with them. Glancing toward the back door, she had half a mind to slip out, take off into town, and sniff out Seth. The way he kissed her last night went beyond trying to make a point. They had unfinished business, and she couldn't wait to finish it.

"I say we form a run and be done with his ass," Haze growled, the middle-aged male suddenly upset enough that the spicy smell of his anger reached Jenna in the kitchen.

She hadn't been paying attention to their conversation until now, too absorbed in her own thoughts. Jenna perked up, suddenly straining to hear.

"I'm waiting on a call. Long will be out of our hair before sundown," Jeremy said calmly.

"You put too much merit in that human," Bruno snarled. "You know he followed your littermate into the bar last night, was right on her tail."

Jenna growled, aching to smack Bruno across the face for trying to refuel their argument. Just because she wouldn't give Bruno the time of day didn't mean he had a right to come howling to Jeremy if another male sniffed after her.

"I don't give the human credit for anything he isn't capable of doing," Jeremy said, surprising Jenna by ignoring Bruno's comment about the two of them entering the bar together, which truth be told wouldn't have happened if she hadn't stalled so he would enter right behind her.

She'd wanted to sniff Seth out, not the other way around. Like she would tell any of them that. Reaching as quietly as she could into the cabinet, Jenna pulled out a coffee cup and poured coffee, straining to hear what else might be said about Seth Gere.

"I'm sure he's capable of doing a lot with your sister," Bruno sneered.

Something crashed and Jenna jumped, biting her lip to keep from squealing when she spilled hot coffee on her hand. If it weren't for the strong emotions reeking in the living room, they would remember she was in the house, and within earshot, and quit talking. Jenna tasted blood, and licked her lip where she'd just bit herself while grabbing a washcloth to wipe up coffee.

"He is capable of capturing Tray Long!" Jeremy roared. "We're going to let him do this. Long is rogue. We don't know if he has affiliation with another pack."

"You must think a lot of this human," Haze growled, his low raspy voice sounding cool and in control regardless of whatever outburst had just occurred from Bruno's crude comment.

"I think no more of him than he deserves," Jeremy explained. "The human keeps a low profile, but he goes after convicts and hunts them down. His track record smells good to me. And I won't have another pack coming forward and claiming we crossed the line punishing one of their own if Long belongs to another pack."

"Has he ever hunted a werewolf before?" Haze asked.

"Not a question I would ask him," Jeremy said, the reasons being obvious enough that no one commented. None of them would do anything to let on to the humans in the area that they were all werewolves. "I will tell you this. When he could have kept my sister at his house, he didn't. He called and did the honorable thing."

"Are you insulting your own flesh and blood?" Haze asked.

Jenna wanted to know the same damn thing. Her brother made it sound as if she would have pranced right into Seth's bed, seducing him until he put out, if Seth hadn't called Jeremy. She hadn't wanted her brother called, but not because she wanted to remain alone with Seth. Jenna wanted to go home on her own, not be picked up as if she were a cub.

"Not at all. Seth made it clear he held her against her will."

"And you let him live?" Bruno snarled.

Jenna rolled her eyes as she leaned against the counter sipping her coffee.

"He held on to her because he believed she needed protection. Tray Long was in the Golden Grill last night and he attacked Jenna. Seth came to her rescue. Seth is one of the best humans I've ever met. And until I know Long is in a cage, my sister will have twenty-four-hour protection—from Seth and from you two."

"I'll help protect her," Bruno barked.

Jenna groaned. The last thing she wanted was that oversized mutt panting around her like he had a right to do so. Jeremy had enough sense not to let that happen though. Bruno's lust toward Jenna was easy enough to sniff out.

She ignored the males when the subject changed and they started talking about someone's property. Pack business usually interested her, but today she was glad to let the males discuss matters and take the conversation off her. After finishing her coffee, she tested waters by stepping out back. If Jeremy had half an ear on the conversation at hand and the other half on her, he'd be outside in a minute, more than likely with the other males sniffing after her. She reclined in the wooden bench alongside their grill, her stomach growling when she got a whiff of the meat that was last cooked on it.

Jenna stared at the mid-day blue sky, glancing at the back door more than once. When a few minutes went by and no one came to check on her, she stood, stretched, and sprinted toward the woods.

She wanted to see Seth again—and help him take
down Tray. It was flattering that this human male
wanted to protect her. Jeremy's reason's for insisting
Seth hunt Tray Long were admirable. Seth didn't
know Tray was a werewolf though. Jenna had no intention of telling him. Seth was human. He would
track Tray Long a lot easier with her help. Her plan
was perfect. A rogue, human-killing werewolf would
be killed. She'd get more time with Seth. Jeremy
would protect their pack without possible bad politics.
Everyone would be happy.

She reached the other side of the trees and headed
into town. Omaha was a decent-sized city, but on the
outskirts it seemed more small-town. Jenna headed
down one of the main streets, narrowing her way in
closer to Seth's home. If he worked, he wouldn't be
there right now. She imagined lying in wait, sniffing
out his den until he returned, then surprising him.
Maybe she would sneak up behind him, take him off
guard, and tackle him to the ground. Jenna didn't
have a clue whether human males liked their females
to be aggressive or not, but imagining wrestling with
him, feeling all of that hard-packed muscle press
against her, made her stumble over a crack in the sidewalk.

"Shit," she hissed under her breath, regaining her
wits about her but overly aware of how swollen her
breasts felt. Her hard nipples rubbed against her bra,
as if suddenly the constraint was too confining. Her
pussy swelled, eager and anxious to try out this human and see if he was as good at fucking as he was
at foreplay.

Her skin prickled, the tiny hairs on her body standing at attention. Jenna imagined Seth somewhere

near, watching her, stalking her while she plotted doing the same to him. There was something about him having the upper hand with her, proving to her he was male enough to take her on, that excited her even further.

There was no bigger turn-off than a spineless male. Werewolves were fighters. They were carnivorous, aggressive, and dominating, regardless of gender. Jenna wouldn't take crap off anyone, not even her littermate, and she respected the hell out of him, loved him more than she loved any other living creature. She honored Jeremy, but spoke her mind when he was wrong. Most of the time he listened, and on a rare occasion even admitted to being wrong. He would be less inclined to listen about Seth. But once she told him, Jeremy wouldn't be able to howl that her plan wasn't solid.

Jenna slowed at the intersection, watched the cars, then hurried across the street. A breeze, warm from the sun, caught her hair and blew it off her shoulder. As she grabbed it at her nape, she walked across a convenience store parking lot. The back of her neck prickled and it wasn't from perspiration. Just as she reached the next sidewalk, the sound of brakes squeaking grabbed her attention.

Jenna turned, knowing it wasn't a motorcycle but still feeling a wave of disappointment when she didn't know the car that pulled up alongside her. It came up next to her on the passenger side and she jumped out of the way when the passenger door opened.

"Get in, little bitch." The familiar snarl made her blood curdle, causing her heart to stop beating in her chest and create a pain that swelled quickly when she couldn't catch her breath.

Jenna stared into the cold, menacing eyes of Tray Long. "What do you want?" she growled, glancing past his car only for a moment as she searched the area. All she saw were humans, but none of them the one she wanted.

"The same thing you do, I'm sure." Tray was a big werewolf in a small car. He leaned over, pushing the door open farther so that it almost hit her. "Get in and we'll talk about it."

"You don't have shit I want," she snarled, stepping around the open door and heading to the sidewalk, at the edge of the parking lot.

She heard the door slam shut but then jumped when a cold, clammy hand wrapped around the back of her neck.

"You give it to that human male, you sure the fuck can give it to me." He squeezed the back of her neck so hard she couldn't catch her breath. As he dragged her backward, his own breath almost turned to wheezing, as if the thought of having her damn near sent him into some kind of asthmatic attack.

"Get your paws off me." Her words were a hoarse whisper, but the rest of her wasn't incapacitated. Kicking backward, she found incredible satisfaction when her heel hit bone and the cracking sound was enough to make her eyes water.

His grip loosened as he snarled behind her, sounding more like an animal than a man, although she knew he wasn't trying to change. Tray might be insane, but he wasn't so far gone he would rip his clothes off his body in broad daylight and drop to all fours. At least she hoped he wasn't. Either way, she didn't want to find out.

The second his grip loosened, Jenna took off

running. Ignoring the stream of curses Tray let out behind her, she darted around the convenience store. She needed to head in a direction where he couldn't follow her in his car.

Jenna cursed under her breath. What the hell was this male's deal? She needed to ask Jeremy if he'd done something to Tray that made the male want to get even with him. Why else would Tray be sniffing her out? Unless it was pure coincidence that he ran into her, which she doubted. The insane rogue had sought her out for a reason other than he simply found her irresistible.

At the other end of the parking lot, she hesitated, shoving her hair over her shoulder as she checked behind her. Then sniffing the air, she didn't hear or see anyone approaching. It would still be a good idea to cut through a few yards, put distance between her and that asshole before he figured out where she ran. A rumbling motor grabbed her attention and she darted toward the street. It was a motorcycle, but it wasn't Seth.

"God, you're an idiot," she cursed herself. What was she going to start doing now, chasing motorcycles?

Jenna didn't make a habit of running through neighborhoods. It was rude and an invasion of privacy trotting across people's property, even if they were humans. She chewed her lower lip, staring at the yards to her right, then glanced again over her shoulder, searching for that small car, a two-door that was a rusty brown color, and swore every vehicle that moved matched that description.

Getting too jumpy would make her senses unreliable. Breathing in a mixture of car exhaust and the rich, greasy smell of chain fast-food restaurants from across the street, she focused on the yards to her right. Jenna needed to remember her reason for seeing Seth. The more facts she gathered on Tray Long, the better job she'd do helping Seth take down the jerk.

"Please be at work and remember that there is a leash law." There wasn't anything worse than a stray dog getting confused by her scent.

Jenna bolted between two houses, using the combined driveway they shared as her path. She headed down the street on the next block, then cut again through yards, very aware that she moved closer to Seth Gere's neighborhood. When she'd made it two blocks from where Tray Long had tried grabbing her, she paused again, breathing in the air and smelling nothing but roses and honeysuckle and the stale lingering smell of humans.

Odd she'd never considered Seth's aroma stale. Maybe he'd managed a way to release his emotions. Most humans didn't possess the ability. They were unable to change like she could, which gave her the opportunity to shift into a more primal state, a condition where only the rawest of instinct prevailed. It was a cleansing state, and one she ached to change into now. The gift werewolves possessed allowed them to release the many feelings and emotions humans carried around with them for life. Hence, the stale smell.

Jenna walked the next four blocks, relaxing as she did, until reaching the intersection and staring down the row of houses where Seth lived. Her attention immediately shot to the motorcycle in his driveway. Seth was home.

"Crap," she whispered, sucking in another breath and creating a game plan. Her idea of lying in wait until he returned to his house wouldn't work. "You could always knock on his front door, inform him we've got unfinished business."

In spite of the insanity of the suggestion, not to mention standing on a street corner in a quiet neighborhood talking to herself, Jenna's insides swelled, an eagerness to explore uncharted territory damn near making her come. There was only one way to handle this matter. Putting one foot in front of the other, she headed to his house. No one ever accused her of smelling shy.

Maybe once or twice her curiosity in the past got her in trouble. But something told her the only trouble Seth might bring her would be emotional. He was human, though. That saved her the worry of losing her heart to him. Seth was a curiosity, an unknown. And he didn't appear the type of male who would fall in love with a female anyway. He was older than she was, and unmated. There wasn't the smell of another female on him, or in his home. So there wasn't anything to worry about.

A car came around the corner when Jenna was a couple houses down from Seth's. Her heart exploded in her chest. She rubbed her palms against her jeans, irritated with how jumpy she was.

"Relax," she hissed under her breath when the car passed her and kept going.

Something deeper gnawed at her. It didn't matter what species he was. Seth turned her on, and she appealed to him, too. She wanted to explore that, and reminding herself who he was didn't make her any less anxious to see him.

She stared at the driver as the car passed her, certain she looked out of place and that was why the guy in his business suit, possibly heading back to work after coming home to eat the same food he ate every day for lunch, stared back at her. Suddenly she couldn't wait to be inside Seth's home. Hurrying across his yard, she came to a halt at his front door and knocked.

Jenna heard him approach from the other side of the door, took deep, long breaths as his scent grew stronger. But then almost choked on the air in her lungs when Seth opened the door and stared at her, with no shirt on, barefoot, and wearing faded jeans that were unbuttoned at the waist.

"Crap. Jenna, what's wrong?" Seth looked past her toward the street and opened the door farther. "Come in. You look like you've been running for miles. Are you okay?"

Her mouth went so dry she couldn't answer him. He thought she ran here because she was in trouble. Seth believed she ran to him for protection. Suddenly her heart hurt. He viewed her as some kind of fucking damsel in distress, unable to take care of herself and racing to him so he would save her.

"Do you want some coffee? Sit down. Tell me what happened." Seth closed the door behind her and already headed to his kitchen. "Do you not carry a cell phone? I guess I can give you my number," he called out from the other room.

She didn't sit but followed him, cautiously, unwilling to let the view of his backside disappear from her sight. It was probably a damn good thing he was human; otherwise he'd trip over himself from the incredibly strong smell of her lust.

Again she battled with how to answer him. Already he thought she ran here *for* help instead of *to* help. If she mentioned Tray Long, Seth wouldn't see how she could help. Jenna needed to show him how strong of a female she was first, then Seth would be a lot more receptive to them running together.

When her parents were still alive, Jenna remembered her mother swearing that in the end, the best way through a situation was honesty. Her mother had been an honorable female, killed in a challenge for another male a year after her sire died in a fire. She'd been fifteen at the time and left with her brother, who'd immediately found work at the age of eighteen, and kept their small den together. Jenna never cowered from any situation, knowing her mother had been the same. She wouldn't take the easy way out now.

"There's no trouble," she announced, standing in the doorway and watching Seth go through the motions of making coffee. He smelled good, better than she remembered him smelling. And with his tousled hair, she guessed she'd awakened him when she'd knocked. "I came by to see you."

CHAPTER SIX

Seth's insides went from being racked with nerves to something stronger, darker, and more dangerous lunging forward. He almost spilled the water he was pouring into the coffeemaker when Jenna spoke. Her soft, alluring tone, telling him she simply showed up at his door to see him, stirred emotions inside him that would be better off left alone.

"Don't worry me like that," he snapped, more irritated with himself for reacting to her words than he was with her.

"Not all females are incapable of taking care of themselves." She leaned against his doorway, her head slightly tilted and that long, dark hair of hers streaming down her back.

"I'm sure you're very capable of taking care of yourself. But already you're showing me signs that you'll step into a situation that could possibly be more dangerous than you're aware."

The way her blue eyes suddenly glowed like sapphires told him she didn't miss his meaning. "There are certain types of danger that are more exciting than others."

"Very true." He liked her natural look, that she

didn't wear makeup. Her cheeks glowed with energy and life. Her thick, long hair wasn't unkempt, but at the same time the slightly tousled look made his fingers itch to mess it up more. "You must not have much excitement in your life."

Her gaze darkened, and he wondered at the emotions he'd triggered with his comment. Seth didn't get the reputation he had of being a damn good bounty hunter by not knowing how to read people. He was very good at it. And Jenna was a wound-tight ball of emotions, each one parading across her pretty face as she experienced it.

"My life is fine. That doesn't mean I won't seek something out if it appeals to me." She shifted her gaze from his to her surroundings. "And it's worth exploring when it's mutual," she added. Her gaze shot back to his just as he was taking in the narrow cut of her blue jeans.

"Are you always this open with men?" he asked, intrigued with her fresh attitude about him, about them. It sure as hell beat playing the games so many women wanted him to play just to get laid.

"Not many males appeal to me." She used an odd choice of words; he'd noticed that about her the other night. "I'm very good at telling if someone is good or bad. The truly bad don't deserve to love."

It wouldn't surprise him a bit if Jeremy insisted Jenna stayed home most of the time, which led Seth to believe possibly her brother didn't know where she was right now. In fact, Seth would bet good money on it.

Her cell phone rang, and she jumped, her expression turning frustrated. Seth turned to focus on the coffee and to hide the smile that threatened his lips.

Jenna wasn't as confident and cocky as she wanted him to believe. He liked her open nature but guessed she experimented with it. That appealed to him even more. She didn't treat all men like this, which meant she wasn't a slut. At the same time she was probably bored and craved excitement, which meant he needed to be very careful.

"What?" she said when she answered her phone, lowering her voice.

Seth glanced over his shoulder, having pulled down two mugs.

Jenna dragged her hand through her hair, pulling it from her face as she stared at the floor. "I can go wherever I want and do what I want," she whispered, her voice taking a deadly tone he hadn't heard out of her yet. "And you know damn good and well I can take care of myself."

Seth fought not to show any emotion when he clearly heard her brother yell into the phone. Every muscle in Seth's body tightened, but if he reacted, the conversation would end. As much as it was a private family matter, he'd been pulled into this, and it was always to his advantage to know as much as possible about those who interacted around him.

"These aren't normal conditions," Jeremy yelled through the phone. "That insane rogue wants your cute ass, little sister, and he can't have it."

"Glad to know we still agree on something," she growled, looking cute as hell when she wrinkled her nose. "Now maybe one of these days you'll smell the truth and realize I'm grown and no one attacks me I don't want to attack."

"Get your ass back here!" he roared.

"Soon." Jenna softened her tone, exhaling and

then speaking, sounding breathy. "Jeremy, don't worry. I'm safe."

"You went to see him again, didn't you? I told you to stay away and you're there right now."

Seth met her gaze, staring into her volatile expression. There was a side to Jenna he was just now seeing. One being she had a temper. Beyond being wild, willful, and damn near the sexiest woman he'd laid eyes on ever, it was more than her craving for an adventure that made her appear a bit on the wild side. Looking at her, hearing her brother yell through the phone, Seth saw deep into those bright blue eyes and saw a woman fighting so hard to be free from her brother's overbearing protectiveness that she was blinding herself to the real danger closing in on her.

"I'm right where I want to be," she whispered, never taking her gaze from Seth's as she pulled the phone from her ear.

"Leave the human alone," Jeremy yelled. Jenna hung up the phone.

Seth raised one eyebrow. "Human?" he questioned.

"He's pissed," she said, shrugging.

"Huh." Seth turned to the coffee, hating that he wanted her here. She was sexy, vibrant, and, whether she liked it or not, needed someone watching over her. Jeremy saw that and so did Seth. What worried Seth was losing a damn good contact, and friend, if he started seeing Jenna.

"You let me in when I knocked on your door," she said behind his back. Jenna moved closer. His backside tightened, every muscle and tendon, every bone in his body acutely aware of how close she stood to him. "You didn't turn me away," she continued, whispering. "You didn't need to hear to know my brother wouldn't want me here. You saw it in his eyes last night. But you let me in. Don't turn righteous on me now. Don't pretend you let me in to protect me. I tracked you when you chased Tray Long."

Seth spun around and she straightened, strands of hair brushing against her cheek and streaming past her shoulders. The shirt she wore hugged large breasts, breasts he remembered pressed against his body when he'd kissed her the night before.

"Do you always say what you're thinking?" he asked.

"Do you ever see something you want and take it?"

"Most definitely," he growled, and lunged without thinking about it.

Jenna drew aggression out of him. She provoked him and he didn't know the real reason why. Seth grabbed her, lifting her off the ground, then placed her on his counter. She didn't fight him but opened her legs, wrapping her thighs around him when he moved in within inches of her face.

Every bit of her appealed to him. He dragged his fingers through her hair, nipping at her lower lip. Jenna opened for him, letting out a slight cry. An unbearable urge to possess her, to take everything she offered and make it his—his to protect and possess. It was such an overwhelming sensation it damn near made him light-headed. An aggressiveness rolled through him, plummeting deep inside him. Seth didn't want to hold back and something inside roared that Jenna wanted everything he needed to give her.

Seth impaled her mouth, letting her sweet moistness mingle with his as her tongue swirled around his tongue. She pulled back when he ached to go deeper, teasing, torturing him. He tore his mouth from hers, dragging his lips down her neck while pulling her hair, drawing her head back.

"Don't stop," she whispered, arching her neck.

Seth felt the vein under her flesh pulse against his lips. She urged him forward, wanted what he needed her to have. "I don't plan on it," he hissed, pulling his fingers from her hair. He dragged her shirt up over her breasts. Her lace bra barely contained beautiful full, round breasts. He exposed them, watching as they bounced with freedom.

Her nipples were puckered, hard, and large. When he took one between his finger and thumb, Jenna jumped, her thighs tightening against his.

"Sensitive," he growled, flashing his attention to her face for a moment.

It damn near took his breath away when he saw silver laced across her pretty blue eyes. Her dark hair was tousled, giving her a wild look. But it was how she panted, her lips parted and her tongue darting out to moisten her lips, that got him harder than steel.

"I liked it," she told him, her voice rough with the emotions he saw in her eyes.

"I can tell." He rolled her nipple between his fingers. Then, he cupped her large breast, loving the weight of so much soft flesh in his hand.

He leaned in to kiss her again. Jenna nipped at his lip, her teeth snagging his lower lip and puncturing his flesh. The metallic taste filling his mouth fueled the already-raging fever roaring inside him. Jenna growled, her thick lashes fluttering over bright blue eyes that glowed with silver streaks. She grabbed both sides of his head and pulled him in for another

kiss, aggressive, passionate, and filled with so much
heat it scalded every inch of him.

He got the strange sensation that they had just
branded each other, the slightest taste of blood in his
mouth bringing them together as her tongue danced
with his. Seth pushed the thought out of his mind,
which wasn't hard to do, since thinking wasn't what
he wanted to do at the moment anyway. Any conscious thought would inevitably lead him to the repercussions of fucking Jenna.

Seth didn't make wrong moves. His line of work
wouldn't allow it. He didn't deny Jenna had been on
his mind since her brother took her away the night
before. Seth had given thought to finding her, learning where she lived. It wouldn't be hard to do. He
found people every day.

Again, refusing to dwell too hard on anything
other than Jenna wrapped around him, the taste of
her, the smooth, silky feel to her hair, and her hot
body pressed against his, Seth took the moment. Let
the repercussions fall where they would. He wouldn't
deny his actions any more than he would deny such
a hot, sexy woman wanting him and not giving her
what she wanted.

Seth had her jeans unbuttoned and unzipped before he knew what his hands were doing. He was un-
dressing her, stripping her, and craving more flesh.
Jenna was muscular, agile, but small-boned. It took
no effort to lift her, drag her jeans down her thighs,
and place her bare ass back on his counter. He heard
the thump of her shoes when she kicked them off her
feet and they landed on the floor. Then her hands
were all over him, exploring his arms, shoulders,

chest, then dragging her fingernails down his stomach to his jeans.

"Take these off before I rip them," she growled and undid the button on his jeans.

As a rule, Seth didn't get along with dominating women. They were headaches and more times than not got themselves into trouble that he didn't want to take time to deal with. But when Jenna moved her lips against his, her lashes fluttering over those sensual eyes of hers, he had no problem doing as she said.

"I want you naked, too," he instructed, lifting her off the counter as he stepped backward. "Everything. Off. Now."

Her closed-lipped smirk and the way her eyes glowed with that odd shade of silver streaking over the blue showed she didn't mind his inability to form complete sentences at the moment. Seth wasn't sure how he managed to strip down when he was sure he was drooling over the incredible view being offered him.

Jenna was by far the most beautiful woman he'd ever laid eyes on. He wanted to know her age, because although her expressions revealed a woman with experience and intelligence, her body was firm, perfect, and full of youth. He loved how those full breasts of hers bounced, so round, large, and firm. Her nipples were perfectly proportioned for her size, hard, puckered, and mouthwateringly delicious. But when she bent over, pushing her jeans off her ankles, all that dark, long hair tumbled over her shoulder. It was a shroud, stealing his view, but he didn't mind. Her narrow back, the slender curve of her waist, and her firm, round ass were just as enticing as her breasts.

"Come here," he said when she straightened, reaching for her hand when she brushed her hair over her shoulder.

For the first time since arriving, Jenna shot him a furtive glance, appearing almost shy. The silver streaks in her eyes were gone, but the sensual deep blue shade of them was equally as compelling.

"Sit here," she said, her voice a rough whisper. "Please." She pulled out his kitchen chair and turned its back to the table. "I want to ride you."

"There are condoms in my room," he said, taking her by the shoulder.

"No condoms. Sit." She pushed his chest, backing him into the chair.

Seth didn't have a problem with the position. "Sweetheart, don't tell me you have unprotected sex," he growled.

"I don't have sex," she told him, her tone louder and more aggressive. "But I am on the pill, and I want to feel you inside me. Or do you go to other women's homes to fuck them?" Suddenly she quit pushing, her face scrunching into a scowl as if the thought of him being with someone else left a foul taste in her mouth. "No other woman besides me has been here."

"I haven't had sex in over a year and it's always been protected. But Jenna, are you telling me you're a virgin?" For some reason it hadn't crossed his mind that she might be. "How old are you?"

"I'm twenty-three, not a virgin, and not a slut." Her expression softened as she dragged her fingers over his bare chest and looked up at him with her hooded stare. "And I wouldn't be here if I thought some female was trying to make this her place. This isn't a one-time thing," she whispered. "Right?"

Seth sat in the chair, convinced she was the most
unusual lady he'd ever met. Yet she stimulated him,
physically and mentally. He pulled her on to his lap.
She stretched over his legs and incredible heat from
her body scalded his cock until he worried he
wouldn't last long enough to satisfy her. Uncertainty
returned in her eyes. She didn't want casual sex from
him. At that moment he understood, Jenna wanted
him. His gut constricted, a faraway voice buried under clouds and a thick fog of lust screaming at him to
run, get the hell away from her. Jenna would be trouble. Such a hot young temptress, so bold in her emotions, so open with what she wanted, had just informed
him she wanted him, all of him.

Jenna dug her nails into his shoulders, more than
likely once again marking him. Her nails were
sharp, the sting noticeable but forgotten in a moment when she sank down on his cock. She took all
of him, arching her back and tilting her head as her
lips parted.

Seth grabbed her waist, holding her in place, and
thrust, feeling her soaked, tight velvety skin shiver
and quake around his shaft, keeping him buried inside her, and suffocating him with smoldering heat
so sweet, so intoxicating, it was as if he experienced
fucking a woman for the first time. Jenna shouldn't be
this appealing. She was hot, sexy, incredible, but there
were many women out there who were pretty and
who'd made offers in the past. None terrified him as
much as what Jenna implied, and none of them made
him crave taking all she offered and ensuring she
wouldn't go anywhere.

Seth held on to her waist firmly, moving his hips
so that he slid out of her heat. When he impaled her

again, Jenna howled, lowering her face and staring at him, appearing amazed. Her mouth formed a perfect circle and her bright eyes once again were laced with silver. He'd never seen a shade of eye color like hers but liked it. He continued taking her, holding her in place and fucking her while sitting under her. Her hair fell over her shoulders, down her back, with thick strands falling around her breasts. And the way they jiggled, bouncing harder the more energy he put into fucking her.

"Seth! God damn," she hissed, her attention fixed on his and not once blinking as she pulled him into her world of sensuality. "Please, I want—"

Her words were lost when every inch of her tightened. He'd taken her to the edge. Her cheeks flushed. She was so close to exploding for him. Seth continued fucking her, keeping the momentum where it was, not adjusting a thing until she whimpered, falling forward against him and her hands sliding over his shoulders.

All those hot muscles in her pussy clenched around his cock, threatening to drain everything out of him, as her orgasm tore through her. He let her ride it out, loving the satiny feel of soaked heat caressing his cock. And although he was damn close to coming himself, he bit down, determined to enjoy this as long as he could.

"Let me," she tried again, panting when she managed to lift her head. "Let me fuck you," she whispered, brushing her lips across his cheek. "Don't move, please."

Her aggressive nature was gone, all cockiness replaced with a sincere desire to give them both pleasure.

"All right," he grumbled, his voice so rough the two words were all he could muster.

Yet it was enough. He felt her smile against his face before she lifted her head and let him see how happy his agreeing to give her free rein made her. More than likely there weren't a lot of times when Jenna felt truly in control. Obviously she had an older brother who cared a lot about her, and with her good looks and spirited nature Seth wouldn't be surprised at the number of men who would try putting a leash on her. For some reason, that thought damn near brought a growl to his throat. He didn't like thinking about any man being around Jenna.

It didn't take long for her to build up momentum until she held on to his arms and rode him hard. Her breasts bounced up and down in front of his face and his cock swelled until he couldn't control it any longer.

"I'm coming," he said tightly, forcing the words out. "Do you want me to pull out?"

"Hell no!" She sank down on him, filling herself with his cock, and allowed him to explode deep inside her heat.

It was the best feeling he'd ever known in his life.

CHAPTER SEVEN

Seth sat across the table at the restaurant where he'd taken Jenna, feeling as if they were doing things backward. He was enjoying her company, though, and loved the sound of her laughter as she finished sharing a story about her childhood. He was giving up an afternoon of work getting to know her, and damn if he cared.

"What is Jeremy going to say when I take you home?" he asked, hating it when her smile faded.

"It would be best if you didn't take me home." She glanced at her plate and the crumbs from her hamburger and began dragging a fry through her ketchup.

"I'm taking you home," he insisted. "And probably soon. There are some things I need to do."

"What?" she asked.

"Work." He leaned back on his side of the booth, stretching his legs. Her eyes flashed an even brighter blue when she rubbed her feet against his. "There are some matters to take care of."

"I'm going to help you." Her expression sobered as her voice turned serious. "I'm not some puppy incapable of taking care of myself. And there are things I know, things that will help you find Tray Long."

"I work alone, Jenna." He wasn't daunted when she narrowed her eyes on him. "Being a bounty hunter isn't just about hunting people," he added. "You research your target, learn what makes them tick. Not to mention somehow I don't think you'd enjoy the amount of waiting and patience required in my line of work."

Jenna made a face at him but then leaned forward, resting her elbows on the table, which caused those wonderful breasts of hers to press together. He dropped his attention to the amount of cleavage she showed off to him.

"You don't know me that well," she informed him, dropping her tone to a sultry whisper. "If you take the time, you'll learn I'm very patient. In my world, hunting is more than chasing and attacking. Sometimes the plotting can be excruciatingly painful in the amount of patience required. Does that sound anything like your world?" She batted her dark lashes, and if she toyed with him, she did a damn good job.

"You say 'your world' as if you live so differently from me."

Jenna opened her mouth, ready to say something, when the waitress appeared at their table. Seth accepted the bill and waved her on when she asked if they wanted anything else. Then sliding out of the booth on his side, he reached for Jenna's hand, helping her stand and feeling her small, soft fingers wrap around his.

"Like I said," she continued, after he'd paid the bill and they left the restaurant. Jenna continued holding his hand as they started across the parking lot to his motorcycle. "There is a lot you don't know about me. I'd like to change that, if you're willing."

He loved her openness, the way she spoke her mind without holding back. A car entered the parking lot and Jenna froze, her grip on his hand tightening so quickly and with enough strength he felt his bones press together.

"What?" he began, searching her face.

Jenna curled her lip and he swore she growled as she narrowed her gaze on the car that had pulled into the parking lot. Seth turned his attention to the brown mid-nineties Honda Accord. There was a fair amount of rust on the thing, and although the windows weren't tinted, the glare of the sun made it impossible to see who drove until the driver turned and started toward them.

"Tray Long," Seth growled, every muscle in his body tightening.

Seth pushed Jenna toward his bike, managing to free his hand and put it on her shoulder, aware of how protective his actions appeared. Tray glared at him, his mouth forming into a cruel sneer as he drove by.

"TR five, six sixty," Seth said out loud. "Remember that."

"What?" Jenna brushed her hair from her face, sucking in a breath. The color in her face returned and she grumbled something he didn't hear, possibly repeating the numbers and letters. "Of course, the tag number."

"How did you know that was Tray?" Seth asked, watching the Honda pull out of the parking lot and turn east into the traffic.

"I saw him." She unstrapped the helmet from Seth's bike, then twisted her hair behind her head. "Let's follow him."

"No." Seth grabbed her wrist.

Jenna looked up at him, holding the helmet as her hair unraveled from where she had twisted it at her nape. "Okay," she said, her features relaxed. Suddenly she was being a bit too agreeable.

"How did you know what kind of car he drove?"

She searched Seth's face. "I saw him enter the parking lot."

"When we left the restaurant, you suggested we get to know each other better. That relationship isn't going to start with you lying to me."

Jenna tried yanking her arm free. "Why do you think I'm lying?"

Seth tightened his grip, yanking her toward him and off balance. She slapped her hand, which still held his helmet, against his chest. The helmet fell to the ground.

"There was a glare on the windows from the sun when he entered the parking lot. So either you have incredible, superhuman eyesight or you've seen that car before and knew what Tray drove. Which one is it, Jenna?"

She tried looking down at the helmet on the ground. Seth gripped her chin, forcing her to remain focused on him. "So you know," he growled, "I'm going to take you up on your offer. I'm going to know you better, a lot better. And since we've established the beginning of a relationship, we're going to promise each other right now that relationship will be an honest one. Do I have your promise, Jenna?"

She closed her eyes, but he didn't see humiliation. Instead, when she flashed those baby blues at him, Seth swore something akin to worry appeared in her face.

"I saw him earlier today."

"What?"

"Tray Long. He tried to take me before I came to your house."

"Why didn't you tell me this before?" Seth demanded, reaching down and scooping up the helmet.

"Because you would have gotten pissed."

"You're damn fucking straight!" Seth roared, slamming his helmet against the seat of his bike. "Tray Long is insane. He killed two women, and went to prison for it. He's been released, is ignoring his parole officer, and now we've got two more murders that fit his profile."

"You didn't hear what I just said. That waste of flesh tried abducting me and failed. He didn't give up. He failed."

She wanted Seth to acknowledge her abilities to take care of herself. Unfortunately, he'd never felt a stronger urge to protect another person in his life. It didn't make any sense. He'd known her two days. They'd had mind-blowing sex and then she lied to him. Granted, her reason for the lie might be justified in her eyes because she didn't want to hear him yell. And that was what he did.

Seth cupped her cheek, watching her stare at him. "When Tray was sent to prison, he openly confessed in front of a jury how he killed those two women. They fought him. The first woman continued attacking even after he broke her arm. There was his flesh

under her fingernails. His blood was found on both
bodies."

"They weren't where . . ."

"They weren't where?"

Jenna exhaled, dragging her finger over the curve
of the helmet. "Go ahead and gave me a ride home."

*   *   *

Seth walked out of the police station glancing at the
sunset and crossing the street to his bike. After running the numbers through the system, he'd learned
the brown Honda Accord was registered to Elizabeth Helo. Heading into the station and running the
tag through the system obviously alerted the cops to
what he'd learned. He wanted to go talk to Ms. Helo
but didn't doubt a car had already been dispatched
to her house. He wasn't in the mood for a party.

Starting up his bike, he pulled away from the
curve, realizing once he headed out he was going to
Jenna's. Within minutes it would be dark, but a very
minor disadvantage to riding a Harley was that it was
difficult sneaking up on anyone. Seth scowled. He
wasn't a coward.

And you're a professional. Which meant present-
ing the facts and putting them in order.

Jeremy Drury was a good man. He had eyes and
ears better than most cops on the force and had
helped Seth out more times than he could count.
Tray Long was after Jenna. Seth could come up with
at least several tangible reasons why Long chose
Jenna, but the reason he'd have to put at the top of
the list was that she was quite obviously the hottest
woman in Omaha, if not the entire fucking state.

Jeremy would love hearing that.

Seth pulled up in front of Jenna's rural home, buried on the outskirts of the forest, and pulled into the long gravel driveway. There were several cars parked there already. He had never seen Jeremy in a car. Jeremy always called where they would meet for information exchange and he was always on foot. A quick glance at the tags on the cars parked in the drive showed they weren't all owned by the same person. Seth's boots crunched over the gravel as he walked up the drive, then along the narrow cement walk to the door.

The house was old, somewhat kept up, the front yard recently mowed, although at the edge of the yard the dense foliage at the base of the tree line made for a natural wall against the rest of the world. Seth knocked firmly on the door, then glanced the other direction, past the driveway at another old farmhouse down the road and across the street. The road curved after that, making it impossible to see any other neighbors. He turned, facing the door, and knocked again.

With all the cars in the driveway, it would appear the house was full of people, yet no one answered. He considered walking around to the back side of the house when the lock on the door clicked and opened. Jeremy stared at Seth, his expression serious if not a bit put out. He stared at Seth for a moment, not saying a word.

"May I come in?" Seth asked, focusing on Jeremy's steel-blue eyes and noticing shreds of silver laced across the blue that he'd never seen before. Obviously the unique eye color was a family trait.

Jeremy continued staring at him, his expression unreadable. Seth never doubted the man would be as grave of an enemy as he was an ally. He held his ground, though, not backing down but waiting for the answer.

"Why are you here?" Jeremy asked, not letting him in.

Someone said something behind Jeremy. It was another man and Seth swore he heard him say, "He doesn't belong here." When Jenna retorted, coming up behind Jeremy and grabbing his arm to move him out of the way, Seth understood. Jeremy knew damn good and well why Seth was there, but he would give the guy something to hold on to, since apparently Jeremy wasn't the only one feeling a need to protect Jenna.

"We can discuss her if you want," Seth said, keeping his attention on Jeremy when Jenna pushed next to her brother. "But I'm here on business."

Jeremy took his sister by the arm and held her next to him when he stepped back and opened the door for Seth.

"Why are you letting him inside?" a stocky, dark-haired man Seth didn't recognize demanded. He had been sitting on the couch and rose when Seth entered the home.

"Welcome to our home," Jeremy said gravely, the meaning in his words heavy. He kept a watchful eye on Seth as he closed the door, then whispered something to Jenna.

"No," she snapped, not whispering in turn. "I've kept nothing from you and you aren't keeping anything from me."

"Do as you're told," Jeremy growled.

Other than the stocky guy on the couch, another thick, tall man who looked vaguely familiar leaned against the wall, his arms crossed as he studied Seth with almost a curious look on his face. Seth was definitely under scrutiny, as if they weren't sure he belonged here. It was an interesting sensation. He definitely had entered many homes where he wasn't welcome. It came with the job. But this was a different sensation. There weren't criminals in this home. That much Seth would swear to. But nonetheless, even Jeremy seemed on edge. If they were all that protective over Jenna, it was a bit extreme.

As the silence weighed heavy in the room, Seth met Jenna's pained expression. Giving her a slight nod, he cleared his throat. "I'll come find you before I leave," he told her, breaking the silence.

All three other men moved, shifting their weight, not appreciating Seth breaking the tension.

"You better." Jenna pushed away from Jeremy and walked up to Seth, touching him.

Jeremy growled, sounding almost like a wild animal, protective of what was his and willing to attack to protect it. The only difference here was obviously Jenna didn't want his protection. At the same time, Seth fought not to grumble in return. Her hand brushed down his arm, her deep blue eyes imploring him to understand and work through the possessiveness embedded in her brother.

Seth hesitated only for a moment, then touched her cheek. "Let me talk to your brother," Seth told her. He wouldn't insult Jeremy by not allowing him to see what he felt for Jenna. The emotions were new, raw, but there. Jeremy needed time to accept them, and seeing the affection, even if it were the slightest of touches, would help the man come to terms with the fact that Seth didn't intend to leave Jenna alone.

"Why did you come here?" Jeremy asked after Jenna left the room and a door closed, suggesting she'd gone to her bedroom.

"Two reasons," Seth told him, remaining standing inside the front door.

Jeremy didn't suggest they sit. He stood in the middle of the living room, facing Seth, while the two other men watched him warily.

"And they are?"

"I ran a tag number on Tray Long before coming over here. Do you know an Elizabeth Helo?"

Jeremy's blank stare showed he didn't. He looked at the other two men, who both shook their heads. "Apparently we don't. She owns the car Long is running around in?"

"Yup. It's a brown Honda Accord, a '96." Seth relaxed some, accustomed to talking shop with Jeremy. Although he didn't know the other two men, if Jeremy was content having them in the room, Seth didn't mind. Not to mention, Long was stalking Jenna and they had a right to know all Seth could offer them to be able to recognize the asshole in case he came around. "It's a two-door with some rust on it. When Jenna and I were at lunch today—," he continued but was immediately interrupted by Jeremy stepping forward.

For a moment he looked as if he'd lunge at Seth for announcing he took Jenna to eat. He'd seen some protective families before, but this was too much. Every muscle in Jeremy's body bulged, his rage so visible the guy almost shook from it. Seth frowned at him and knew this needed to be discussed. He would broach the situation as soon as he finished telling Jeremy what the guy needed to know about Long.

"And left the restaurant," Seth continued, keeping his focus on Jeremy in spite of the guy's intense irritation over him mentioning Jenna, "Tray Long entered the parking lot. I then learned he'd tried abducting Jenna before she came to me today."

Jeremy roared, unable to hold his rage in any longer. Instead of pouncing on Seth, Jeremy turned and slammed his fist against his wall, creating a dent in the wall and causing a wall hanging to crash to the floor. Ignoring it, he spun around, his blue eyes so silver it was fucking eerie.

Jenna raced into the room, her look wild as she came to a stop, her eyes wide as she stared at her brother. "What did you say to him?" she asked Seth, whispering.

Seth didn't answer her. He kept his attention on Jeremy. "I plan on going to Elizabeth's when I leave here but want you to know what I've learned about Tray, as well as discuss your sister's insistence that she can walk around town by herself."

"Why didn't you tell me Tray Long tried attacking you?" Jeremy turned his fury on his sister.

She shot Seth a condemning glare. "Thanks a lot."

Jeremy didn't strike Seth as the kind of man who would hurt a woman, but he moved to Jenna without thinking about it. Pulling her to him, he kept his attention on Jeremy, who looked more than put out that Seth would openly show affection toward Jenna in front of him. Jenna relaxed against Seth, though, wrapping her arms around his waist, her hair and the rest of her smelling so damn good it was hard not to physically react to her even though her brother looked ready to attack.

"Jenna is convinced she can take care of herself," Seth continued, tightening his grip on her when she tried creating distance and looked up at him, ready to argue with him. "And I'm sure she has tons of experience fending off men. But this situation is different. She can't continue walking around town alone."

"Seth!" she cried out.

"Agreed," Jeremy said, also ignoring Jenna's outburst. "She didn't tell me Tray Long got that close to her."

"I hesitate in speculating on his motives, but Tray Long is stalking your sister. I've tried telling her what this jerk does to women, the atrocities he inflicts before killing them."

"Jeremy!" Jenna yelled, spinning around in Seth's arms when he wouldn't let her go. "Tell him I can take care of myself."

"He will kill you," Jeremy said, his suddenly quiet tone more disturbing than when he was yelling. "Even more so now that you've fucked him." He gestured at Seth.

Seth was surprised Jenna had told her brother they'd had sex, but didn't blink, unwilling to show any remorse over his actions or surprise that Jenna had decided to confide in her brother what level her relationship with Seth had moved to.

"Seth, come outside with me." Jeremy moved to the door. "There is something I am going to explain to you."

"What?" Jenna slid out of Seth's arms, hugging herself and suddenly looking so pale she looked sick.

The other two men stepped forward. "What are you going to do?" the large man who looked vaguely familiar demanded.

Jeremy held his hand out, silencing the group. He held weight as the head of this household; even the two men respected his commands. "I trust this one. You will all accept that." Then turning to Jenna, the transformation in his expression, the rage dissipating as compassion replaced it, he cupped her cheek, like a father would to a daughter he loved very much. "This is for the best, Jenna," he whispered. "Better for him to know now than for you to be so hurt later."

Jenna hugged herself, backing away from Jeremy as she bit her lip. She looked ready to cry but then shook her head frantically. "Let me tell him then."

"No." Jeremy opened the front door. "Seth, come with me."

CHAPTER EIGHT

Jenna raced to the back of the house, knowing Jeremy would take Seth to the backyard.

"You can't go out there," Bruno called after her.

"Shut up!" She ignored him, hurrying to the back door, her heart pounding a thousand miles an hour in her chest and her palms wet when she gripped the cold metal handle on the door.

Why was Jeremy doing this? Seth would run so fast if he learned they were werewolves. She couldn't accept that Jeremy wanted her to be hurt. And he knew she had feelings for Seth. Even though he didn't approve of her being with a human, Jeremy liked Seth. He'd said as much. They were friends.

She was ready to rip the handle out of the door when the lock suddenly wouldn't cooperate with her.

"Would you want a relationship with someone that you could never be yourself around?" Bingo said from behind her.

She'd always liked the older werewolf. Her parents had been killed when she was fifteen, leaving her under the protection of her brother and their pack. Bingo sometimes felt like the sire she no longer had. And more than once when she wanted to shred Jeremy's skin with her claws, she'd run to Bingo, unloading on him until he helped her feel better. But Jenna didn't want his words of wisdom right now. She rested her forehead against the smooth wooden door, her heart refusing to settle in her chest.

"You don't understand. He is different." Even as she spoke, though, Bingo's words sank into her system, creating a nasty bile in her throat. "I can't let Jeremy destroy this."

Somehow she yanked the door open without crushing the lock. Then as she closed it behind her, both Seth and Jeremy, who were at the edge of the yard by the trees, where no one would see them in daylight, turned and stared at her. The concern and confusion in Seth's eyes ripped at her heart.

"Jeremy, no. Not like this," she said, running to them.

"It is time." Jeremy was all business, his cool, determined smell assuring her he wouldn't be swayed on the matter.

Jenna wouldn't cry. She wouldn't lose it in front of Seth. Throwing a fit would make her look like a cub. "Then let me show him."

"Show me what?" Seth demanded. "Neither one of you are making any sense."

"We aren't human," she stammered, blurting out the words.

"Jenna. Silence," Jeremy ordered.

He was her brother, the elder in their litter. Years of honoring him, of following his lead after their parents died, made it almost impossible to completely defy him. Jenna had already told herself, and him in so many words, that she'd continue seeing Seth regardless of what Jeremy ordered her to do or not do. But in this matter, in breaking their laws, in allowing a human to know the truth about them, she obeyed without thought and shut her mouth.

"There are laws," Jeremy said, voicing her thoughts and shifting his attention to Seth. He pulled off his shirt as he spoke. "They are very clear and written for the safety of our pack, as well as for all packs."

Seth took a step backward. "Man, what are you doing?" He smelled so confused it was hard not to reach out to console him.

"Jenna is right. We aren't human. More times than you realize I've smelled your bewilderment when I've given you pieces of information on a case you've been working on and known you couldn't figure out how I knew what I did."

Seth didn't say anything but took another step backward when Jeremy kicked off his boots, then reached down and pulled off his socks.

"Okay, that's enough," Seth ordered when Jeremy reached for his pants. "You've lost it, Jeremy. And you aren't making any sense." He turned from Jeremy, walking to Jenna and then gripping her arm. "What's wrong with him?"

"Nothing." Her mouth was so dry she could barely speak. It was too hard to move. She wanted to grab Seth and run, take him somewhere no one would interrupt or ruin the wonderful thing that had begun between the two of them.

"Seth," Jeremy said, his voice garbled as he stood naked in his and Jenna's backyard, the change already boiling strong in his blood.

When Seth turned around and saw Jeremy, the

expletives that left his mouth turned Jenna's blood cold. Her brother transformed before them, his face altering and contorting while fur spread over his flesh, the change in full force and taking over him with rapid speed.

"Get in the house," Seth ordered, gripping her arm and almost lifting her as he took long strides away from Jeremy.

"No. Seth!" Jenna put more than a little muscle into the effort of keeping Seth outside. "Seth, look at him."

When he again turned his attention to Jeremy, Seth froze, pulling Jenna into his arms with enough force all air left her lungs. "What the fuck?" he hissed.

"Seth, we're werewolves."

Seth paled noticeably, the smell of fear overwhelming in spite of how he stood his ground when Jeremy fell to all fours and took a step toward them. He walked slowly, his head held high, and his features relaxed. Jeremy was a noble creature, his dark, coarse hair reflecting the sunlight. It wasn't often Jenna saw him in his fur in the daylight, but she sucked in a breath, suddenly feeling a wave of pride over what her brother was doing. He was bringing Seth closer to them, bridging a gap that had always been there up to this moment.

"There's no such thing," Seth said firmly.

He might as well have stabbed her in the heart. "How can you say that?"

She laughed although there wasn't anything funny said. Pointing to her brother, she grabbed Seth's arm, looking at him as her gaze riveted to the scratches still visible on his neck. For some reason, a strange sensation washed over her. If Seth were a werewolf, those scratches would be long gone by now. The realization of how vulnerable he was, of how easily he could be marked and hurt because of his species, created mixed emotions inside her she didn't understand.

Jeremy once again began transforming and Seth's jaw dropped, his pallor turning so pale he looked like he might get sick. When Jeremy stood, naked, then walked to his clothes, Seth started shaking.

"I don't believe it," he whispered, noticeably upset.

"It's okay," she whispered, pressing her palm against his chest and feeling the steady beat of his heart.

Seth looked down at her, the smell of his fear gone and anger filling the air between them so quickly its spiciness almost made her sneeze. "Can you do that, too?"

"Yes," she whispered, searching his face. "But now you know. I don't have to hide it from you."

"No," he said, not elaborating but letting go of her and storming around the side of the house.

"Seth, wait!" She ran after him, catching up as he reached his bike. "Where are you going?"

"I've got work to do," he said, not looking at her when he climbed on his bike and caused it to roar to life.

"I'll come over later."

He looked at her, his expression so cold and distant and the strong, spicy smell of outrage scaring her. Seth stared at her as if they were strangers. He backed his bike up without saying anything, then turned it around, causing his tires to send gravel flying when he tore out of her and Jeremy's driveway and took off down the highway.

Tears burned her eyes as she watched Seth leave. She hugged herself when Jeremy came up behind her, the smell of him not strong enough to drown out the lingering anger still hanging heavily in the air.

"He's mad," she said unnecessarily, almost choking on the words.

"Come inside." Jeremy put his arm around her, guiding her to the house.

Jenna was so numb she barely felt him touching her.

"You can't just let him leave," Bruno complained the moment Jeremy closed the door behind Jenna.

"He needs time." Jeremy placed his hand on Jenna's back.

"And what if he runs to the cops, announces we're monsters, and starts a panic?" Bruno yelled.

Jenna didn't want Jeremy comforting her right now. She sure as hell didn't want Bruno, or anyone, yelling and throwing a fit about how Seth had reacted to learning who she was. She didn't want to think about it at all. And at the same time, she wanted to race out the door and hunt Seth down and not leave him alone until he admitted he was cool with who, and what, she was.

"Go to your den." Jeremy opened the door. "No one is going to turn anyone in. No one is in danger."

"How do you know that?" Bruno wouldn't let it go.

Jeremy walked up to the stupid brute, glaring at him when he stood inches away from him. "Because I know," Jeremy growled, his voice low and venomous. "Now return to your den. Don't discuss this with anyone and everything will be fine. The only way what happened here today will become a problem is if you start howling about it."

Bingo slapped Bruno on the shoulder, nodding to the door. "Let's go." Bingo walked past the other males and to Jenna, who stood hugging herself and almost jumped when he touched her hand with his rough palm. "You know where to find me if you need me, sweetheart."

She nodded dumbly but then turned into the older male and gave him a fierce hug, her body shaking as tears soaked her face.

"Don't start smelling around for a situation you don't know is there," Bingo whispered into her hair. "Give him time and sniff him out. If he is the one, he'll understand and accept. If he isn't the one, it's best to know now."

Jenna wiped her eyes and sucked in a deep breath. "He looked so pissed."

"No male, regardless of his species, likes being thrown off guard."

Jenna nodded again, her heart still weighing so heavily in her chest she could barely breathe.

"You're going to make her stop sniffing around that human, right?" Bruno asked, after moving to the door.

"Leave," Jeremy barked. "And if I hear anyone howling about this at all, I'll know whose ass to kick."

Bruno started mumbling something, but Bingo shoved him out the door, closing it behind him without saying good-bye. Bingo would take care of Bruno, though. And Bingo would be there if Jenna needed another good cry.

*   *   *

Seth parked his bike in front of Elizabeth Helo's house. Never in a million years would he have believed what he just saw if he hadn't seen it with his own eyes. And at that, he questioned his sanity. He wasn't one for fairy tales; hell, he wasn't even that religious. Hard, cold facts. That's what he lived by. Jeremy had sure as hell laid some facts on him just now.

"Crap," Seth hissed, rubbing his eyes and slowly climbing off his bike. He was still a bit shaken, and that sucked. "Get a grip, Gere," he ordered himself. He needed information out of Elizabeth Helo, and if she was willingly allowing Tray Long to run around in her car she wasn't going to be cooperative. Not to mention, she'd just been questioned by cops. They weren't here now, but Seth would bet they'd just left.

Seth tugged at his shirt, staring at the house while getting his thoughts in order. Later, he'd think about what happened out at Jenna's house. Right now, he had work to do. He wasn't going to get paid until he brought Tray Long in, and that wouldn't happen if he freaked out on a man who changed into a wolf before his eyes.

Didn't Jenna say she could change into a wolf, too? *God. Shit.*
Think about it later.

Call it advantage, or disadvantage, but driving a Harley made his presence known. More than likely Elizabeth stood just inside one of the several windows facing the street, staring at him right now. He couldn't stand out here appearing awkward. Seth strolled up to the front door and knocked.

The door opened and a woman, maybe thirty at the most, with straight platinum hair and breasts he would bet weren't real, gave him a wary once-over.

"Yes?" she asked.

"Are you Elizabeth Helo?"

"Who wants to know?"

Seth pulled one of his cards out of his shirt pocket and handed it to her.

" 'Fugitive Apprehension'? What the hell is that?" She wrinkled her nose and handed his card back to him, shoving it at him as if it would burn her if she continued holding it.

"I find people," he offered, accustomed to the questioning and knowing the words "bounty hunter" often made people nervous. He was on familiar ground now, and set the ball into motion. "Ms. Helo, you're good friends with Tray Long. I need to find him. Where is he right now?"

"I don't know Tray Long," she told Seth, sucking in her lower lip and batting lashes thick with mascara at him.

"Ms. Helo, he is using you, using your car. The tags are registered to you. Now he is going to hurt you, hurt you very badly. I'm not a cop, but I can protect you. Tell me where to find him."

She stared at Seth with wide green eyes, assessing him. A car drove down the street behind him and she shot it a furtive glance before rubbing her hands together and taking a step backward.

"Come inside."

He was in. She didn't need to tell him she knew Tray. She didn't need to admit knowing him. They both knew she did, and now to get her to talk.

"Is Tray staying here?" Seth asked, walking past her into a cluttered, dark living room and taking in the surroundings. He continued walking, finding the kitchen off the living room. It was just as messy and hard to tell how many people were eating here.

"Hey, I didn't say you could search the place," she complained, hurrying around him and facing him, crossing her arms under her large breasts.

"Do you know what Tray has done?" Seth asked, ignoring her accusation. He continued taking in his surroundings, moving to the sink and noticing two coffee cups, among other dishes, before leaning against the counter and pinning her with a hard stare.

Elizabeth Helo stuck out her chin, matching his stare with a chilling glare. "Tray hasn't done a damn thing," she hissed. "You're trying to frame him, just like the cops. He did his time and isn't going to hurt anyone else."

Seth grunted. "What time will he be home?"

A car door closed out back and both of them turned their attention to the back door. Elizabeth hurried to the door and then squealed.

"Shit. Oh, shit. Crap, crap, crap," she groaned. Her hands started waving in the air in front of her as she looked at him frantically. "Get the hell out of here," she hissed. "You've got to leave now!"

"Or what?" Seth leaned so he could see out the back door window as well. Talk about timing. Tray Long was walking across the yard to the house.

"God. Please!" She actually started shoving Seth out of the kitchen. "You've got to go."

They made it as far as the living room. Seth wasn't exactly helping her move him. The back door opened and Elizabeth froze, turning whiter than a sheet.

"Where you at?" Tray bellowed into the house, his words sounding somewhat slurred.

"Coming. I'll be right there," Elizabeth called out, her pitch so high there was no way she'd be able to pull off lying to Tray about anything.

She put her finger over her lips, her expression so frightened, Seth knew she didn't believe Tray incapable of violence. Seth had seen this same look on way too many women in the past. Fear and panic over what their man might do. Seth matched her motion, putting his finger to his lips, and gestured for her to go to Tray. He wouldn't need to hear much before taking the guy down.

Elizabeth ran into the kitchen, leaving Seth standing in the living room.

"What the hell is wrong with you?" Tray demanded.

"Nothing. Nothing," she said, not sounding convincing at all. "Did you have a good day?"

"What the fuck do you think?" A cabinet opened and closed. "You ever plan on washing any of these dishes?"

"Sure. I'll do that right now. I'll make your drink, too."

"Who the hell is here?"

"No one. They were. But they're gone," she added, talking so fast it was hard to understand her.

"They're gone?" he hissed. "I smell fucking humans. Who the fuck was here?"

Elizabeth squealed and Seth fought to hold his ground. His head was spinning, though. Tray said he smelled humans. Everything that happened at Jenna's house came rushing at Seth faster than a freight train on a collision course. He couldn't wrap his brain around it fast enough.

Seth looked up when Tray stormed into the living room, holding Elizabeth by the arm and damn near dragging her along with him. He flung her away from his side when he sneered at Seth.

"Jenna Drury not enough pussy for you, asshole?" Tray growled, his voice even more garbled than it was a second ago. "You got to come after my bitch, too?"

"I'm here to see you," Seth said, tensing for an attack.

"You and what army?" Tray laughed and his eyes flashed silver.

Seth remembered staring into the eyes of the wolf—no, werewolf—he'd faced in Jeremy's backyard. Eyes that were silver. Eyes filled with more knowledge and understanding than any he'd ever seen in an animal before. Eyes that weren't human.

"I don't need a fucking army," Seth growled.

Tray laughed. Maybe if he hadn't laughed Seth would have been able to hold his ground. Possibly if Tray hadn't glanced toward Elizabeth, acting as if he might lunge at her instead of Seth, he would have stayed where he was. But he had his man, or whatever the fuck Tray Long was. Seth leapt, taking Tray down.

Seth barely registered being thrown across the room. The crashing sound didn't come from him landing on the edge of the couch. He made it to his feet, but not before someone raced into the living room from the back door with enough speed it was just a blur. The growling and screams that followed didn't hit him as fast as the bloody battle that played out before him. He stared, dumbfounded, when Jeremy released Tray and the man slumped to the floor, blood pouring from his mouth and nose.

"I forgot to tell you before you left," Jeremy told him. "The only way you're going to kill a werewolf is by breaking their neck."

CHAPTER NINE

Seth didn't feel like being inside. It was so dark; barely a star shone and there was no moon. The blackness somehow was comforting. It had been a whirlwind of a day. Hell, it had been a crazy week. Beyond crazy. Insane.

Jeremy had wanted Seth to take credit for killing Tray Long, out of self-defense, so Seth could get paid. Jeremy also mentioned something about pack politics that hadn't made a lot of sense. Seth didn't take credit for shit he hadn't done. Besides, he brought them in alive. Always had. So he'd turned his back on that case, let the cops find him, which they inevitably did. Elizabeth Helo had long since split, taken off to find a pack that would accept her, according to Jeremy.

Seth went after Elaine Gold. At least she was human. He'd turned her over to the authorities earlier that day and gone home. After moping around in his house for a few hours, he grabbed a beer and headed out back to lean against his stoop. Out here he felt he was alone in the universe. And after the past few days, alone was cleansing.

At least he hoped it would be cleansing. If only he could get rid of the image of Jenna standing in her

drivenway, looking terrified, as she watched him
leave. She'd been so upset, scared to death, and he
believed it was because she didn't want him walking out of her life. It wasn't the only image of her
that stubbornly refused to leave him alone. He saw
her glistening with perspiration while racked in the
throes of passion. He saw her entering his home,
determination etched on her pretty face, when she
sought him out after their first meeting. Seth sipped
his beer and stared at the dark, black sky, void of
moon and stars, and surrendered to the many pictures in his mind of Jenna.

He should seek her out. They needed to talk. There
was something between them, and now that he'd
brought in Elaine Gold and the police had found Tray
Long, Seth had some downtime before his next case
would be dropped in his lap. Tray's death was under
investigation, but no one suspected Seth as having
anything to do with it. Damn good thing, since he
didn't kill the motherfucker. There wouldn't be any
connection to Jeremy either. The man was a ghost.
Make that a werewolf.

There would be time soon to see what John Payton was up to, which was more than likely nothing.
Hannah was level-headed. Seth was willing to bet
what she was picking up on was a PI who was ready
for some serious downtime. But Seth would look
into it, after he took care of some personal matters.

Something stirred in the trees and Seth squinted
into the darkness, listening for the sound he'd heard a
moment ago. It was suddenly too damn dark and tiny
hairs prickled at the back of his neck as he straightened, willing whatever it was to make another sound.
At least if he couldn't see into the trees, whoever it

was out there wouldn't be able to see him. Seth didn't have a back porch light on his house.

He stared, not blinking, until his eyes burned. Waiting sucked, but he was damn good at it. Taking his time and not once diverting his gaze, Seth raised his beer to his lips and took a long sip of the cold, refreshing brew. He almost choked on it when he heard the sound again, this time accompanied by a shadow.

Seth set the beer down on the cement slab outside his back door and moved to his feet, willing the shadow to take form. After a minute he wondered if his eyes had played tricks on him. The shadow seemed to fade into the darkness. Seth stepped off his slab. Let whoever was out there know he'd spotted them. Dare them to come out of hiding and present themselves. He remained rooted with the cement at his heels, again waiting, watching, searching with his eyes.

The shadow hadn't moved, and it reappeared where he'd last seen it. Seth took another step toward it, his heart suddenly pounding hard enough in his chest to drown out any other noises around him. The shadow took shape, dark grays and browns and blacks covering the deadly-looking creature that stared at him with intense silver eyes.

In a different life he would be kicking his own ass for not having his gun on him. But that was before— before he knew people weren't always who they appeared to be. Seth stared at the creature moving closer, its hesitation and wariness apparent not only in its movements but also in its face.

This wasn't Jeremy.

"God damn," Seth whispered under his breath, and the creature stopped.

It was so dark outside. The blackness of the night suddenly irritated the crap out of him. He wanted to see, to understand, and God help him for suddenly becoming so fucking insane, but he wanted to accept.

"Jenna?" he whispered, then cleared his throat.

She raised her head. He wouldn't go as far as to call her gorgeous. There was an elegance about this creature, though, that he hadn't seen a few days ago when Jeremy had changed before his eyes. The creature before him stood taller than a dog, possibly larger than a wolf, although he hadn't seen many wolves up close and personal in his lifetime. He noticed fangs, long, white teeth that were pressed against her jaw and contrasted with the dark fur. Her coat looked silky and thick. She was muscular yet lean. But it was what he saw in her eyes, in those eyes that glowed with no source of light other than an inner warmth that stole his breath. He saw fear, uncertainty, and pain.

Did she see that in him?

Seth sucked in a breath, daring to take a step closer. He kicked the thought out of his head that this creature could kill him. No way would she sense fear in him. Not now. Not ever.

"We need to talk," he said firmly.

She stood still as a statue, her head held high. This wasn't going to be a one-sided conversation.

"Unless you can talk like that, I suggest you change."

Her mouth opened in what he could only guess might be a grin. But then her face contorted in an odd expression.

"What?" he asked, frowning.

She started panting and her body puffed out, her shoulders appearing to arch as if she were trying to stand on her hind legs and couldn't quite master it. When she started panting, her eyes ablaze, Seth understood what he was witnessing. She was changing forms.

And it didn't appear to be a pleasant experience. Suddenly he wondered what the hell he was thinking. He didn't even know what Jenna was. Even as he stared, seeing with his own eyes, part of him was convinced this was all a terrible dream. Gorgeous women didn't turn into deadly creatures, or vice versa.

Jenna's long, thick dark hair was damp and clung to her naked body as she straightened. God. Naked. His brain needed a good kick-start. Seth almost stumbled forward, ripping off his T-shirt and then shoving it over her head. It fell down her body and halfway to her knees.

"Thank you," she whispered, her voice scratchy. "And you're right. We need to talk."

It was odd how the thought suddenly hit him that one of the reasons Jenna appealed to him so much was her appearance of being so strong, yet how apparent it was that she needed him. Had he been a fool? What kind of protection did a woman need who could turn into such a deadly creature?

"I didn't think you wanted to talk to me," she added, her voice a bit softer.

"I wasn't sure I did, either," he admitted, feeling something cold inside him surface, and at the same time a heat swelled throughout him like a drug, making him ache to reach out and touch her.

There was still a hint of silver streaking across her pretty blue eyes. "I've come by your house every night," she admitted, her tone dropping to a whisper. "Tonight you were outside."

She wanted him. He'd known that from the beginning, the first time he laid eyes on her when she walked into the Golden Grill with him. God, that seemed years ago. It had been a week. In one week Jenna had turned his life upside down and made him consider the possibility that he wanted a woman in his life full-time. He wanted her in his life full-time.

"Does your brother know you're here?"

"Does it matter?" she asked.

He didn't want to piss Jeremy off. But if that meant talking to him, assuring him he wouldn't hurt his sister, Seth might consider doing that. "Let's go inside," he said, knowing in a way he'd just answered her question. "I might have some sweats that would fit you." He seriously doubted it. Not to mention, she was sexy as hell wearing only his shirt.

"Do you really want to put more clothes on me?" She followed him inside.

Seth would bet there was a grin of pure female satisfaction on her face. "If we're going to talk, then yes," he growled. He faced her when she entered his kitchen, the lights off, yet somehow it appeared brighter than it had been outside. He closed his back door and locked it. "And we're going to talk." Except he wasn't sure how to begin.

Saying he wanted to protect and cherish her but might have a problem if she proved to be stronger than he was seemed an odd way to start the conversation.

Jenna watched Seth down his beer, then reach into his refrigerator and pull out two more bottles, handing one to her and snapping the lid off of his. She twisted her cap, following his actions, and tossed her lid into the trash can alongside the refrigerator. She was in his house. That was a start. Jenna knew in her heart and in her soul there wouldn't be any leaving. Not now. She would stay here until Seth saw and understood they were supposed to be together.

"I was really mad at Jeremy for telling you we were werewolves. But when he told me without you knowing I was simply playing with you, it got me to thinking," she blurted, breaking the silence and daring to pause, catch his reaction.

Seth held his beer halfway to his mouth, his lips parted, watching her. This was her only chance. He had let her in his home. Humans couldn't be that different from werewolves. If he invited her in, there was interest. He wanted her. Jenna stared into that brooding stare of his, seeing the aggressive, sexy, and intelligent male she was falling head over paws for. She took a gulp of the cold beer, then placed the bottle on the table behind her.

Jenna held her ground, fighting not to fidget when she didn't know what to do with her hands. His bare chest called to her; her fingers itched to run over all that perfectly toned muscle, feel his chest hair under her fingertips. She held her ground, determined to make him see she was the female for him.

"The night Tray Long was killed, I came by. You were here and I watched your house. I did that the next night, and last night. I wanted to celebrate your joy of the kill," she said, feeling as if she was speaking way too fast. She sucked in a gulp of air.

"I didn't kill him," Seth told her, his low baritone sending shivers over her flesh. "I'm not a killer. I'm a hunter."

She nodded once, remembering Jeremy describing what had happened when he plowed into Tray

Long's house earlier this week. Jenna had argued that Jeremy didn't give Seth the opportunity to show he could take down the rogue werewolf. Jeremy had insisted Seth wouldn't have killed him. He'd been right.

"That is what I do, Jenna." His voice was calm, but his body was wound tight. Every inch of him appeared ready to pounce. "I'm paid money to hunt, and deliver, whatever criminal is out there and wanted by the authorities."

"I know that," she whispered, wishing he would pounce. It was too much standing and staring at him, half-naked, while breathing in his scent, which was wrapped around her while his shirt hung over her body. "Our laws are different from yours, though."

"There's only one law, Jenna," he growled. "As we speak they are searching for the murderer of Tray Long."

"Why would they care who murdered someone who has killed so many?"

"Because that's the way the human justice system works, Jenna."

"Does that mean Jeremy is wanted for murder?"

"The only people who saw what happened aren't coming forward—and that includes me. Though I don't approve of what Jeremy did, I understand his reasons." He clasped Jenna's hand. "Your brother will be safe."

The last thing Jenna wanted to do tonight was discuss the differences in beliefs between werewolves and humans. She knew human laws. She walked among Seth's kind every day. She wouldn't let the conversation sway to whose laws were right and whose weren't. Running her fingers through her hair, she lowered her gaze, exhaling slowly.

"We're always going to be different," he grumbled.

Jenna's mouth went dry as she focused on the bulge in his jeans.

Right or wrong, in spite of their differences, Seth wanted her. She wouldn't believe it was just physical. A male like him could have any female he wanted. Jenna was going to make sure the only female he ever wanted from this point forward was her. She started to move toward him but then looked up quickly when he gripped her jaw.

"We are different," he stressed, his voice rough, deep, and his fingers hot against her oversensitized flesh. "That will never change."

"I want you." It slipped out. Jenna couldn't stop the words she'd ached to say to him every night she'd lain outside and watched his home, watched him.

"You have me," he told her. Then pulling her against him, he impaled her mouth, his hunger unleashed and demanding.

Jenna's heart exploded. She couldn't keep her hands off him, needing to feel all of him at once, claim every inch of his body and put it to memory. Her male. Her human. Seth was right. There were differences. There were with any couple. But he would be her mate, no matter how different they were. They were also the same. They were meant for each other and she'd known it since the first night she'd lain in the woods, watching him talk to her brother.

"There is so much to talk about," she said on a breath when Seth's mouth left hers and seared a burning path down her neck.

"There's plenty of time to talk." Seth lifted her in his arms, cradling her like a cub, and carried her to his bedroom.

And as they made love, the fiery passion igniting in her veins and setting her free, releasing all of her inhibitions and empowering her with the strength to make this relationship work no matter what, Jenna wanted to cry from the happiness enveloping her.

Seth rose over her, their naked bodies united and his cock buried deep inside her. "You answer to me now, not to your brother," he growled, thrusting deep into her heat.

Jenna growled, taking all of him as she wrapped her legs around roped muscle and dragged her nails down his chest. "I never answered to Jeremy," she managed, her voice rough as she fought not to pant while he fucked her. "If I had I never would have met you."

It sounded as if he laughed, although his dark stare never left hers.

"We answer to each other. You and me," she said, gasping, which made it hard to talk. "Seth!" she cried out, pulling him to her.

He thrust again, burying himself inside her. She never wanted him to leave. Never wanted it to end. There were tough times ahead for them. Not with his kind; they wouldn't know who she was. Jenna didn't care what her pack thought, though. In her heart, in her soul, she knew Seth was always meant to be her male.